Mariposa Intersections

To Mati,
friend, neighbour,
enjoy the story;
it will take you to
a different place.

Mariposa Intersections

a novel

Bruno Huber

GRANVILLE ISLAND
PUBLISHING

ISBN: 978-1-926991-92-4
ebook ISBN: 978-1-926991-93-1

Book editor: Maureen Phillips
Book designer: Omar Gallegos
Cover designer: Daniel Colmont
Proofreader: Rebecca Coates

Granville Island Publishing Ltd.
212 – 1656 Duranleau St. Granville Island
Vancouver, BC, Canada V6H 3S4

604-688-0320 / 1-877-688-0320
info@granvilleislandpublishing.com
www.granvilleislandpublishing.com

Printed in Canada on recycled paper

Dedicated to all who get involved, either in community or in activist groups, to all the David's fighting the Goliath's of this world.

I want to thank Sandra and Molly and all of my friends who urged me on to pursue this story.

Contents

Prologue   ix

Chapter 1
Rafael   1

Chapter 2
Gabriela   13

Chapter 3
In Between   29

Chapter 4
Radio Libre   41

Chapter 5
ELL and NNN   53

Chapter 6
Karen and Jason   67

Chapter 7
Dissent   73

Chapter 8
Carmen   83

Chapter 9
Morelia   93

Chapter 10
Bernard   107

Chapter 11
Randall   117

Chapter 12
Parker   119

Chapter 13
Confrontation   125

Chapter 14
Aftermath   137

Chapter 15
Fallout   147

Chapter 16
Regroup   157

Chapter 17
Positioning   165

Chapter 18
Changing Sides   181

Chapter 19
The Day Before   189

Chapter 20
Day of the Living   201

Chapter 21
Endings   213

Chapter 22
Beginnings   221

Author's Notes   225

Prologue

Professor Frederick Urquhart from the University of Toronto and his wife, Norah, researched the migration of the monarch butterflies from southern Ontario for over forty years. Their dogged persistence and tenacity would not let them rest until they found where they migrated to. Fred and Norah knew that the butterflies ended up somewhere in central Mexico, high up in the Trans-Mexican Volcanic Belt — but just where exactly eluded them for years. They found traces of the monarchs in Florida and then again in Mexico, but in the sparsely inhabited mountains in central Mexico the butterflies suddenly vanished. From 1940 on, Fred and Norah and thousands of volunteers tagged hundreds of thousands of monarchs with a specially developed tag.

The story goes that Ken Brugger and Catalina Aguado, his Mexican wife, were working for Dr. Urquhart in Mexico when they met a Mexican *campesino* in the silver-mining town of Angangueo.

The farmer told them about the clouds of mariposas (butterflies) high up in the mountains, in a ten-acre section of pine forests near the small village of El Rosario.

Professor Urquhart arrived on the 3000-metre-high plateau above El Rosario on January 9, 1976, dismounted from the old mare he was riding, and as if in a dream, gingerly stepped into a living cloud of gold-and-black butterflies. By the millions they hung, in dense clusters like beehives, from the branches of every pine tree, filling the silence all around him. He sat down on a log, overwhelmed by the wonder of it, and was incredulous when he looked down and saw an expired monarch. He gingerly picked it up, and there on its delicate wing was the tag that he himself had affixed four months earlier, back in Ontario. He finally had the empiric evidence he had searched for all his adult life.

What remained a mystery to Urquhart, though, was how the butterflies returned to the same patch of pine forests year after year. The ones that flew to Mexico every autumn had never been there before. No single butterfly ever makes the round trip from Ontario to Angangueo. In Mexico at the end of winter, the mature male butterflies mate copiously and then die, leaving it to the now pregnant female butterflies to fly north to Texas and Florida. They look for milkweed to lay their eggs on, as it's the only plant that sustains the caterpillars. After laying the eggs, they die without ever seeing their offspring. The caterpillars pupate and metamorphose into young monarchs, which now continue their migration north, all the way to Canada, repeating the cycle: find milkweed, lay eggs and die. In the fall, only these — the great-great-grandbabies, the super generation — will make the tremendous journey all the way to Angangueo, in the Michoacán mountains, where they've never been.

It is a true phenomenon of nature; somehow the information is built into their DNA, compelling the insects that hatched three thousand kilometres away in Ontario to make that epic journey all the way to this remote pine forest in Michoacán's section of the Trans-Mexican Volcanic Belt. Here they rest for the winter before repeating the cycle: from egg to larva to caterpillar, pupating and metamorphosing into the black-and-orange butterflies. It may take up to five generations for the monarchs travelling north to reach Point Pelee in southern Ontario, where they reverse direction and return to El Rosario in a timeless, perpetual relay across continents.

The discovery of the migration destination of the monarch butterflies prompted the founding of the Santuario de la Mariposa Monarca in El Rosario and spawned a whole new industry in this impoverished region. After the closure of the Trojes silver mine, the people who stayed behind subsisted on a bit of agriculture and some logging. The discovery of the butterflies led to a tourism boom, especially after an article appeared in National Geographic. This prompted all kinds of spinoffs for the local economy. Most residents became engaged in hospitality, transport or guiding. They also started crafting numerous versions of monarch butterflies as art and souvenirs.

Chapter 1
Rafael

R afael Pascual Monrovia was born in 1970 and grew up in El Rosario. Being the youngest sibling, behind two elder brothers and two sisters, he was forced to be innovative and look for gains outside the scant conventional family resources. Rafael's family lived and worked on their primitive homestead, with no running water or electricity, halfway up the mountain, about an hour by horse from Angangueo. The whole family was engaged in the arduous task of putting enough food on the table from their small patch of blue maize and beans, as well as their few goats and chickens. Rafael's two elder brothers worked the harsh land, while his mother and his two sisters stitched and embroidered monarch napkins, doilies and shawls, and his dad carved and painted wooden butterflies. Rafael helped paint the souvenirs and became adept at this tedious task. The crafts helped subsidize the Monrovia family's poor existence, enabling them to send their youngest boy to high school in Angangueo.

Primary education in the state of Michoacán was provided for free up to Grade 6, but for any further schooling, Rafael's parents, Arturo and Maria, had to pay a monthly fee, as well as buy the books and provide transportation to and from school, or arrange lodging. By sheer luck, Rafael found room and board with the warden of the Mariposa Santuario, which resulted in Rafael's first summer job: guiding tourists up and down the steep two-kilometre hike from where the trucks and buses dropped them off.

One warm January morning on the Monday after a hectic weekend, Rafael was hanging around the guide shack, as he did every morning, grousing about his predicament. No matter how many times he went up and down the dusty track through the pine forest to the centre of the mariposa habitat, his weekly pay remained the same paltry few pesos, which he immediately handed over to his dad. The only bonuses were his tips, which Rafael for the most part also passed on to his dad.

Rafael had dreams of owning things and going places — vague dreams, because he didn't know a whole lot about the world outside Angangueo or El Rosario. But one thing he knew, even at fourteen: He didn't want to be like his dad and had no interest in scraping a living off the barren patch of land his family owned. This fate was reserved for his two older brothers, not him. Rafael spent some of the tips he had squirrelled away on a snazzy new pair of Onitsuka Tiger sneakers, to replace his worn-out huaraches, but he only wore the tennies at work, never at home. He also sported a pair of cool new sunglasses, through which the world appeared richer and softer. He kept a growing collection of foreign bills and coins in the Onitsuka shoebox, and he would look and feel the dollars, francs and marks and imagine himself travelling to the exotic places these bills represented.

On that balmy morning when he was sitting in the entrance shack, a young American couple came in and asked him to be their guide. Maybe it was because he was the youngest, or maybe because he greeted them with a bright and hearty "Hello, good morning!" or maybe because el espíritu intervened. Who knows these things? Rafael didn't believe in coincidence. His mother taught him early on that in life things always happen for a reason: "God makes the choices and we live with them." Some call it luck, some destiny, but for Rafael, life's incidents were just jewels on a string — some bigger, some smaller, some real, some fake, others glittery and polished or dull and unrefined, some common, some precious.

The man introduced himself and his companion in proper schoolroom Spanish: "*Hola, me llamo Brian y mi esposa se llama Clare, Clara en español.*"

Rafael grinned and said in heavily accented English, "My name is Rafael. Welcome to El Santuario." That and a few other words, like *money*, *tips* and *butterfly*, was all the English Rafael knew.

In the course of their hike, Brian became very inquisitive in his rudimentary Spanish and got Rafael to talk about himself, his *pobre familia* and his *hermanas* and *hermanos* and how they struggled to keep food on the table. Clare could have listened to the young Mexican's velvety voice for hours, and she commented about it to her husband when they fell a few paces behind the nimble-footed guide.

"I wonder if he sings," Brian mused.

When he asked him later, Rafael just laughed. "Everybody sings," he said.

"Rafael," the American insisted, "it's important that you go to school and learn English. It will open so many new doors and opportunities." Brian also emphasized that school was a lot more important than this job on the mountain, despite the much-needed extra income. He impressed on Rafael that if he did well in high school, he could go on to university, and then he could really help his family. Rafael didn't see how that was possible — he had never considered himself or any of his peers from El Rosario going to university. He might as well have aimed for the moon.

Rafael had no illusions about his position in life. He now earned money guiding tourists, most of which he handed over to his papa, and then the time would come when he would marry one of the girls in the small town or in Angangueo in order to increase the family holdings. There was no point explaining this to the gringos, because they didn't know how life in a small Mexican village functioned. They had no idea what it was like to be a poor Mexican *campesino*'s kid. The tourists who came to El Rosario were rich by virtue of the simple fact that they could afford to travel so far from home to view some bugs on a remote mountain.

Brian asked Rafael, "How much do you make here guiding us tourists?" Rafael was taken aback, not sure how to respond. Brian saw Rafael's hesitation, but, being curious, he pressed on. "Okay, Rafael, *cuántos pesos por una semana?*"

"*Doscientos o trescientos,*" Rafael answered, embarrassed, and when Brian asked him what he did with the tips, Rafael said untruthfully that he gave them all to his dad. Brian looked down at Rafael's sneakers and then admired his sunglasses.

Clare explained in stilted Spanish, "You must save your tips for your future, for an education fund for yourself. Your dad doesn't need to know. When you have a good job in the future, you can pay him back many times."

Rafael looked at the two tourists and then raised up his eyes. "*Dios sabe todo.* God knows everything." He didn't really believe there was anybody watching, but sooner or later his dad would find out, and then the punishment would be swift and severe. "Neither God nor my dad like lies," he said, pointing his index fingers towards heaven.

Brian shook his head. "You would be doing your papa a favour. The money you save can get you to a bigger school, maybe even to university. Your dad will never be able to raise that himself, and what he doesn't know won't bother him, Rafael."

Something in Rafael's mind clicked. Maybe the gringo was right. It could just be between Dios and himself; leave Papá out of it. As long as he kept his tips for an honest purpose, it was the right thing to do, surely, was it not? As long as Papá didn't find out, that was.

When they emerged from the trees into an open meadow, Clare spread her arms wide with total enchantment. "Oh my god, look at this!" Brian and Clare stood still, mesmerized by the orange and black spectre of the mariposas that suddenly engulfed them. They danced with their arms outstretched, as if wanting to join the silent, timeless, wondrous ballet of the thousands of butterflies filling the air and the open sky all around them.

"Isn't this wonderful!" Clare exclaimed, completely in awe of this miracle of nature. They walked through the open meadow, inside a swirling cloud of monarchs, back into the pine grove and to the end of the path. They gazed in wonder at the beehive-like clusters hanging by the dozens off the pine trees. Millions of monarchs huddled together for warmth, fluttering loose as the sun penetrated the trees with bright shafts of light. Brian was snapping pictures, which could never convey the feeling of awe and wonder. To Rafael this was a daily sight, but still every time he was struck by the same wondrous feeling as when he first stepped into the large church in Angangueo.

They retraced their steps back across the meadow, through the thousands of butterflies filling the air, and returned to the shack, where they thanked Rafael for his guidance. Brian pulled out his wallet and discreetly handed a two-hundred-peso bill to Rafael. "Learn to speak English, amigo."

Rafael mumbled *"Muchas gracias"* and *"Buena suerte."* He watched the American couple disappear amongst the souvenir stands and taquerías. *"Entre yo y Dios."* Rafael looked from the two-hundred-peso bill to the blue sky and stuffed the money in his pocket.

Over the next few months Rafael took Brian's advice to heart and improved his English by way of a couple of dog-eared books he borrowed from the school library, as well as by listening and talking to tourists. He also developed a knack for culling out the lucrative *turistas* for himself, mostly gringos from America with loud voices and big cameras. Rafael's tips increased dramatically, and between *Rafael y Dios*, the shoebox started filling up with pesos and dollars. Rafael still handed over a good portion of his tips to his dad, but when he mentioned his desire to go to university, old Arturo just shook his head. "Your future is your family. Don't get any high-flying ideas in your head," he said with finality.

For every tip Rafael received, he crossed himself like a good Catholic, which always made his donors feel twice as good about themselves, and he regularly gave thanks to the Virgin of Guadalupe and the village saint, Santo Rosario, for his good fortune. In the same breath, he would ask for forgiveness for any sins or transgressions he might have committed. That way he covered all the bases, just in case.

Rafael finished high school at the top of his class, which earned him a scholarship from the state of Michoacan. But his parents didn't want to let him go, because losing their son's income from his guide position would threaten their status quo, which now included one of five television sets in the village, as well as a fridge and a sewing machine for his mom.

Rafael's dad's secret wish was to buy a truck, so he could get into the business of ferrying tourists up and down to Angangueo. Losing Rafael would be a major blow to Arturo's ambition to claw himself and his family out of poverty.

Rafael naively took it upon himself to solve the problem. The day after he graduated, he came into his house giddy with excitement and proudly handed his papa a set of truck keys. "Here, *Papá*, this is for you. I saved the money myself, and this is my goodbye present to the family."

His papa stared at the battered old Ford crew-cab, which Carlos the mechanic had assured Rafael was in fine condition. He then turned his attention to Rafael and without a word, threw the truck keys back at his feet. "How could you cheat me out of all the money that rightfully belonged to all of us, to the *familia*! You are a cheater and a liar, an ungrateful son, and no fancy university degree can right the wrong you did to me. I want all the rest of the money you stole from me, right now, and you can return that truck and bring me that money too. I will be the laughingstock of the village! *Oh, your boy bought you a truck, Arturo. Does it come with a gas allowance?*" Arturo mimicked. "You are an ungrateful son. Not only do you steal from the family but now you also want to take away our main income. It was me who got you that job. I should have let one of your brothers have it and never let you go off to that school. But you would have stolen and sold the eggs and the milk from the goats so you could buy fancy sneakers and then think you could bribe your *papá* with a truck." Arturo spat on the ground and turned on his heel, leaving his son standing at the threshold of his own home.

Bewildered, Rafael slowly bent down and picked up the keys. He thought he had done the right thing by helping out his dad and his family. That way, he would feel better leaving the homestead and going to Morelia to study. But his well-intentioned charity had the opposite effect, causing his dad to lose face. Rafael returned the truck and took a considerable loss, and then shamefacedly handed over the shoebox with the rest of his money in several denominations.

But his dad still wasn't happy. "I know there is more. I know how much money those gringos give you for tips. I talk to the other guides and know exactly how much money you make."

"No, *Papá*, I swear by the Virgin and all the *santos* that I have no more. I gave you everything."

"You lied once, you stole twice and now the third time you insult the Virgin and the *santos*, which will surely land you in hell for all eternity. You are no longer welcome in this house and are my son no longer."

In order to re-establish his authority in the eyes of his peers, he thus cast Rafael out of his parental home, despite the laments from his mother and sisters. Rafael couldn't understand the world anymore. Not only had he underestimated his papa's fierce pride and undermined his authority as head of the family, but he had also jeopardized the future he had envisioned for himself. Rafael left, penniless and outcast from his own home.

Luckily, Rafael's high school teacher was aware of what had happened and took Rafael under his wing. His teacher told him that although he had done the right thing by saving the money for university, he had made the wrong decision in buying that cursed truck for his papa.

The teacher had a sister in Morelia, and he assured Rafael he would have room and board in return for some menial work around the place, and with his scholarship in place, he could at least get through his first year of study. If he excelled, the rest would follow.

Rafael clandestinely said goodbye to his *mamacita* and his sisters, who were equally heartbroken at this turn of events, and took an awkward leave from his brothers, who wished him well.

He sat in the back of a battered old pickup truck, looking at the receding hills and cornfields of El Rosario through a lens of hot tears. In Angangueo he boarded the bus to the big city of Morelia.

Seven long years were to pass before Rafael would return to El Rosario.

Rafael took to life at UNAM, the Universidad Nacional Autónoma de México, in Morelia, like a fish to the sea. The vibrant and stimulating atmosphere on campus was a new world compared with his sheltered upbringing in El Rosario and Angangueo. The language remained the same, but every other aspect was markedly different. Rafael enrolled in some English, history and social studies courses, not yet sure where his ambitions would lead him. He was shy by nature but determined to succeed.

Students came from all parts of Mexico to study in Morelia, mostly from well-off families in the city itself, while a few made the leap out of some small village by way of bursaries and scholarships, like Rafael. In the intellectual enclave of academia, parental status meant little, and Rafael was accepted as an individual. It spelled a newfound freedom. No more kowtowing, no more submission, no more small-town restrictions and jostling for social status.

In this cosmopolitan atmosphere, even the stature of the Virgin of Guadalupe and Santo Rosario diminished, and they were to a large degree left behind in the recesses of his boyhood psyche and in the pious, rarefied air of the Sierra Nevada of central Mexico. There was nothing to be ashamed of and nothing to ask forgiveness for. All that mattered was the new relationships, the endless discussions about Mexican and international politics and, of course, girls. Never in his life had Rafael seen so many beautiful girls all in one place. In the first eighteen years of his life, the women around him were his mother, his sisters and the village girls, few of whom were his age and none of whom meant anything more to him than another sister or cousin.

But being poor limited his social activities, so Rafael immersed himself in his studies and took walks around the old city of Morelia. *Señora* Álvarez, his old professor's sister, lived in a narrow flat on the third floor of an old colonial building in the historic part of town. Rafael loved the old town. *Tía* Ana, as she insisted Rafael call her, worked as a law clerk for the city. Unmarried and childless, she took pleasure in showing the young man around. Rafael became particularly enamoured of the murals of Alfredo Zalce, tableaus of Morelia's history that graced many public buildings in the historic part of town. Rafael thought Zalce's earthy, vivid colours and harmonious compositions captured the essence of the Michoacán aesthetic.

• • •

On July 2, 1988, less than seventy-two hours before the Mexican presidential elections, the bloodied bodies of Francisco Xavier Ovando and Roman Gil Heraldez, political aides to the presidential candidate of the Party of the Democratic Revolution (PRD), Cuauhtémoc Cárdenas, were found by the police in Ovando's car in the Tránsito district of Mexico City. Ovando had died instantly from five bullets to the head, Heraldez from a single shot. These brutal slayings sent shock waves through Mexico, and Rafael and his fellow students talked about nothing else.

"This is what happened," Hernan, a politically savvy classmate explained to Rafael. "The four opposition parties formed an alliance in preparation for the election, running only one candidate — Cuauhtémoc Cárdenas — to avoid splitting the vote." That made sense to Rafael, but after the election, the government shut down the Federal Electoral Commission computer systems and refused to broadcast the results. A member of the Cárdenas coalition cracked the code from the government computers and shared the election results. A week later Carlos Salinas de Gortari, the head of the Institutional Revolutionary Party (PRI) was awarded 50.2 percent of the vote. Tens of thousands of partially burned ballots marked for Cárdenas were found floating in rivers or smoldering in garbage dumps. Salinas de Gortari was a Harvard-trained economist known to be connected to the illicit drug trade. The doctored figures stating that he won incensed every student on campuses across Mexico. Numerous reports of fraudulent election practices kept turning up, but Salinas de Gortari remained el *Presidente*[1].

Demonstrations erupted. Rafael, like many of his fellow students, felt betrayed and enraged by the hijacking of the president's office, and he joined the numerous protests on campus and in downtown Morelia. He was appalled by the way police kicked and lashed out indiscriminately with batons at the mostly young demonstrators. When tear-gas grenades exploded with a dull thud just behind Rafael, his eyes instantly flooded with searing tears, and he ran blindly along with the rest of the screaming crowd, until he found himself in the Plaza de Armas and pressed himself against one of the big old trees for protection.

After he witnessed his friend Hernan get brutally beaten by police for doing nothing but holding an election poster of Cárdenas, Rafael lost his appetite for mass political protests. He thought them necessary but futile, and he had no stomach for violence. Across the country the demonstrations were brutally squashed. In universities, students were threatened with expulsion. Over the next two years, more than sixty journalists and opposition figures were murdered. Rafael vowed to work for social and political justice through other means and to avoid the adrenaline-fuelled front lines.

"Is political upheaval and violence in Mexico, and for that matter in all of Latin America, as certain and at the same time as unpredictable as the annual hurricanes and floods?" Rafael later wrote in an essay. The question was rhetorical. Some blamed the hot Latino blood, others the scorching weather and the spicy chilies, and some unfailingly pointed to the imperial might of the industrial north as a catalyst for the persistent cycle of violence in

---

1   According to a deposition ten years later by a Colombian drug dealer at a Swiss inquiry into the $132 million the president's brother, Rafael Salinas, had deposited in Swiss banks, members of a Colombian drug cartel allegedly funnelled $200,000 into the campaign of Carlos Salinas de Gortari. The money was given to his brother Rafael to protect drugs shipped through Mexico, and Rafael received $300,000 for each cocaine shipment he protected.

Mexican history. Rafael's own speculations were a lot more cynical. He knew from personal experience that money and greed ruled the grand political arenas as well as the family barnyards.

Rafael resolved to keep his head down and concentrate on his studies. After two years, halfway through his liberal arts degree, he switched to journalism, with a major in communications and broadcasting. Rafael had found his niche, where he could apply his interest in language, politics and history and his newfound passion: radio. He spent many hours listening to broadcasts on Señora Alvarez's short-wave radio, which received signals from as far away as the US, as well as most of Latin America and Mexico. Rafael had a voice, deep, resonant and smooth. When he spoke, people listened, no matter what the subject — it was the tone of his voice that seduced his audience. It was a gift that set Rafael apart, a sleeping talent that he needed to develop and embrace, but he was more interested in politics than music, and being a shy mountain boy, he was not comfortable being the centre of attention.

Chapter 2
Gabriela

Gabriela María Ramírez was born five minutes ahead of her brother, Lionel, in the Manzanillo General Hospital, in the midst of the hurricane season in the summer of '69. Gabriela's father, Rodolfo Eduardo Ramírez, was well known in the town of Punta de San Juan, a hundred kilometres south of Manzanillo, just inside the boundary of Michoacán. He was a businessman who had transformed his destiny through his own will.

Rodolfo had started his working life the day his dad took him out on the boat and let him help sort the fish, disentangling the catch from the tight net. Rodolfo's father had also been a fisherman, following in the footsteps of his own dad, who had inherited the baton of responsibility in a timeless relay through the generations. Rodolfo's father's boat had capsized in a vicious February storm. The fourteen-year-old Rodolfo had been on the boat but had managed to lash himself to an empty fuel barrel. The other men on board, including his father, drowned while Rodolfo bobbed up and down like a cork for many hours, hanging on. He was picked up by another fishing boat, exhausted and dehydrated but miraculously alive. Consequently, Rodolfo's mom moved in with her brother-in-law's family, along with young Rodolfo, whose days as a fisherman were over, breaking a tradition that went back many generations.

Instead, Rodolfo helped his uncle Carlos mend boats and motors, and developed a knack for spotting opportunities. He convinced his tío to purchase unwanted motors and leaky boats for a pittance. Rodolfo then restored these derelicts, and Carlos sold them and pocketed the profits. That way Rodolfo earned his keep and kept his mother safe.

But Rodolfo wanted more out of life than fixing boats and engines for his uncle, and when he was only eighteen, he recognized his chance when an ice plant opened up in his village. He knew that most of the fish ended up in markets in the larger centres and that most fishermen were beholden to their primary contacts, middlemen who bought the daily catch at rock-bottom prices straight off the boats and then sold it for large profits to their own contacts, merchants and restaurants up and down the coast, sometimes even destroying part of the catch to drive prices higher. Those were the days of abundant fish and easy hauls, and by the time the fish ended up on the family's dinner plates, the price was ten times what the fishermen earned.

Rodolfo knew the way the system worked, but nobody questioned the status quo, afraid of inviting unpleasant repercussions. Whenever Rodolfo pointed out to his uncle the unfairness the fishermen were subjected to, Tío Carlos always dismissed his concerns, pointing out that that was the way it had always been, and why fix a working system? "Leave it alone, Rodolfo. Don't tickle the sleeping serpent."

Rodolfo didn't just want to tickle the serpent, he wanted to kick it in the head. He made no secret of his opinion that the fishermen were getting ripped off by the dealers and middlemen.

"Don't start something you cannot finish," his uncle warned him more than once. But Rodolfo, with his youthful impatience and rebellious nature, wouldn't keep quiet about the injustice. Nacho (short for Ignacio), an old grizzled fisherman and friend of his dad, warned him, "If you don't shut up, the *terceros* (middlemen) will do it for you."

These threats and intimidations had the opposite effect on the young man. They made him furious. But he swallowed his pride and kept his cool, not because he was giving in but because he didn't want to jeopardize his uncle and by extension his family. He knew his time would come. Now, more than ever, he was determined to climb out of his economic and social trap.

When the *hielo* (ice) plant opened, Rodolfo called a clandestine meeting with some of the village's young fishermen. They met at the Sala de Pescadores, the ramshackle fishermen's hall behind the church, and Rodolfo presented his plan of cutting out the middlemen. "We cut out the *terceros*, we double our money. That's the bottom line, *compadres*." Despite misgivings and fears of reprisals, everybody liked the concept of independence and better returns for their labours. They collectively raised enough money, which they lent to Rodolfo.

Rodolfo finally convinced Tío Carlos, and with his uncle's blessing and a loan from his peers, he bought a second-hand two-ton truck and a pallet jack. He had half a dozen strong wooden crates built, which he loaded onto the back of the truck. Then Rodolfo drove it to the *hielo* plant and bought his first load of ice, which he evenly distributed into the crates and then covered with straw. Very early the next morning, long before daybreak and before any of the other fish buyers were around, he was parked on the beach waiting for the first boats to come in.

When the orange sun climbed into the pink and blue eastern sky, Rodolfo's truck, full of fresh fish and ice, was en route to Guadalajara, a long, dangerous climb up a winding, narrow road. He sold his first truckload of fresh fish to a local distributor, who promised to buy all Rodolfo could bring in. When Rodolfo returned a day later, he paid the fishermen double what they usually received for their labour. He himself kept a hefty percentage for his operation.

He bought up fish not only from his village but from all the other neighbouring villages along the Michoacán coast. At first some of the local fish merchants and middlemen threatened war, but instead of fighting them, Rodolfo won them over by treating them as partners on a percentage basis. "Sell me the fish you buy from the boats and I'll distribute it. Less headache and work for you finding customers and transporting the fish, losing half of it to the heat and unsold leftovers. I'll pay you less per kilo, but I'll buy all you bring me." Fairness was the key to his success, and that way nobody lost out. For every fish caught and sold, Rodolfo got his few pesos, and over the next ten years Rodolfo Ramírez became a very wealthy man.

Before too long he had made enough to repay all the borrowed money with interest, and he had enough left over to buy another truck, and then another, until he had a whole fleet of trucks. Two years later he opened his own ice plant.

Rodolfo married Isabel, the oldest daughter of his Guadalajara distributor, and thus cemented a union that shaped the fortunes and lives of both families. Nine months after their lavish wedding, Isabel gave birth to Teresa; then followed Amanda, and two years later a set of twins, a girl and a boy. They named the girl Gabriela María, after her grandmother, and the boy Lionel, in honour of Rodolfo's father.

The Ramírez children never lacked anything materially. They were brought up in a strict Mexican tradition, taught to fear and obey their father and God, in that order, respect their fellow man, and learn all there was to know, because, as their mother repeated over and over, "Knowledge is the key to freedom, especially for a woman."

Rodolfo's steadfast, strict morality and adherence to fairness made him a popular man, in stark contrast to other wealthy Mexicans who bribed and cheated their way to the top. Many Mexicans believed wealth was a privilege bestowed upon the rich by divine intervention, with no social or moral responsibilities attached. Gabriela's father imparted a different philosophy to those close to him. He rejected the belief that wealth begat power and that the poor had only themselves to blame for their shortcomings. The Mexican mandarin class, mostly of Spanish descent, had come to power with the cross in one hand and the sword in the other. Eventually the sword was replaced by the *mordida* (bribe), by which politicians as well as bureaucrats were controlled. Power and wealth were passed down through the generations, as were the relationships between the powerful and wealthy families, creating and maintaining a rigid class structure.

Rodolfo Ramírez had the pride of a self-made man, though he never saw himself as privileged and treated other people as equals. What mattered to Rodolfo was their honesty and their desire to make the best of their resources, and their sense of community and family. Rodolfo built two schools and sponsored a medical clinic. He fronted business loans and donated money to help renovate the old church in Punta de San Juan, on the Michoacán coast.

His wife, Isabel, was small of stature but big of heart. She'd never had a chance to fulfill her own dreams, which were known only to her. She was mostly devoted to raising her three girls and one errant boy, Lionel, the black sheep of the Ramírez family.

While benevolent and tolerant with strangers, Rodolfo was a tyrant with his own family. He had no intention of letting any member of his family slip back into the muck of poverty. He placed all his offspring into private schools, where they could mingle with the aristocracy. When Lionel was reprimanded for missing classes, Rodolfo was livid. "I've raised my family from poverty to respectability, and I intend to keep it that way!"

Lionel had shown his wild streak when he was still a boy, always in trouble and fights. In high school, gambling became his vice, which soon landed him in debt. Rodolfo grudgingly bailed his son out more than once, hoping against his better judgment that Lionel would snap out of it once past adolescence, but Lionel's habits just got worse as time went on.

Lionel's only confidante was his twin sister, who helped him out of trouble more often than she cared to recall. Lionel wasn't malicious or evil. To the contrary, he was good-natured and big-hearted, like his twin, but he loved the lure of easy money, and in time he became hooked on the adrenaline rush a win — or a loss, for that matter — supplied.

While Gabriela was studying in Guadalajara in her first year of law school, Lionel, only nineteen, began his short career running cocaine up and down the coast between Punta de San Juan and Manzanillo. He went all the way to Puerto Vallarta and from there eventually to Tijuana, and even across the line to San Diego, where the real money was. When he came home for Easter in 1989, flush with cash and driving a brand-new black Jeep Wrangler, Rodolfo lost his temper and took a baseball bat to the Jeep. "You will not disgrace this family any longer with your drug money and gambling debts! You are no longer my son!"

Gabriela drove her brother to the bus depot, imploring him to consider changing his renegade ways.

"I'll be all right. Don't worry about me. I don't need *Papá*'s money. I have one very big job to do, and after that I can buy a business, maybe a dive shop in Puerto Vallarta or a charter boat. I'll be in touch with you and *Mamá*."

On a hot August night that summer, Lionel was found dead — shot in the head and tossed over the bank along the main road north of Puerto Vallarta.

Gabriela's world crumbled. She dropped into a black hole of despair and self-recrimination, walking for hours on end along the rugged shore and then lying on her bed staring vacantly at the ceiling. She didn't eat or talk and avoided the silent, morose spectre of her papa.

"I could have saved Lionel if I had been a better sister," Gabriela cried desperately while her mama held her to her bosom and quietly stroked her head. Only the unwavering love of her mama, whose inner strength held the family together, kept Gabriela from falling over the edge herself.

Rodolfo walked through the large house not speaking to anybody, filled with silent rage, shame, and grief, and he refused to speak his son's name.

Slowly over the long hot summer, Gabriela regained some of her former strength, and by September, instead of returning to the

Universidad Panamericana in Guadalajara, she opted for a change in direction, wanting to dedicate her life to a more worthwhile cause than the dry and exalted study of the law.

Gabriela had inherited her father's compassion and tenacious nature, and she became a sworn enemy of organized crime and big government, which in Mexico was often one and the same. She believed her ambitions would be best served through the established media, believing in the old adage that if you can't fight them from the outside, fight them from the inside. Gabriela Ramírez enrolled in a two-year program for communication and broadcasting at the Universidad Nacional Autónoma de México (UNAM), in Morelia.

• • •

Gabriela's mane of blue-black hair suggested Indigenous ancestry, her onyx eyes and long lashes betrayed a Moorish influence, and her bronze skin and high cheekbones were evidence of her Spanish genes. Like her mama, she was small of stature but large of spirit. *She is beautiful*, flashed through Rafael's mind when Carlos, a fellow student, introduced them on the steps of the library. It was an overcast day in early October — October 4, 1989, to be exact — but when Gabriela stood before Rafael, with her slim hand in his for a greeting, Rafael's whole mental state underwent a phase shift into a higher gear of awareness. Suddenly the colours appeared brighter, as if the grass, flowers, and tile roofs had been recently washed by rain. Carlos must have said something funny, but it escaped Rafael, whose senses were taken over by the petite, vivacious young woman in front of him. Her throaty laugh at Carlos's joke was celestial music to his ears, and her smile lit up her face and radiated warmth and passion that enthralled him completely.

Gabriela also took an instant liking to the handsome young man from the Michoacán mountains. His eyes shone like obsidian and his voice flowed like honey when he introduced himself, his firm hand lingering just a fraction longer in hers than was customary. They seemed to meet everywhere on the extensive grounds of the campus: in the library, the cafeteria or the lecture hall, on the grassy knoll behind the citadel, or in the vast courtyard full of exotic plants and multi-tiered clay fountains where she often sat and read. When their eyes met across the hubbub of activity around them, she quickly averted her gaze, turning crimson and feeling like she had just been touched, but in a pleasant way. She could recognize Rafael's slender form from a long way off by the way he moved, without any shifting in his upper body. He glided like a dancer or a skater, which enabled him to move through crowds and spaces unnoticed, like a shadow. They had some friends in common, but they deliberately avoided being alone together out of fear of not knowing what to say or how to act. And yet they always found themselves in proximity to each other.

Rafael didn't know anything about Gabriela's family. According to Carlos, she came from one of the wealthiest families in the state of Michoacán, "without being tied to the drug trade or politics." Neither did Gabriela know anything about Rafael's background. It wouldn't have mattered to her that Rafael came from a poor mountain village with nothing but his dreams, his will to succeed, and a basic scholarship. Gabriela didn't consider herself rich, just lucky, and Rafael didn't consider himself poor, just strapped for cash.

Rafael was standing at the checkout counter in the library with a book in his hand, when Gabriela suddenly appeared behind him and pointed at the book. "Oh, I came to check that book out too. What a coincidence."

Rafael felt the blood rush into his head and spluttered, "Oh, I'm sorry. I'll let you have it. I mean, if you really need it."

"Oh no," Gabriela said brightly. "But that's very nice of you. Maybe we can share it and study together here in the library." Gabriela had a natural, straightforward way about her, a trait she had her dad to thank for.

"Yes, we could do that. In fact, I would like that very much," he stammered. "I'm not sure if you remember my name."

"It's Rafael, I remember," she said with a sunny smile.

"Yes, Rafael Pasqual Monrovia. And you're Gabriela."

"Gabriela María Ramírez. Pleased to meet you again."

They sat in the library together and looked at the book they both needed to read for their broadcast journalism class. It was written in English, and Rafael was able to show off his language skills.

"Where did you learn English? Surely not up in the mountains," Gabriela teased him.

"I've taken English since I came to Morelia, and I learned a little bit from the tourists in El Rosario," Rafael admitted. "But you're not bad yourself."

"My dad insisted on all of us learning English. 'English is the language of money,' he would say, 'and Spanish is the language of the soul.'" Gabriela consequently was enrolled in English classes from an early age, and her dad used to bring home American comic books and always had American newspapers lying around the house.

When Gabriela told this to Rafael, he just shook his head and said, "I'd like to meet your dad someday."

"Yes, that would be nice," Gabriela said, turning away, embarrassed, when the implications of her remark dawned on her.

Luckily, her discomfiture escaped Rafael, whose mind wandered back to his mountains, thinking how much he would like to bring Gabriela to El Rosario and show her the miracle of the butterflies.

From that day on, they studied and hung out together as much as their busy schedule allowed, balancing the social high-wire act of their porcelain love. Gabriela loved listening to Rafael. His golden voice with its resonant timbre enthralled her. They also shared a passion for the underprivileged in society, and both wanted to do their bit to make Mexico a more equal society, though they came at the problem from opposite directions.

Rafael's conviction sprang from his rural roots and from a deep well of resentment against authority and government, who only and always seemed to stand in the way of his people's trying to better themselves. The mountain *campesinos*, many of them with Indigenous ancestry, were like the forgotten tribe. They tilled the soil and tended the livestock, they worked the mines and in the mills, and often the men had to leave home to toil in the *maquiladoras*, the American-owned assembly plants in so-called free zones up along la *línea* (the US border), which paid minimum wages for back-breaking, monotonous labour.

"My people are the modern slaves," Rafael explained to Gabriela. "I want the rich employers to contribute to Mexican society, pay their fair share in taxes so we can build schools and hospitals and provide health care and education. They could start by supplying running water and electricity to everyone."

Even slaves had it better, Rafael had passionately argued in a paper on social inequality before he knew Gabriela. *At least the slave masters had to house their chattel and make sure they were healthy and reasonably fit. The sweatshops provide no such basics. They pay poverty wages and provide no security, no opportunities, no way out of the misery trap, just threats of retaliation and empty promises.*

His professor gave him only a C+ and added, *Excellent writing, but substantiate your claims, verify and quote your sources and reserve judgment. Too much passion — not enough facts.*

When Rafael showed Gabriela these comments, she just laughed. "The professor liked you, otherwise he wouldn't have made those remarks."

Gabriela didn't disagree, but her passion sprang from a more personal source. She had witnessed poverty in her village, although from afar; she had witnessed how people used and exploited the weakest in society. She believed that her brother's death had been caused by people willing to exploit and even kill others for money, but she didn't tell Rafael about Lionel; those scars had not yet healed enough. Despite her privileged upbringing, her passion to make the world a better place was as real as Rafael's.

Gabriela's social conscience had its roots in the simple convictions her father had instilled in her. Rodolfo had never missed an opportunity to point out that he would still be a fisherman if not for his own tenacity and determination. "If I had waited for the government or anybody else to change things for the better, I would still be a poor fisherman, dependent on the weather and the middlemen."

Rafael disagreed with her father's libertarian philosophy, which enshrined the basic law of the jungle: Only the strong survive, and the weak go under. "If everyone was a fighter, society would be pure chaos," Rafael said. "Your dad believes in a society where the strong can win and be successful. That's because of what he did with his life. We have to go one step further and provide opportunities for all."

But Gabriela saw how her dad had been able to better the lives of the villagers and fishermen in her town, not by sharing or distributing his money but by providing them with jobs and opportunities, and she held firm to her conviction that in order to succeed one had to forge one's own destiny.

Although modern and educated, both Rafael and Gabriela remained old-fashioned and morally grounded by tradition. Gabriela's upbringing had been shaped by the strict morality and righteousness of her dad, while Rafael wanted to break free of the traditional bonds of rural poverty and religion. These parameters guided their physical relationship into virtuous and quaintly romantic territory. Rafael's fantasy and desire for Gabriela remained forbidden fruit for a couple of reasons. The first one was their differing beliefs. Gabriela had been raised a strict Catholic and was a believer, while Rafael professed himself to be an agnostic, not having any love or respect for the power of the cross, and the Catholic Church in particular. He'd studied the bloody history of the Church's Mexican conquest, the spread of diseases, the spilled blood of Indigenous people and the sanctimonious Book offered as solace to a decimated and enslaved population. Rafael had given up on God a long time ago, but he tolerated Gabriela's beliefs because he knew how much hold the Church had on his compatriots.

The second impediment to their love lay in their class difference. Gabriela would never admit that money or class had any hold over her true feelings. She insisted in her own mind that her dad, although strict and traditional, was also fair; but would he accept a poor *campesino* from the mountains into his family? Gabriela chided herself for even thinking thoughts like this, because she knew the answer.

Rafael didn't trust Mexico's elite — even its self-made elite. He knew the fervour with which the wealthy guarded their kin, often to the point that many an unacceptable suitor had mysteriously disappeared. Rafael quietly became convinced that if he ever acted on his infatuation, only tragedy would follow. They steered clear of these conflicting personal differences but argued passionately in general terms.

Gabriela didn't fully understand Rafael's reservations about religion, which he didn't like to talk about. He remained respectful and never criticized her beliefs or social standing. Although they never openly talked about their mutual feelings, she could sense his devotion and adoration, as well as his reluctance and distance. She would have scoffed at the idea that her father's money or her beliefs would come between them. She wanted to believe that if she ever met the right man for her heart, both her father and God would accept her choice.

But she didn't say anything like that to Rafael. Their mutual love was a delicate matter, kept in a bubble. Many a night both of them lay awake in their separate beds, thinking of the other. Gabriela would dream about Rafael, would find herself floating with him across the silvery surface of a lake, the two of them twirling and turning into each other, their faces and bodies touching and melting together. Then she would wake up in a state of confusion, sweaty, lonely, sad.

They spent a lot of time walking the university grounds, and often sat on a favourite bench underneath an ancient beech tree with a traditional white-painted trunk. They talked about their hopes for the country's future and always the politics of the day. It was on a warm Friday evening when most of the students had already left for the weekend that Gabriela told Rafael about her brother's tragic life. "I could have been a better sister," she concluded, unable to help the tears spilling down her cheeks.

Rafael had just listened, and he draped a protective arm around her shoulders, holding her close and letting her cry. It was then that Rafael confessed his harsh breakup with his dad and how it had all come to pass.

"He'll come around when he sees what you're achieving, Rafael," she tried to reassure him, but Rafael just sadly shook his head.

"You don't know my dad, stubborn like a mule and proud like a bull."

Gabriela took his hand in hers. "Your *papá* sounds a lot like mine." They sat there for what seemed like an eternity, and when Gabriela turned her head to look at her friend, he awkwardly moved to kiss her.

It was not a kiss of passion but one of restraint, however full of desire and longing. Gabriela squeezed his hand and then they both let go.

Tradition and religion, status and naiveté were formidable hurdles in the way of their young love, and sacrifice was part of their inbred discipline. They did not stray as easily from their traditions and conventions as their American or European contemporaries who valued libido over customs and doctrines. This was Mexico, where the most revered saints were virgins.

One of their class assignments involved pairing each student with a partner, and together they had to pick opposite sides of a historical subject, person or situation. Good against bad, old against young, yesterday against today. They could choose to present their treatment as a play or in the form of a live broadcast or as a historic oral review in front of the class. It had to be half an hour long and would be judged by their peers as well as their professors.

Naturally Rafael and Gabriela teamed up, and after discarding several ideas they chose a historic theme and settled on something close to home. They picked two historic figures and presented them in the form of an alternating "black and white" dialogue, presenting their actions, their philosophies and their conclusions.

Both Nuño Beltrán de Guzmán, a former captain in Hernán Cortés's army, and Vasco de Quiroga, the visionary Spanish lawyer and bishop, were well-known protagonists in Mexican lore, particularly in Michoacán.

The first was a bloodthirsty, brutal *conquistador* who hacked a trail of misery like a deep wound across central Mexico, the latter a benevolent philosopher whose utopian experiment in socialism saved the decimated Indigenous people from extinction. Those two characters provided perfect opposing subjects for their project.

Their collaboration stood as a fine example of making Mexican history relevant to the present and provided an analogy to the struggles going on right now in many parts of the modern world. Rafael read Nuño Guzmán's part — the "black" side — while Gabriela took the "white" side — Vasco de Quiroga's history, deeds and philosophy. The conclusion, which took into account the impact both men had had right up to the present day, was presented by Rafael in his golden, irresistible voice.

Gabriela and Rafael's presentation, embellished with pictures and maps, both historical and current, was a great success. They were given a standing ovation, complete with hoots and whistles, from their fellow students and received the highest accolades from their professor.

Both Rafael and Gabriela had been raised in the state of Michoacán, although she by the tropical seashore and he in the rugged mountains. Morelia, the state's capital, with its bustling atmosphere, suited them. They felt at home in this historical city and proud of its colonial and precolonial architecture, evident in the government buildings, the opera house and of course the university buildings, which were vibrant and alive with young people like themselves. They felt part of the city's tapestry, but remained anonymous. Nobody but their fellow students, their landlords and professors knew them. They enjoyed this freedom and frequently wandered the city's old streets together, often along the old viaduct.

They spent many hours just sitting in the cafés lining the Plaza Melchor Ocampo, where they had a perfect view of the Palacio de Gobierno, which used to be a seminary in the mid-1700s. They sat incognito alongside local and foreign visitors, and Rafael always walked Gabriela home. Gabriela had found lodging with family friends who lived in a stately mansion not far from the university, while Rafael lodged with Tía Ana on the east side of the city. They always parted at the gate to the grounds, not with a kiss but with a promise to meet up again the next day.

They both graduated with honours, and the summer, as well as the rest of their lives, loomed before them like a vast blank canvas. They decided to prolong their companionship and go for a one-week sojourn to Pátzcuaro, to explore the area of their "black and white" project on the ground. Such went their intellectual excuse. The truth, of course, was that they wanted to spend time together, away from everybody who knew them.

Chapter 3

In Between

Rafael and Gabriela got off the bus in Pátzcuaro next to the bustling Plaza Gertrudis Bocanegra, named for the heroine who was tortured and executed for supporting the independence movement in 1817. Her statue and the black stump of the tree she was allegedly shot against still grace a corner of the plaza. This pretty, tree-lined square was filled with shoe shiners and street vendors, clowns, buskers and hawkers, while all around cars jockeyed for position, guided by the shrill whistles of traffic cops.

The two young friends were immediately charmed by the town's colonial character, the uniform brown and white colour scheme and lettering of business names in the centro histórico. Under the high arches covering the sidewalks, vendors of pastries, records and magazines crowded each other in makeshift stands. Indigenous Purépechas, the women in their traditional blue and black striped shawls and braided hair, the men with felt hats and

mingled with businesspeople in suits, school kids in
ns, young women in high heels and fashionable clothes,
go tourists and local townsfolk.

"Look at this." Gabriela pulled Rafael by the arm and pointed
to one of the many shops surrounding both main plazas, selling
traditional weavings.

"Let's sit down here," Rafael said, pulling out a chair for
Gabriela in one of the many sidewalk cafes. They ordered a hot
chocolate, a specialty of the town, and took in the colourful bustle
around them. Rafael could see himself idling away the hours just
watching people.

They walked into the Biblioteca Gertrudis Bocanegra on the
north side of the Plaza Chica and were fascinated by the powerful
mural by Juan O'Gorman that takes up the whole back wall, depicting the violent history of Michoacan from the time of the Conquest
to the present day. Much of the graphic renderings of slaughter,
upheaval and conversions, as well as the tall, saintly figure of Don
Vasco de Quiroga surrounded by the Indios, was familiar to both of
them from their recent research for their project. From the library
they ventured into the mercado and looked at the local pottery,
masks, and hand-carved wooden kitchen implements. "Look at all
this stuff," Gabriela said, amazed at the cramped and lively space.
"And here you can get any kind of fruit or vegetable," said Rafael,
pointing to precarious pyramids of tomatoes, onions, oranges and
avocados. To the west of the library, they checked out Pátzcuaro's
Teatro Emperador Caltzontzin, which had been converted from a
former convent in 1936. They felt like regular tourists, fascinated
by all the foods and crafts, and giddy with excitement.

They held hands, comfortably and automatically. They had to
decide on lodgings, and found themselves standing in the front
lobby of the Hotel Los Escudos, stammering and feeling like kids
trapped in the adult section. They hadn't rehearsed this part, and
when Gabriela insisted on paying for the double room — she
emphasized two beds — Rafael protested feebly but to no avail.

They stood in the doorway, surveying the large room with
the traditional high, woven-wood ceiling interspersed with ancient

hand-hewn timbers. The room was appointed with traditional local furniture and fixtures. Their eyes were drawn to the centrepiece, a carved wooden four-poster bed with a colourful painted headboard depicting intertwining flowers and birds. The woven bedspread was a bright red, yellow and blue, and on each side stood an intricately carved pine night table. A round painted wooden table and four leather chairs sat against the window overlooking the lush courtyard with a large fountain in the centre. Local woven rugs were spread over the wooden plank floors, and a red brick fireplace added to the joyful colour scheme. The bathroom was finished with hand-painted tiles, with an ornamental ceramic sink and terracotta floors. Neither one of them wanted to point out that there was no second bed.

The hotel and the lovely room were an extravagant luxury for Rafael, but Gabriela didn't want to talk about money or Rafael's lack of it, and that was that. They were both starved, and after dropping off their bags they headed straight for the restaurant downstairs, adjacent to the courtyard. They dined on *sopa tarasca* and *pescado blanco*, both local specialties, accompanied by a celebratory bottle of red wine.

After dinner they strolled across the lively plaza, listening to the music emanating from the various cafés and restaurants spread out along the cobblestoned perimeter, underneath the tall arches supporting the Spanish colonial-style mansions. The twelve graceful palaces surrounding the plaza Don Vasco de Quiroga were built by a dozen noble Spanish families that had been invited by Don Vasco to make their homes in Pátzcuaro. The two young friends sat on the whitewashed stone benches, taking in the lively atmosphere. Over on one side, dancers dressed like old men with masks and sticks danced a circular pattern in wooden clogs; young lovers, hand in hand, old men and whole families strolled by; shoe-shine boys on wooden crates waited for customers; one man in a clown suit sold balloons, and kids were trying out their bicycles and latest toys. Rafael and Gabriela walked hand in hand around the plaza in silence, enjoying each other's company but at the same time delaying the inevitable.

After a couple of glasses of Don Pedro brandy — more than they had ever drunk — they returned to their hotel room with most of their steadfast self-control melted away and their inhibitions drowned. After fighting the temptation for so long, they finally succumbed with equal zeal and passion and crashed into each other with all the abandon of their youth and innocence. They tore off each other's clothes and fell onto the ornate bed, socks and shirts, belts and hairclips strewn all over the floor, all inhibitions melting away. They made love with wild enthusiasm, clumsy and impatient, then more slowly, exploring with pleasure, laughing and cajoling until they lay there, exhausted, happy, draped around each other, arms and legs intertwined like vines, and fell asleep.

When they woke up, it was noon. The sun filtered into their cozy room through the heavy curtains, and rather than talk, they made love again. Later, they stepped into the sunny afternoon like astronauts who had landed on a new and exciting planet. They had discovered youth's panacea, the fountain of pleasure, the nectar of the gods. The pure ecstasy of lovemaking and exploring each other's thresholds of pleasure was indeed heady medicine. They walked around town in a trance, floating on a cloud through the narrow streets and alleys. Their senses had been recalibrated. Colours were more intense and food tasted better. Touching and feeling each other sent electric tingles all through their bodies.

They visited the tomb of Vasco de Quiroga in the Basílica de Nuestra Señora de la Salud, and later they stood hand in hand before the figure of Nuestra Señora de la Salud, sculpted out of *tatzingue* (corncob and honey paste) by Purépechas in the 16th century.

They clung to their dwindling days in Pátzcuaro, spending hours in bed or wandering aimlessly through the narrow streets, talking about their precious and tenuous love. But neither one dared talk about a future.

Gabriela knew deep down that her father, even though he saw himself as a tolerant man, would never let one of his girls marry a poor campesino, no matter how educated and noble. The stronger her love for Rafael grew, the harder it was for her to picture herself introducing him to her father. Rodolfo Ramírez had every intention of bequeathing his daughters to members of the first class, not the lowest, contrary to his proclamation that status and class didn't matter. "I worked too hard and long to let some gold-digger into the family. No matter how noble, the poor always want what we have," her stern father had preached to his daughters more than once. Only her mama would understand, but she could not go against her husband, even in matters of the heart.

During their ecstatic week in Pátzcuaro, they hoped against all reason that the more they drank from the fountain of love, the less they would crave it in the future. Time stood still and reality remained suspended.

On their last day they took the small, crowded boat to the Island of Janitzio in Lake Pátzcuaro. From the boat, they saw the villages nestled around the lake. They passed the occasional fishermen, who demonstrated their famous butterfly nets, oversized hoops raised and lowered in graceful unison. Besides craft shops, which all sold the same merchandise, and some restaurants, the main attraction was the giant statue of the Independence hero José María Morelos, Mexico's first Indigenous general. Inside the statue a circular stairway led them all the way to the raised fist, past an endless historical mural that amazed them in its scope and artistic execution. The raised fist had room enough for half a dozen people and offered a panoramic view of the island and the lake.

It started out as an idyllic day, but increasingly the spectre of their separation and departure loomed large. They held on desperately to each other in the main square, with the statue of Don Vasco de Quiroga standing in the large central fountain. Gabriela cried and Rafael clutched her in a tight embrace and never wanted to let her go.

"You don't have to go, love. We can start a life together, just us. We can do it if we really want to," Rafael pleaded.

"We promised not to go there," Gabriela said, shivering inside.

"I know, I know, but I can't help myself. You're everything I have now."

Gabriela couldn't speak. She thought of her father and felt that she should not have fallen for this lovely, sweet boy, this Peter Pan from the mountains, this guardian of the butterflies. To go against her father would fracture the family, but it would be breaking Rafael's and her heart to please her father. She shut down and became morose and distant.

Rafael didn't need her to tell him what she was thinking. He had long ago understood what she was only now coming to realize. She could not go against her father, who was still bitter about losing his only son. He would lash out with a fury that would subject her sisters and mom to a world of hurt she did not want to be responsible for.

They sat on a stone bench facing the large fountain. Pigeons were pecking the ground at their feet, and children happily splashed water on each other. Somewhere in the corner some performers danced the Old Men's Dance, but neither one of them was in the moment.

Time of course did not stand still, and it was time for them to fetch Gabriela's luggage. They moved as if in a dream. They took a cab to the bus station and Rafael took hold of her hand, but she suddenly dropped it and had to dig in her purse to find her ticket. In a state of shock, she boarded the bus that would take her first to Morelia, where she had an interview for a position at *El Sol*, the leading newspaper in the state, and from there to her village on the coast.

Rafael's bus left a couple of hours later, taking him in the opposite direction — not home to El Rosario, because his father still would not accept him, but to Oaxaca, where he had been offered a job at a radio station. Under normal circumstances, Rafael would have been thrilled with his prospects, but all of it was overshadowed by leaving behind something more precious than life itself.

• • •

In a guest bedroom at the Ramírez estate above Punta de San Juan, Bernard opened his eyes. Slowly and painfully, his surroundings came into focus through the haze inside his head. He recognized the white ceiling with the fan lazily casting strobing shadows. He quickly shut his eyes again and started wading through his foggy, doughy consciousness, not remembering much of anything.

"Water, please," he managed to croak, and again, "Water." Suddenly, even before he reopened his eyes, he felt a presence looming over him, and when his lids fluttered open, he looked into a dark-skinned, round face framed by two long thick braids, and round black eyes full of surprise. The woman instantly withdrew, yelling, "*Señorita Gabriela, está vivo!* He is alive!"

Bernard tried to move his head, but his whole body felt like a rusty Meccano set, numb and dull. He could wiggle his toes and curl his fingers, although a dull throbbing pain emanated from his right leg and his chest. Then the angular olive-skinned face of a young woman appeared in his field of vision. Her charcoal-black hair was held behind her ears with lacquered hairpins. Blue highlights danced through her hair when she moved her head. She looked worried. "Are you awake?" she asked in accented English.

"Water," Bernard croaked again through cracked lips. Magically, cool water trickled down his throat. With one hand, the woman held the glass to his lips, while the other lifted his head gently towards the precious liquid. Bernard drank greedily and then sank back, exhausted from the exertion.

"My name is Gabriela Ramírez, and you were run over by one of our trucks near Bucerias," Gabriela informed him gently.

"Oh my god," Bernard stammered. Suddenly an image of a white panel truck taking up his entire field of vision flashed through his mind. "Is this a hospital?" he managed to ask.

"No, we think it's better if you stay at our family home. We have the best doctor, and to travel to Guadalajara, where the next hospital is, was impossible for you. You would have died. I'm sorry," Gabriela said in her best English.

"How long ago?" Bernard asked. He had absolutely no sense of time or place.

"Six days ago. You have been in a coma. We thought you'd never wake up. The doctor said fifty-fifty chance. You are very lucky."

"I don't feel so lucky," Bernard groaned, and Gabriela laughed.

"I'm so happy you are awake. You will be healthy again as soon as your broken leg is healed."

"My broken leg?"

"Yes, your right leg is broken badly, but Dr. Sánchez is a very capable doctor and he made you a professional cast. Also, you broke three ribs and collapsed one lung. You also suffered a concussion; that is why the coma. Dr. Sánchez ordered at least three weeks' bed rest. No worry, Bernard, everything is in control. If you need something, Consuela will help you. She is a nurse, just for you."

"Three weeks. Oh boy. What about my truck?" Bernard was suddenly worried about his camper.

"No worries, your truck is safe. We picked it up and parked it here at the hacienda. Like I said, everything is fine. We could not find any name or address to notify anybody. Are you alone?"

Bernard thought about that for a moment. "Yes, I'm alone. No relatives, no wife, nobody."

Gabriela digested that and thought it strange. Nobody was that alone unless it was by choice. "I'm sorry to hear that," she said, and meant it. "Now I must go, but if you need anything, Consuela will be here for you. *Bienvenido a mi casa.*"

With that she left the exhausted Bernard alone to ponder his fate. His mind drifted and he fell into a deep, healthy sleep.

Bernard recovered slowly under the attentive care of Consuela. She couldn't speak one word of English, but Bernard enjoyed the chance to improve his Spanish. She fed him *pozole* and wonderful corn dishes, *tamales* and plenty of beans. Before too long Bernard was able to hobble around his room on a crutch, dragging his heavy cast around. Dr. Sanchez looked in on him regularly and insisted that bed rest was the only option with his concussion. Bernard got to know the view from his window like a familiar painting. It looked down into a Mexican courtyard with a large fountain in the centre and pathways laid out in colourful mosaics, enhanced by a dizzying array of plants and flowers, from fuchsia and cascading bougainvillea to birds of paradise. There was something soothing and comforting about a courtyard like this, and the covered verandas opening onto it made it all so private and intimate, like a sanctuary from the hectic world outside.

Gabriela dropped in over the next few days, but then she had to return to her new job in Morelia. She was writing a weekly political column for *El Sol*, propagating a rather conservative line, not at all the heady, socialist stuff of her student days, which she had pushed firmly behind her, along with her tempestuous affair with Rafael. She laboured hard to dismiss that relationship, compartmentalizing it as an episode of wild and wayward days, something surely everyone had in their closet. She tried to force herself to forget, pushing those confused feelings of love down into the furthest reaches of her heart, which sadly left it feeling empty and hardened.

Bernard liked Gabriela and was sure her tough outer shell contained a soft inner centre. She was civil to him but remained reserved and aloof, as if she was afraid, not just of him but of getting close to anyone.

She assured Bernard of all possible help from her family and made sure he lacked nothing under the Ramirez roof. When he told her of his initial plans to go to Pátzcuaro, her eyes clouded over for just a moment, but long enough for Bernard to notice.

"It's a beautiful town and you will love it. I'll be in Morelia for the next little while. I'm covering a story for the paper there," she said.

"Oh, what kind of story?" Bernard asked, his curiosity awakened.

"Well, it's a complicated affair. The Mexican Electric Utility has plans to build a nuclear power plant on Lake Pátzcuaro," Gabriela said, sounding evasive and professional.

"Sounds like a controversial issue. I guess nobody likes a nuke plant in their neighbourhood," Bernard offered lamely. He wondered if the Canadians were supplying their CANDU reactors as part of the deal, thereby spurring on the Mexicans. He didn't speak his mind, though. He saw that Gabriela represented a conservative view, and he didn't want to thwart his chances with her.

"If we want to advance as an industrial nation," Gabriela went on, "we need the energy, and it has to be generated somewhere. The Pátzcuaro region is not heavily populated, and the construction and operation of such a plant would mean a major economic boom in the region, which lives mostly off agriculture and some tourism. Anyway, it's just in the preliminary planning stages, and I'm assigned to cover the topic. If you are headed that way, I'll gladly show you around."

She abruptly got up from the chair, already regretting the spontaneous offer, and gave Consuela some rapid-fire instructions.

Bernard reflected on this strange journey that had landed him on the Ramírez estate with a broken leg. Fate had put him here, he was convinced. He had left a mundane career as a history and English teacher, an unhappy marriage and an undeserved seedy reputation behind in Ontario. This accident had surely ended his former life and marked the beginning of a new existence, a new beginning.

Dr. Sánchez eventually allowed him to read a couple of hours a day. Bernard had access to the vast family library and tried to read up about Pátzcuaro and Morelia. Thus, he learned about the bastard Nuño de Guzmán and the Renaissance man Don Vasco de Quiroga. Fascinating stuff for a history buff like Bernard.

He also read the newspapers, including Gabriela Ramírez's column. His Spanish had improved considerably over the term of his convalescence. Six weeks after his accident, Dr. Sánchez replaced his initial cast with a lighter version that enabled Bernard to hobble around the extensive *hacienda*, still on crutches, always followed by his faithful shadow Consuela, who cared for him like a mother. If it hadn't been for the discomfort of a broken leg and a smarting chest, he would have enjoyed his stay a lot more. But in a way, he was grateful, if not for the accident itself, at least for the chance to live in a Mexican household, even though the Ramírez family was not ordinary.

He met Rodolfo a couple of times. The old man was brusque, like a general, but polite and courteous, offering Bernard the run of the place. He also met the rest of the family over his long convalescence, and thus temporarily became an accepted member of the busy household.

The time came when he felt well enough to travel on. He finally took his leave, and despite being the victim of an accident that could have easily killed him, he was a bit sad to leave the comfortable surroundings of the Ramírez household and the pampering care of his personal nurse and servant Consuela.

Dr. Sánchez gave him the thumbs-up and supplied Bernard with the address of a physician in Morelia, since that's where he was heading. After saying goodbye to everybody, he clambered into his pickup truck with its piggy-back camper, which he had purchased in LA shortly after disembarking from his one-way flight from Toronto. He tucked his left leg, still in a cast, to the side and drove out of the gate, towards the coastal highway, excited to be on his way again. It was two months later than he had planned, but he was armed with a better knowledge of the language and the history of the region. He now had a destination and a purpose.

First, he would try to meet up with Randall, the camera operator from Vancouver whom he had met on the ferry from Cabo and again in San Blas on his way down the coast. They had spent a couple of tequila-fuelled nights together, and it was Randall who first told him about Morelia and Pátzcuaro.

"It's a different Mexico from the touristy coast. It's a step back in history, and the architecture and landscape are a bonanza for a camera nut like me," he said.

It now almost seemed predestined to Bernard, who had another motive to go to Morelia — he wanted to make an effort to get closer to Gabriela. He felt he had a good chance, since he already knew her whole family. Despite his recent accident, life suddenly seemed to have new meaning and spark.

Chapter 4
Radio Libre

For the first time in his life, Rafael hated his own poverty. After the painful, heart-wrenching parting with Gabriela, he cursed his roots and background. For the first couple of days after he arrived in Oaxaca, he locked himself into his Spartan hotel room, claiming a stomach ailment that made it impossible for him to leave. But he knew if he scuttled this chance of a broadcasting job because of a broken heart, his whole future would be jeopardized. After three desperate days coddling his bruised heart, he forced himself to leave his self-imposed exile. He resolved to remember the few days of bliss in Pátzcuaro as a precious treasure that belonged to him alone. Instead of succumbing to the bitterness his loss inspired, he tried to focus on the task ahead. It was the future that mattered most, he kept telling himself over and over. In time, Rafael landed back on terra firma with at least one foot on the ground.

Enrique Ortega — Rico to his friends — radio commentator, writer and activist, formally headed Radio Alban in Oaxaca, a state-sponsored experiment in "free" broadcasting. Enrique, along with his work and live-in partner Paula Sandoval, from Morelia, had hired Rafael on the basis of his entry in an essay contest at UNAM, which had been circulated amongst the students in Rafael's graduating class. Rafael wrote about the value of radio to the poor of Mexico, who often were illiterate and had no TV. Their only source of information was the radio, which gave the broadcaster a lot of power and responsibility.

Enrique finally met the mysteriously enticing voice over a cup of coffee, around the corner from Rafael's hotel. Unlike Rafael, who was unsure of who to look for, Enrique knew right away that the somewhat lost-looking slender young man had to be Rafael, their new recruit from Morelia.

"*¿Como estás?* I'm Enrique, but everyone calls me Rico," he introduced himself, curious as to what ailed the young man, who didn't seem to notice any of the pretty girls in the café. He suspected an ailment of the heart, but for now he refrained from teasing his young new associate.

Hiring a new grad was one of the station's grant stipulations. They offered Rafael the job in their government-sponsored radio station, which was supposed to devote itself to spreading the Institutional Revolutionary Party (PRI) message. But Rico and Paula had other ideas. That's why Rafael's essay, which championed the struggle of the poor and of the Indigenous peoples, seemed exactly the right fit for the two activists. That's what they planned to do with their broadcasts: expose the government's failure to improve the lives of the Indigenous and underprivileged peoples of Mexico and the state of Oaxaca, as well as the neighbouring regions of Chiapas and Michoacán. Enrique and Paula planned to feature interviews with *campesinos* and Indigenous people, as well as to have a lot of fun playing contemporary Mexican and English folk music — but they did not expect their mandate with the Mexican government to last. They had a unique opportunity and vowed to make the best of it.

Rico explained the station's official, and their o'
official, mandate to Rafael over a hearty meal of chicke
a couple of *cervezas*, improving Rafael's mood and ;
noticeably. Rafael took an immediate liking to the anin _____,
who wore his black hair in a ponytail and whose long, bony fingers
constantly tapped out an internal rhythm on the wooden coffee
table. The next day, Rafael also met the confident and outspoken
Paula, so different in her up-front modern sassiness from Gabriela.

Rafael liked his two new partners right away and felt that
this job and his new situation in Oaxaca could be exciting and
engaging. Maybe it was enough to help push his constant thoughts
of Gabriela to the back of his mind. When Enrique and Paula
confided in Rafael that they basically wanted to further their own
socialist philosophy rather than be a mouthpiece for the PRI,
Rafael became fully alert. This was indeed a fantastic opportunity,
a dream job for Rafael.

"Isn't this going to cut my job fairly short?" Rafael asked, not
with worry but with a twinkle in his eyes.

"No worries. We're good for a while," assured Paula, a natural
optimist. "It will take them some time to catch on."

The state of Oaxaca is bordered to the north by the states
of Puebla and Veracruz, to the east by Chiapas, to the west by
Guerrero, and to the south by the Pacific Ocean. Its great valleys
are located between the Sierra Madre del Sur and the Sierra Madre
de Oaxaca.

Rafael fell in love with the city of Oaxaca, which reminded him
of Pátzcuaro, only bigger, with colonial architecture and squares
rivalling those of Guadalajara and Mexico City. When he wasn't at
work up on Mount Alban, Rafael hitched a ride or took the bus
into the city and walked for hours, looking for distractions from
memories of Gabriela. He went into the imposing Santo Domingo
Temple or the massive cathedral. He gazed for hours at the striking
murals in Government Palace.

He also explored Mount Alban and the region surrounding
Oaxaca. Civilizations had flourished in this area and attained
great splendour before the arrival of Columbus. Despite the

conquest and colonization by the Spanish, the Mixtecs and the Zapotecs maintained their language, their culture, and their social organization, the products of a unique Indigenous civilization. Subsequently, all of Mexico's, and indeed Mesoamerica's, Indigenous populations were decimated by slaughter and disease, and the surviving ten percent occupied the bottom rung of the economic and social ladder to that day, despite Oaxaca being one of the richest states in Mexico. The region's expressions of culture and history were vital tourist draws, and visitors and travellers flocked there from around the globe, attracted by the state's mix of pre-Hispanic treasures and colonial patrimony, as well as by its music, dance, painting and culinary arts. But more than anything, it was the people that made Oaxaca what it was.

At nights, Rafael watched a public folk-dance performance at the venerable Macedonio Alcalá Theatre, and he stared mesmerized up into the high ceiling of the *Basílica*. He often sat on a bench in the *zócalo* (main square), listening to traditional music played by a band on the bandstand in the central gazebo. On Sundays the whole of Oaxaca came out dressed in their Sunday best, with the children along, running and playing. In short, he was a tourist and did all the things he knew Gabriela would have enjoyed as well. She was always on his mind.

• • •

The old 100-kilowatt tube transmitter (double the allowable size) was a "border blaster" — a pirate transmitter near the border, broadcasting into the US — that had been made available to Radio Albán by the federal government, who had confiscated it from whoever had owned it before. The three amigos were going to broadcast on the AM band from an old stone house on Mount Alban, near the ancient Toltec ruins high above Oaxaca. Enrique figured they could be heard all the way to Mexico City.

Rafael didn't know much about the imposing ruins of Mount Albán, with their large ball courts, pyramids and carvings, but Rico, who had studied history, knew all about them and loved the chance to show off his knowledge. "The Zapotecs completed Monte Albán, the great ceremonial centre on this flattened mountaintop, which is about 400 metres above the valley floor," he explained as they walked together through the site. "The oldest structures date back to the Formative Period and are known for the bas-relief sculptures of the Olmec dancers. The builders were obviously influenced by other cultures in Chiapas, by the Maya, and by the Teotihuacáns, who built the Pyramids of the Sun and Moon near Mexico City. The Zapotecs brought Monte Albán to its zenith somewhere between 600 and 900 AD, and because of its altitude and remoteness, it remains one of the most attractive and intact ancient sites in Mexico."

This location, away from the hubbub of the big city, couldn't have been more ideal for Rafael. A Spartan flat in the same building as the transmitter, with a cold-water tap, a fireplace and a propane stove, served as his home. The only luxury came in the form of a flush toilet. The nights could get quite cold, due to the altitude, and Rafael liked the ritual of lighting a fire; the crackling of the dry wood could often be heard in the background during live broadcasts. Practically living in the station, Rafael could guard the equipment as well as man the phone lines. Being isolated suited him just fine. The pay was minimal, but at least it was guaranteed, coming from the government, and since he had no real expenses, Rafael steadfastly saved every last penny he could.

"How did you bamboozle the Mexican government into subsidizing a radio station?" Rafael had asked Enrique the first day on the job.

Enrique had grinned. "Paula's uncle is a Member of Parliament for the PRI, and she was able to convince him that sponsoring a 'free' radio project would look good on his record, as well as being the perfect propaganda tool for the party."

"What a con!" Rafael laughed. "He fell for that?"

"Hook, line and sinker. Pedro Alvarez, that's his name, is a typical macho Mexican and proved easy prey for the beguiling charms of his niece Paula. It also helps that he has no idea that once a station is transmitting and has been granted a bandwidth, there is no controlling the contents. We will simply submit fake broadcast reports, and he will pay the bills and salaries through his party's propaganda accounts, thus subsidizing his own subversive counter-revolutionary radio program, including the most recent punk, rock and blues from America, England, Mexico and Latin America. But most importantly, we will broadcast regular interviews with local *indios, activistas* and *revolucionarios*," Enrique finished with a flair.

Rafael was dazed. Not only was he going to have fun and be paid for it, he was actually going to be involved in upstaging the notoriously corrupt PRI with one of their own scams. He under-stood that a project of this nature could only be in operation for a limited time until the game was up. But for now, here was Radio Alban in Oaxaca, broadcasting for the people, to the people!

Rafael embarked on one of the most stimulating times of his young life. He was able to play the music he liked, to broadcast his and his friends' philosophy over the airwaves and most of all, he got to talk to the people about their lives. He interviewed guests and read fan letters — yes, fan letters, because in no time at all, Radio Alban, and in particular the silky voice of its night broadcaster, had built a substantial following. This popularity didn't go unnoticed by the local political authorities, who didn't quite understand how this obviously left-wing radio station could have been allowed to come into existence in the controlled environment of Mexican politics. Who else would have handed out the broadcast licence? This was no pirate station, no sir; this was Radio Albán, officially sanctioned by the PRI.

Paula faithfully submitted monthly reports to the government, which they promptly paid for. She diligently shored up commercial support for the station by selling advertising and even courting the opposition parties to come onside. The more popular support they could muster, the harder it would be to shut them down. For the time being, they took full advantage of their opportunity to broadcast uncensored and unconstrained programming.

Rafael turned the dials and manned the open mic from 4:00 p.m. until midnight, highlighting plights and complaints, opinions and diatribes, mostly against the ruling authorities or the police.

His slot became very popular and attracted callers from all over Mexico, some of whom just wanted to talk to "the voice." Enrique found his main audience amongst the young people, because he played the hippest tunes this side of San Diego and alternated between American and Latin music, as well as Indigenous music from all over the world. He called his music show *Pop del Mundo*. It broadcast afternoons and repeated again after midnight.

Paula hosted the morning show, which included news from all over the world, and a popular Saturday show that mixed cool tunes with alternative and natural medicine. They also pre-taped their own commercials for clients and used the revenue to sponsor worthy local causes, like the local orphanage and a couple of local artists.

It didn't take long before the Sunday dinners at the Álvarez's table became very strained and all controversial topics were avoided. Paula wasn't exactly as popular a niece as she used to be, but she steadfastly defended her right to free speech, although Pedro Álvarez could barely contain his fury. He had been duped and used, not by an enemy but by a member of his own family. Paula tried to placate him, using all her natural charm, telling him he could turn the whole thing around in his favour by arguing that the PRI was proud to sponsor a controversial radio station. It would make him look liberal and probably make him more popular. Pedro mulled this over for a while and did find some merit in the argument, but he had no illusions about convincing his ultra-conservative and corrupt colleagues of this point of view.

Rafael found himself once more living in a place that was mostly frequented by gringo turistas — the ruins of Mount Albán — which enabled him to use and improve his English. He often wandered around the ancient Zapotec ruins in the mornings during Enrique's shift, and he soon became a well-known fixture around Mount Albán. He got on well with the local guides, featuring them often on his broadcasts. He was familiar with their lot in life, having been a tour guide himself. More than once he ended up befriending some visitor, mostly young travellers laden with backpacks, tramping from one end of Mexico to the other.

He was able to persuade a few of them to give him an interview. Rafael always tried to juxtapose the American way of life with that of Mexicans. The standard of living and the many dollars it took to live a decent life in the *Estados Unidos* stood in stark contrast to the lousy wages Mexicans were paid there. But Rafael always emphasized that despite the gaping differences in income, living and working in Mexico could be just as fulfilling as in the US, and more dignified in many cases. To be a minimum-wage agricultural labourer in California was definitely less prestigious than working a family farm in the Oaxaca valley. He translated the interviews and broadcast them.

Rafael interviewed most of the local Indigenous leaders and was able to lure some local *campesinos* into the studio. The shy old men, small in stature but tall in spirit, were not easily convinced to speak their minds, but Rafael spoke their language. He convinced one couple, Jesús and Huitzilin (meaning Hummingbird) — him in an old worn poncho and a felt hat and her in a heavy black skirt, a colourful shawl and long braids — to open up about their hard lives, their need for more teachers, medical aid and infrastructure. They worked a small patch of dirt, grew some corn and owned a couple of goats and chickens. Sometimes during harvest, they got hired by the bigger farms. They had no electricity, no telephone and no running water in their adobe hut — a tenuous existence at best. These kinds of people had never been included by commercial radio before.

One time, Rafael received a phone call from a guy who called himself Subcomandante Marcos, a Zapatista from San Cristóbal. He asked some strange questions about the nature of the station and if their broadcasts were censored or if they were scrutinized and controlled by the government. He seemed very suspicious, but Rafael assured him that Radio Albán was the freest of the free and that he could say anything he liked on air apart from blasphemy and foul language. "Radio Albán is the one and only station to tolerate political dissent and advocate change," Rafael said, adding, "We are particularly concerned with the plight of the poor and forgotten Mexicans, most of whom are Indigenous."

Two days later, Marcos showed up at the st
accompanied by two other Zapatistas from San
were all dressed in green army fatigues. Subcon
wore a black balaclava, wanting to remain anony
"If nobody knows, it adds an air of mystery," he said misch...

Subcomandante Marcos turned out to be a very well-spoken man, obviously educated. He sat across from Rafael, smoking his pipe, speaking calmly into the microphone, painting a devastating picture of the underprivileged and disenfranchised Zapatistas. "They're treated no better than modern slaves and serfs: exploited, underpaid, under-schooled and blatantly ignored by the powers that be." Marcos's voice was beamed out from Mount Albán in the dim light of the studio, his dark eyes glinting, the rest of his face covered by the black balaclava. "There will be trouble ahead if the Mexican government continues to ignore the plight of its Indigenous people."

"What kind of trouble?" Rafael asked. "An armed uprising?"

"I wouldn't rule it out."

After the interview, the phone lines at Radio Albán glowed red hot, so many calls were coming in, wanting to know who this Subcomandante Marcos was. Rafael couldn't tell them anything except that he was a pipe-smoking Zapatista from San Cristóbal.

During the day, Rafael often listened in on the police band and tended to find out what was really going on from the head of the dragon itself. He would then use the information to broadcast warnings about political raids or possible intimidation of certain in-dividuals. It was here that he first heard the rumour of a proposed nuclear power plant on Lake Pátzcuaro. He intercepted a trans-mission from the Pátzcuaro police about breaking up a gathering of some upset farmers and fishermen. He had a hard time believing these rumours. *A nuke plant in Pátzcuaro — how insane is that?*

Just the mention of Pátzcuaro made Rafael wince, and threatened to open the barely healed hole in his heart. He kept listening for more news about this item but failed to hear any more about it. Rafael convinced himself that it must have been a misunderstanding, gossip gone wild without any facts to back it

For the time being, he pushed that information to the bottom of his mind. The Sunday after the Marcos interview, Paula's uncle was furious. "I'm under fire from my superiors!" he said to her. "They want this communist station shut down. You're putting my political future in jeopardy and by extension the well-being of my family, which includes you," Pedro railed at his niece.

Paula knew their days were numbered. To string out their chances, she took a risk. "Come to Enrique's open-mic morning show," she said. "Talk to the real people and explain a few things to them, including the PRI's position on free speech. You will have a bigger audience than you've ever had. Your voice will reach the ears of people who've never heard of you."

Pedro's ego was too big to pass up such an opportunity, and his vanity got the better of him. He took her bait. He marched into battle, head held high. But not for long. By the second phone call, which demanded a position on the rights of children who had to work alongside their parents as farm labourers, some as young as seven and eight years old, Pedro started to sweat. Then a woman, obviously educated, called in and asked him straight out what his salary was. "How do you justify the PRI's lack of money for infrastructure and new schools in rural Mexico?"

Pedro wanted to kill his niece and Enrique, who left the mic wide open, broadcasting his mumbling, incoherent excuses. Pedro had made an absolute fool of himself and he knew it. The disastrous broadcast spelled the beginning of the end.

Pedro stormed out of the station. "You and your communist scum friends need to shut down the station now!" he shouted at Paula. "Unless you want to suffer some very serious consequences."

The three conspirators knew their time was up. They kept Radio Albán broadcasting, even changed the name to Radio Libre. But without the government funds, which stopped the minute Pedro Álvarez got back to his office, they were hard pressed to pay the power bills and rent, never mind their own meagre salaries. The advertisements also dried up pretty quickly, and it wasn't hard to figure out why. Just a simple phone call from the PRI to Radio Libre clients would do the trick.

Then on a warm spring night in April during Rafael's show, he heard the approach of roaring vehicles. When he stepped outside, he was instantly caught in the glare of several headlights. Half a dozen black-clad figures jumped out of the jeeps, silhouetted and surrounded by a cloud of dust — like in an action movie, Rafael thought, while he was roughly turned around and slammed against the wall. Out of the corner of his eye, he saw several of the armed combatants kick open the door, despite its being unlocked. Then he heard the awful noise of clubs and machetes smashing up the equipment. "Please don't destroy the equipment," Rafael pleaded, but in vain. The commandos had a mission to accomplish, and they strictly followed their orders. Without speaking one word, they destroyed the station, kicked Rafael to the ground and left with tires squealing, in a dense cloud of flying rocks and dirt.

The nightmare was all over in a matter of minutes. Rafael surveyed the destruction and decided there was nothing worth saving. He packed up his meagre personal belongings and, since there was no bus at that hour, started the two-hour walk into Oaxaca to inform his two partners. He arrived after midnight, and after waking them up with the bad news, they sat around the kitchen table with a bottle of mescal until the horizon turned pink with the rising sun.

Officially, the three friends were wild-eyed subversives, portrayed as anarchists and communist sympathizers by the PRI-controlled media, which was inundated with queries about the sudden demise of Radio Alban or Radio Libre. The destruction of the station was blamed on the three broadcasters, who were said to have done it in order to save themselves from a mountain of rising debts. The PRI denied any involvement, as did the Oaxaca police. Paula's family, although somewhat sympathetic in private, didn't help any. Paula accused her uncle Pedro of cowardice and betrayal, but he insisted he'd had no idea this would happen. Either way, their relationship came to an acrimonious end.

The three friends were determined to take their experience, their commitment and their physical presence out of the politically unfriendly situation in Oaxaca, where they were branded as outcasts and outlaws. With their present pariah status, they could be of no help to any political contra movement, like that of the emerging Zapatistas around San Cristóbal in Chiapas, or indeed the local Indigenous people.

Over many late-night beers, they brainstormed new ideas. Another radio station? Nobody would sponsor them now. "What about a language school?" Rafael suggested. All three friends were fairly fluent in English, and a language school for tourists sounded like a good idea. Just where they could open such a school, they didn't know. Rafael suggested Pátzcuaro, because he knew it was a popular tourist destination where a language school could flourish. Paula, who also knew the town, having grown up an hour away in Morelia, liked the idea. It was in a different province, not unlike Oaxaca but smaller.

Within a couple of days, they packed Paula and Enrique's old Ford Bronco and headed out across the Mexican plateau into the mountains of Michoacán. Paula suggested a side trip to Angangueo to see the butterflies, but Rafael put them off until later. He hadn't seen his family since he left El Rosario for Morelia under a black cloud all those years ago. He wasn't ready to return quite yet. He had nothing to show for all his schooling and dreams that would impress his family, especially his dad. He couldn't return home, broke and branded as an outlaw by the government.

Chapter 5
ELL & NNN

The three young *activistas* drove Rico's battered Bronco, loaded with all their worldly belongings, into the town of Pátzcuaro. Rafael's prize possession was a guitar he'd bought off an American tourist at Mount Albán. He had started learning to play during the long solitary hours at the radio station. Everybody told him he had "the voice," so he learned to sing some traditional songs and became quite enamoured of the rich treasure of Mexican and Spanish folk music. He was too shy to play in public and didn't deem himself at all ready to be an entertainer. His two friends encouraged him and were his biggest fans, but Rafael would have none of it. He felt the music was a private affair with him, sort of like prayer.

They followed the bumpy two-lane road, meandering along the shore of the large, pale, jade-coloured lake that lay like a gigantic mirror at the feet of several prominent surrounding volcanoes. A few small islands dotted the lake, with the distinctive cone shape of Janitzio lording over them all. At the top of Janitzio, the massive statue of General Morelos, with its fist raised to the heavens, was clearly visible from miles away. The air was pleasantly cool because Pátzcuaro sits at an altitude of over two kilometres, amidst pine forests and volcanic cones.

"How many people live here?" Paula asked.

"About 80,000, *más o menos*," Rafael answered.

Each of the three friends was inspired by the vistas and the location, and all of them had an affinity for the place, but for slightly different reasons. For Paula it brought back fond memories of childhood visits to "the heart of Michoacán" with her parents. Rico simply looked forward to a new adventure with his two friends in a place they all felt very excited about. For Rafael, Pátzcuaro was already evoking strong memories and images from his happiest time and his greatest sorrow.

They found temporary lodgings at the Villa Pátzcuaro Campground on the outskirts of the town. The campground included cabins and a tennis court, of all things, and the owner happened to be a respected local historian as well as a former state tennis champ — hence the court. Arturo Pimentel Ramos, known by everybody simply as Turo, thought their idea of a Spanish-English language school a worthy endeavour. "You need to advertise your language and teaching services at all the local hotels and tourist spots," he advised them.

Within a couple of weeks, they had attracted some Europeans and Canadians who wanted to learn Spanish. Turo rented them two rooms to serve as classrooms, in addition to the two adjacent rooms for lodging. A central kitchen building with a large dining table served all the campers and was the hub of the campground.

The foreign tourist business slowed down considerably in the summer months, so instead of teaching Spanish to tourists, they offered English lessons for locals. Their lessons became quite popular once word got around. The three entrepreneurs didn't refuse any students, even if they couldn't pay. Some just wanted to learn some English phrases like "How much?" and "How long?" and "What is your name?"

At first they met their students at the library adjacent to the Plaza Gertrudis, but it was only open to the public a few days a week. One of their students turned out to be the owner of the perfect building, two blocks from the Plaza Vasco de Quiroga, right in the centre of the pueblo histórico. "It's too large for a family and too small for a hotel," Francisco said with a shrug, "but it might suit your purpose."

As in most colonial buildings, the numbered front door was set in a long common wall that lined both sides of the street. You never knew what was behind the entrance door, a pigsty or a palace. This particular door led into an open courtyard, with two stories of rooms on the left and against the back wall. Not only could it house their school, but there were enough rooms for their own needs, as well as some they could rent as a traveller's lodging. The ground-floor rooms were easily converted into classrooms, and the large kitchen functioned as a communal gathering place. The former pantry had a door leading out back into the overgrown patch of walled-in garden. The vaulted entrance room became the information centre, where lodgings and goods for trade or sale were advertised, as well as political and ecological facts about the area.

For the first few months all three lived upstairs, sharing meals and working on schedules and plans while teaching as much as possible. But their incomes were meagre. This lack of money created tensions among the three friends that threatened to derail their enterprise. Rico, who had the least English, spent a lot of time hobnobbing and fraternizing with local activists, while Rafael taught the younger students and Paula spent time with the older students, most of whom paid better than Rafael's kids.

"We need more income," Rafael complained to Rico over breakfast one day in July when only a couple of students were scheduled.

"I know, I know," Rico answered defensively, taking the complaint personally. "What do you want me to do?"

Rafael just shrugged his shoulders and concentrated on his *huevos rancheros*. Paula, sensing the tension, came up with an idea. "How about if Rico and I moved out? That would give us two more rooms to let."

"That's a great idea, but where would we get the rent money?" Rico said, dismissing the idea out of hand.

"I made a friend, one of my students, who lives in a big house. Actually, it's her parents' place, but both of them are working up north, so she has it all to herself. I could ask her if we could rent lodging from her for free lessons. I know she doesn't have much money," Paula said.

Rafael and Rico looked at their friend, and for a moment nobody said a word. "I think it's a great idea," Rafael said. "We would have more rental income, and you would have your own space, sort of."

Rico asked, "What's her name?"

"Marlena Moreno. You all know her. She's the one with the birthmark on her throat. She always wears a scarf around her neck."

A couple of weeks later, at the beginning of October, Paula and Enrique moved in with Marlena, whose house was uphill from the school. It had plenty of room and a view of the town all the way down to the lake. Rafael retained his small bedroom upstairs at the school, and therefore had the building all to himself at the end of day. People who walked by could often hear a distant, soft guitar and an enchanting voice singing songs of loss and love, floating as if on angels' wings into the balmy night air.

They settled into a routine of teaching and structuring and developing their school. They needed a recognizable name — a brand, as Paula called it — and after some lively discussions, settled on Escuela de Lengua Latina, or ELL. Rafael lived for free but was in charge of the rentals, since he was the one who lived in the building. They saw less of each other, since Rico and Paula often left soon after their respective classes were over.

Rafael liked to stroll around the old town and listen to the buskers, of whom there were plenty, mostly trying to make a few pesos from the tourists. All three friends loved to sit in one of the many cafés off the main square, and often they were able to recruit new pupils, since these lovely outdoor restaurants under the medieval arches were also frequented by the tourists who flocked to Pátzcuaro from all over the world. And so their heady days of activism on Mount Alban seemed long in the past, and the three renegade broadcasters were embarking on the road to becoming respected members of society.

Rafael had heard about the construction of a nuclear power-generating plant on Lake Pátzcuaro as far back as his time in Oaxaca, but nobody took this rumour very seriously at the time. It had sounded like such a crazy idea. But now the gossip turned to fact, as the controversial proposal was introduced and heralded with much fanfare by the local and state governments. The behemoth of a project was lauded in the local paper as an unprecedented economic opportunity for the whole lake region, and indeed for all of Michoacán. *El Sol*, one of the two Morelia dailies, carried a feature article wholly in favour of the project, extolling the benefits of an economic boom and riches flowing into everybody's pockets. It also identified the proposed site, on the east end of Lake Pátzcuaro, on the land formerly owned and farmed by a character everybody knew as el Viejo (the Old Man).

Rafael brought the paper to the school and excitedly pointed out the article, written by a G. M. Ramirez. "Remember when I told you that rumour about a year ago? I guess it was right. Look at this!"

"Who is G. M. Ramírez?" Paula asked, scanning the article. Nobody knew. "One of their editors, I presume," Rico said. Rafael shrugged his shoulders. Ramírez was a common name.

"This is going to destroy the lake and the whole area. This means a concrete cone the size of Janitzio," Paula said.

"Economic boom, my ass," Enrique said disgustedly. "This will bring in hundreds of migrant construction workers with all their boozing, gambling and whoring."

Paula gave her boyfriend a look that said, *Simmer down.* "Let's do some research on this before we jump to conclusions," she suggested. "We need to make sure we get the facts straight before we start shooting from the hip."

Rafael called the Comisión Federal de Electricidad under the guise of a news reporter, and it confirmed their worst fears. This new plant on Lake Pátzcuaro was the next step in their ambitious program, following on the heels of the activation of Laguna Verde II, Mexico's second nuclear generating plant. All this new energy would transform Mexico, unleash the jaguar and bring undreamt-of wealth and economic potential, especially to poor rural areas like Michoacán.

Rafael, Paula and Enrique started gathering facts and then displayed them at their school. Since most of their clients were Americans, Canadians and a smattering of Aussies and Europeans, as well as the odd Kiwi, they all were, without exception, against nuclear power in any shape or form and were easily convinced of the folly of such an endeavour But the challenge was to convince the local populace, and in particular the local government, of the negative impact this project would have.

When the flow of tourists abated at the end of summer, the three partners decided to act. They founded an ecological activist group and called it No Nuke No, or NNN, complete with phone number and logo. They turned the former library/living room into the NNN's office and headquarters. They also opened a bank account for donations, which one of the Canadian tourists advised them to do. It had been a year since they first arrived in Pátzcuaro.

At the beginning of October, Rafael travelled to Morelia to listen to some music and to drum up support for the NNN at his old alma mater, UNAM. He also wanted to check out the possibility of a future rally in that city. He stood at the entrance to the university and handed out a simple pamphlet that said (in English):

SAY NO TO A NUCLEAR REACTOR ON LAKE PÁTZCUARO!
NO NUKE NO

His message found plenty of eager eyes and ears, and approval from the students at the university. But when he handed out the flyer at the Plaza de Armas, the working poor, who were afraid to oppose anything the government proposed and approved, met it with scepticism and outright opposition. Also, the lure of jobs was an attraction that Rafael couldn't counter with his argument about sustainability for the fragile lake. Not much money in that.

That night Rafael happened to hear Joaquin Pantoja, a young guitarist and singer from Uruapan, who held his audience spellbound with his virtuoso guitar playing and treasure trove of Mexican folk songs. Rafael came away elated and also humbled. He had lots to learn, and he vowed to spend at least an hour a day on his guitar.

Rafael took the bus back to Pátzcuaro and found himself sitting across the aisle from a young couple who were presumably from Canada, based on the small maple-leaf pin on the young woman's lapel. She had the most incredible mane of wavy red hair Rafael had ever seen. He introduced himself, and his English impressed the couple, whose Spanish consisted of some nouns and verbs they were able to string together.

"You will need some Spanish lessons, no?" Rafael asked, not wholly without an ulterior motive.

"That's for sure," said the young woman. "Any idea where we could find a language school, one that's not too expensive?"

"I happen to teach at just such a school," Rafael said mischievously, feeling a bit like a salesman.

"Oh, really? That's great!" she enthused.

"You need a place to stay also?" Rafael asked.

"Well, yes," she answered, a bit embarrassed. Was it that obvious? "By the way, I'm Karen and this is Jason. We're from Toronto, and we are actually looking for lodging, but, eh . . . we're not rich."

"You are in luck. I am also a partner in the Pátzcuaro Travellers Lodge, which is attached to the language school, ELL, short for Escuela de Lengua Latina, and I would be happy to show you," Rafael offered with a grin, immediately convincing Karen and Jason that this was indeed a lucky encounter.

"Great," said Karen. Both she and Jason took an immediate liking to the sympathetic young Mexican.

Karen and Jason followed their new friend to his lodge, where they were given a tour of the premises and quartered in an upstairs room. They were thrilled to have landed so perfectly.

"Karma," Karen said. "It's meant to be."

Karen, always the keener, immediately wanted to enrol in classes, while Jason reminded her of their dwindling funds.

The next morning the two Canadians took a walk through Pátzcuaro and fell in love with the quaint town, its two plazas, the stone buildings with their timbered and vaulted roofs overhanging the busy sidewalks, the old churches and cobblestoned alleys, the cafés and restaurants, and the bustling maze of the mercado.

Karen especially delighted in the local Indigenous women who sat in front of their colourful stalls in their blue-and-white striped shawls and skirts, with their braids reaching to their waists, their friendly, open smiles enticing them to buy and barter. They sat down at a picnic table in front of the *mercado* and across from the old *biblioteca*. The inexpensive lunch was prepared by a small, stocky woman who fried the chicken, potatoes and peppers in sizzling oil in a large steel pan and then, bare-handed, tossed, turned and served the piping-hot chicken onto plates while her husband collected the money and opened the soft drinks.

This is the true Mexico, Jason thought, mesmerized by the din of Mexican music emanating from tiny speakers, the noise from shouting vendors and the palaver from the groups of diners like themselves, all drowning in a cacophony of blaring horns and rattling mufflers from the incessantly congested traffic around the *zócalo*. Uniformed policemen were blowing their shrill whistles at what seemed arbitrary intervals, gesticulating wildly at pedestrians and impatient motorists.

The two young Canadians explored the region by *colectivo* (bus), which cost one peso to go just about anywhere in town. One of their first trips was to Santa Clara del Cobre, where every shop in town was dedicated to the art of beating, bending, forming, polishing and selling copper. The shops were crammed from floor to ceiling with everything from household utensils to high vases and sophisticated artistic vessels of all sizes. The shelves of the shops and the sidewalk stands were all bursting with copper wares, and even the central gazebo in the small *zócalo* sported a shiny copper roof.

At one time there used to be an actual copper mine near Santa Clara, but these days the raw materials came from primitive backyard smelters of discarded electrical wires and plumbing pipes. The couple watched horrified as a bunch of grimy *muchachos* who should have been in school laboured in the backyard, burning the plastic coating off the wires, releasing toxic fumes and plumes of black poisonous smoke. Inside the smithy, the copper was melted in a steel vat over hot coals, then poured into ingots and waltzed and hammered into sheets and forms. They observed the black sooty coppersmiths, who looked like vaudeville performers with only their red eyes and pink lips showing in their black, grinning faces, some of them no doubt children. It was a grim, medieval scene behind the glittering storefronts.

They travelled around the lake and stopped in several villages, each known for a particular specialty: unique carved and lacquered masks, furniture, weaving, pottery and straw ornaments, carved wooden furniture painted in yet another town. They walked through markets and squares, all bursting with the region's artifacts, which were a living testimony to the utopian vision of Don Vasco de Quiroga, who over 400 years ago organized the local Indigenous people into self-sufficient trading communities.

Jason had to ask Rafael, "How can all these stores exist, selling the exact same goods right next to each other in all these towns? This is not just competition, it's blanketing the market."

Rafael laughed. "You have a point, my friend, but you must remember that most of the shopkeepers are related. Instead of looking at it the American way as competition, look at it as the whole town being one big family copper or pottery market. Instead of each one working against the other, underselling and competing, they all are a small part of the same big enterprise. Did you notice a big difference in prices?" Rafael asked.

Both Jason and Karen had to admit they hadn't.

"It's all part of Don Vasco Quiroga's philosophy of communal enterprise and social equality. It works well. On the other hand, competing with one another would make them enemies and destroy the social and economic fabric of the town. Instead they all remain friends and marry into each other's families. They also export their wares all over Mexico and beyond."

Karen was curious about this socialist prophet Don Quiroga, who had lived to be ninety years old, and this in the mid-1500s. Rafael told them about the Spanish lawyer and bishop who took the devastated Purépechas under his wing after the conquistador Nuño de Guzmán had laid waste to the region in a campaign of death and destruction. The two young Canadians were visibly impressed when Rafael described Quiroga's accomplishments and revolutionary vision that was five centuries ahead of its time, and most of which was still evident in every facet of life in and around Pátzcuaro.

The more Karen and Jason found out about Pátzcuaro and the region around the lake, the more they felt this was where they wanted to stay for a while. They were also intrigued by their teacher's activist group and their political battle for the survival of the lake and indeed the town and region of Pátzcuaro.

Karen and Jason met Enrique and Paula during their first week at the lodge, while they were busy organizing an upcoming rally in the Plaza Don Quiroga, the first public event for NNN.

"What's this about?" Karen asked Rico, who was scrutinizing a map on the table.

"Well, it's about educating the public about the Mexican Utility Commission's proposal to build the nuclear power station. And this map shows where they plan to build it."

"A nuke plant on Lake Pátzcuaro?" Jason cried, horrified.

"This will destroy the whole region," Karen said.

"We know," Rico replied, shaking his head. "That's why we formed the No Nuke No campaign. We have to stop them."

"This can't be true!" Jason cried. "How could they?"

Rico just laughed at Jason's naiveté. "Because they can, just like a dog can lick his balls," he said, laughing at his crass metaphor, which earned him a funny look from Karen.

"I'm sorry," Rico said, "but you must understand that there is a lot of money involved in a massive project like this, and the payoffs alone are reason enough to build such a monstrosity."

"But what about the people of Pátzcuaro? Don't they have a say in this?" said Karen, directing her question at Paula.

"This is Mexico, Karen," Paula replied, "and the people's opinion does not count for much in the corridors of power. That is why we started NNN. It's all about educating the public, and we would be happy if you wanted to help."

"What can we do?" Jason asked eagerly.

"You can help distribute these pamphlets."

The two Canadians retired, and as soon the door closed behind them, Rico turned to his two friends and said between clenched teeth, "Why are we inviting them to join the NNN and distribute pamphlets for us? They are foreigners and have little investment in this town, in this lake. We need to stick together as locals, as Mexicans. Before we know it, we'll be taken over by the gringos."

"Come on, Rico, you don't mean that," Paula said. "We need people from everywhere to support us — locals, tourists, gringos, the more the better. What do you think, Rafael?"

"I know where Rico is coming from, but I agree with Paula. This is not just a local issue, it's an international or even a global issue. I think involving concerned foreigners is a good idea. It adds clout to the NNN. I don't think it takes away power."

Rico shook his head, not happy with his friends' point of view. "You may be right, but I'm not putting my life, my career, my future on the line just to be relegated by some gringo who knows better."

"We'll be careful who we let in, Rico. But for now, Jason and Karen are perfectly suited to help us. They are genuinely concerned, just like we are." Rico got up and left the table, obviously not happy.

The next day Karen and Jason were handing out flyers in the tourist community in Pátzcuaro, in the hotels, the campgrounds and amongst the cafés under the arches around the two plazas. They already saw themselves as active members of the fledgling protest group. They genuinely supported NNN's cause and couldn't possibly picture a nuke plant on the pristine shores of Lake Pátzcuaro. But the irony of their position didn't escape them. They came from a part of the world — Ontario — that lived off nuclear power. But here in the heart of Mexico, in the sacred land of the Purépecha? No way!

They also joined the nightly get-together around the large kitchen table, which often included residents of the lodge. They drank coffee and *cervezas* and talked about a lot of issues, from the plight of the local people to the effect of NAFTA on Mexico, but always the matter of the proposed nuke plant on Lake Pátzcuaro galvanized everybody's opinion. Visitors and locals were unanimous in their condemnation of the project.

It was during one of those discussions that Paula suggested to Karen and Jason, "You could write to your own government and find out if they are somehow involved here. I heard a nasty rumour that the cores of the two proposed generators are CANDU reactors, and since we now have this wonderful free-trade agreement with Canada, Mexico is getting a very good deal from them."

"Jason," Karen said, "I bet your dad could find out if that's true."

Jason didn't like the idea of involving his dad at all, and he gave Karen a look that said as much.

"You just have to ask him, that's all," she said.

"My dad happens to be a Conservative MP who is most certainly in favour of exporting technology, even of the nuclear kind, to Mexico," Jason explained to their puzzled Mexican friends.

An awkward silence fell over the room, and then everybody wanted to speak at once. Rafael pleaded for calm and sane conversation. "No point going all crazy," he said, holding up both his hands like a conductor. "We need facts and information and quiet heads."

"You mean calm heads," Karen corrected him.

"Excuse me," Rafael said, bewildered.

"Calm heads," Karen repeated, "not quiet heads. Calm like the water on Lake Pátzcuaro."

"Yes, calm like the water of Lake Pátzcuaro," Rafael repeated, laughing.

Jason promised they would try to find out what they could, but he doubted the Canadian government would give out classified information to two twenty-somethings tramping through Mexico, even if one of them happened to be related to an elected Member of Parliament.

"This is important for Pátzcuaro, isn't it?" Jason asked, knowing the answer already.

Rafael looked at Jason. "The cost of not fighting this would be much higher than anything we stand to lose."

Rafael couldn't know at the time that one of them would have to pay the ultimate price.

Chapter 6
Karen & Jason

While riding her bicycle home from the studio on a balmy autumn evening, Karen, two days after her 19th birthday, was cut off by a spiffy little red sports car targeting a parking spot just ahead of her. She rammed into the rear of the car and was catapulted over her handlebars and onto the pavement. She broke her wrist, fractured her kneecap and tore ligaments on both sides of her left knee. Before the operation, the doctor said, "This will take me about an hour; it will take you half a year."

She eventually returned to Rosa Matisse's dance school and continued taking ballet classes. It took a few weeks of gritting teeth and tearful nights before it became clear to her that she would never dance the lead in Giselle. Instead, she started helping out Ms. Matisse, who guided her towards working with the younger dancers. After high school Karen enrolled in a dance program at the Ryerson's Polytechnic Institute, where she discovered her passion for folk dancing. She joined a group of dancers and together they formed a small company called Folk Ballet. Within a year they were performing throughout Toronto, at Ontario Place and at various conventions, and became a hit at Caravan, an annual multi-ethnic festival.

A couple of months before Karen's final exams, a leggy blond male dancer joined Folk Ballet. Jason Neumann could dance a Hungarian czardas or a Polish mazurka like nobody else. He was also very good-looking, and just as much in love with dance as Karen. It was inevitable that before the school year was out, Jason and Karen would discover more common passions than dance. Karen passed her exams and was offered a summer job at Ontario Dance magazine by a friend of Ms. Matisse's, and Ms. Matisse also kept her on as a part-time teacher for the youngest kids.

Jason had a funky one-bedroom apartment on Pape, off the Danforth, not far from Ms. Matisse's school, and held down a part-time job at Globe Travel, the travel agency his mother owned. His dad was a Conservative Member of Parliament, something Jason didn't like to talk about. He didn't agree with his dad's politics and had reduced their relationship to Christmas dinners and birthday phone calls. Jason was an only child. Growing up, he saw little of his dad and was basically raised by his mom. She was the glue that kept the small family together, and it was his mom who supported Jason's passion for dance.

After they'd gone steady for three months, Karen decided to move in with Jason. Financially, it was a prudent choice, but hanging out in a one-bedroom apartment was entirely different from living in that small space together.

She liked Jason and at times even thought she probably loved him, especially when he danced or they made love. But she also knew that unless he stopped smoking and started cleaning up after himself, they would have a major blow-up. Karen demanded changes, and Jason promised but never did much about it. Karen tried very hard to fit into Jason's life, but he didn't do very much to accommodate her. His mom had cleaned up after him all of his growing years, and he somehow assumed it was natural that Karen would take over that role.

After having made love one morning, Karen, coming out of the shower, couldn't find a clean towel anywhere. She burst into the bedroom, stark naked and dripping wet, while Jason was still lounging in bed with a full ashtray beside him, blowing smoke rings at the ceiling, listening to Guns N' Roses.

Karen lost it. In a flood of hot, angry tears, heaving and crying hysterically, she screamed at Jason, "You're a fucking pig!" She began throwing stuff at him, whatever was within her reach — books, clothes, even a wet bar of soap. "I've had it with your goddamned mess, Jason. I can't even find a towel, and I hate the stink of your fucking cigarettes, and I hate Guns N' Roses and I hate you! I want out of now!"

Jason just lay there, completely overwhelmed by Karen's barrage of accusations. He wisely turned off the ghetto blaster and put out the cigarette, just before he held up his hand to stop a toothpaste missile coming straight at him. He scrambled out of bed and headed for the kitchen, stark naked, with Karen, naked as well, in hot pursuit, yelling, throwing stuff and crying hysterically. Jason was trapped, and in his desperation, he handed her a dish towel. "Please, Karen, I'm sorry. Here take this. It's better than nothing," he pleaded.

Karen stopped in mid-flight, just before heaving an apple at Jason, and the absurdity of their situation suddenly overwhelmed both of them. They started laughing, haltingly at first, but then with ever more hilarity, until they both dropped to their knees onto the black-and-white chequered linoleum floor, shaking and laughing, tears running down their faces. Jason then held Karen close, futilely trying to dry her with the tea towel. "Oh, my god," Jason said. "I must buy some more bath towels. Otherwise I'm going to be killed."

Jason did buy more towels, but Karen gave him two choices. "Either I move out, or we find a new two-bedroom apartment, one with a balcony so you can smoke outside.

Jason had a better idea. "Let's go to Mexico instead for the winter. My mom can get us cheap tickets, and with the Mexican peso being way down, we could live well on a small amount of cash."

Karen had never been anywhere west of Sault Ste. Marie or east of Quebec City. Travelling sounded like the best thing ever, and after she mulled the idea over and looked at some glossy posters of Mexico through a travel agency window, she grew more and more enamoured of the idea.

Mexico! It sounded so exotic, warm and sunny, especially when she considered the miserable Toronto winters. A couple of days later, over a half-priced pasta lunch at Mario's, their favourite Italian restaurant, she blurted out, "Let's do it!"

Karen's summer job at the magazine was over, anyway, although they promised to keep her in mind if a permanent job came along. Jason booked two open-ended flights to Mexico City. They stored most of their belongings with their parents, sold what they could in order to raise more money and gave away the rest. "Free at last!" Jason proclaimed, surveying their few belongings, all of which fit into their two new backpacks.

Jason nervously brought Karen along to a farewell dinner at his parents' house. His mom insisted on it, and Jason gave in. Karen found Jason's dad rather reserved and aloof, but Jason said, "You made a good impression on the old man."

"Don't be so damn hard on your dad, Jason. At least he tries to do something about the state of this country. I'm sure at your age his philosophies and politics were different as well."

Jason just shrugged his shoulders and dismissed the matter. Karen suspected there was more to their estrangement than just differing politics.

After surviving a week of "going-away parties," they were finally seated on a flight to Zihuatanejo, Ixtapa — according to Jason's mom, the latest exclusive beach resort just around the corner from a charming fishing village on a spectacular bay. The two young adventurers watched the vast sprawl of Toronto recede below them.

• • •

They had been in Zihuatanejo for over a week, during which they had walked hand in hand along the la Ropa and Madeiro beaches, getting sunburns and drinking margaritas the size of goldfish bowls, when Karen happened upon an article about Michoacan, and Pátzcuaro in particular.

"Look at this, Jason. It sounds like a beautiful place. I looked it up on the map, and it's not very far from here, only about 400 kilometres. They call it a *Pueblo Mágico*."

"How are we gonna get there? By bus?" Jason asked.

"I don't know, but I'm sure we can find out," Karen said.

They boarded a bus to Morelia, which took them from the beach up and up, to Mexico's Terra Alta, at an altitude of 2500 metres, through small adobe towns clustered alongside the narrow road, through Uruapan and into the colonial city of Morelia. There they changed to a local bus that took them into the land of volcanoes, traversing some of Mexico's most beautiful country, close to the pale blue sky and cotton-ball clouds, through pine forests and along lakeshores. On the way, Karen struck up a conversation with a friendly young Mexican sitting across the aisle. He had longish wavy hair, a short beard and dark puppy eyes. He travelled with a guitar and introduced himself in accented English as Rafael.

Chapter 7
Dissent

When Enrique boldly called the Commission's head office, posing as the mayor of Pátzcuaro, gushing with praise and enthusiastic support for the project, he was put through to a public relations officer, who disclosed the proposed site for the forty-acre facility. Rafael followed the thread and traced down the local corn farmer known as el Viejo, Jesús Xavier. When Rafael asked him about the proposal, el Viejo glibly told him about the very generous offer he had accepted from an *hombre de gobierno* for his practically worthless land.

"Here is the proof!" Rafael excitedly exclaimed, dramatically waving a section of the newspaper in the air, while Rafael and Paula sat at the kitchen table going over bills and trying to figure out how much they were in debt. In the newspaper was the Commission's first public mention of their intent to build a 700-milliwatt nuclear fission plant, in a short press release in September 1994.

The massive plant was to be situated between the small lakeshore towns of San Andrés and Oponguio, exactly where el Viejo had sold his hundred acres of flood-plain farmland to a "man from the government," as the old man put it. The two-paragraph article that appeared towards the back of *El Sol* briefly outlined the Commission's plans to build an ultra-modern, safe and ecologically viable generating plant that would greatly strengthen the region's, and indeed Mexico's, economic clout and provide much-sought-after employment and unending streams of revenue, flowing into Pátzcuaro and Michoacán.

Seeing their ultimate fears spelled out in plain black and white made the three friends jump into frenzied activity. "Now the fox is out of the hole," Rico proclaimed, slamming his fist onto the table.

On the strength of these new facts, the three young founders of the NNN organized their first public protest rally in the Plaza Don Vasco de Quiroga on a balmy Saturday afternoon in late September.

Naive and enthusiastic, they erected a makeshift podium and hand-painted a number of banners and placards, all decrying the proposed evil deed of the Electricity Commission, which their new friends from Canada helped distribute.

The NNN attracted curious onlookers rather than instant converts, and ended up entertaining rather than lecturing. However, they were unprepared for the vicious response from the local police. El Capitán, locally known as el Loco, flanked by his lieutenant and half a dozen black-clad police and brandishing his billy club, confronted the three teachers. He threatened them and the dozen tourists, followers from the school, with jail if they didn't immediately cease their unlawful activities. El Loco underlined his serious intent by having his goons smash the makeshift podium and the small PA system, and had all the literature and banners confiscated. The whole affair got only a mention in the local paper, as "an unlawful disturbance by communist agitators."

The school and the backpacker's lodge served as the main recruiting ground for supporters of No Nukes No. Although most of the students and travellers were foreigners, their international connections were vital to the novice activist group. They also needed to build a local consensus amongst the ordinary people of Pátzcuaro, the Indigenous people, university students, businesspeople and even local politicians.

Although Enrique, Paula and Rafael were university grads, only Paula came from a well-to-do family with conservative political connections, whose relationship with her at this time was still rather icy.

The three friends saw themselves only as genuinely concerned citizens who shouldered the collective burden of social responsibility in order to stop the destruction of one of the most pristine parts of Mexico. They seized the moral high ground because of their honest concern for the region and its people, who were kept in the dark and lived in constant fear of the corrupt authorities. Generally, people would only find out about a proposed project like a bridge, a highway or the invasion of a superstore like Walmart, long after the decisions had been made behind closed doors. The NNN needed support from shopkeepers, farmers and workers, nurses, teachers and students, grandmothers and housewives, and this could only be achieved by means of public education, not just in the classroom but in the plazas and mercados.

They found a new friend in Carmen Landenberg, an expatriate Swiss businesswoman who lived in Pátzcuaro and took a liking to the three young activists. She was shocked by the proposal of a nuke plant and also by their treatment by "el Loco," a man she knew well.

Their new friend and supporter helped NNN organize an information meeting, which they advertised by means of photo-copied invites plastered all over Pátzcuaro and distributed among the hotels, campgrounds and restaurants. She also helped with the design of their logo; No Nuke No around a red circle with a diagonal red stripe through the nuclear symbol symbolized loud and clear the aim of NNN. The poster proclaimed in both English and Spanish, "Information meeting about the proposed nuke plant on the shores of Lake Pátzcuaro. This is about your lake, your future and your lives!" Time and place of the meeting: Saturday 3:00 p.m. at the *biblioteca*. The library, a former 16th century church, overlooked the Plaza Gertrudis Bocanegra, and was known by everybody.

"This way, we look at least halfway legitimate," Rico reasoned when Rafael voiced his doubts about the location.

"Isn't it a little misleading to rent the library through the school?"

"Well, it does concern education," Paula argued. "After all, we are just informing the public of the facts, aren't we?"

"Paula is right," Rico said, "and I doubt the police will come into the library."

"Let's hope not," Rafael said.

The long, tall nave of the bibliotheca was almost full when the trio arrived, armed with papers and posters. Crowds attract bigger crowds, and word had gotten out that something vital for everybody's future would be discussed at the library.

Rafael took the microphone and introduced himself and Enrique and Paula as the principals of the language school, as well as the founders of the movement NNN, "under whose banner we are all gathered here today for the benefit of the people of this region." Silent stares met his introduction, and nervously Rafael shuffled the papers in front of him. He was not used to speaking in front of a live crowd, but his velvety voice resonated with the people, and soon they were enthralled by the young man.

"Some of you might have noticed the article in last month's paper about the proposed generating plant the Comisión Federal de Electricidad is proposing to build on the other side of Lake Pátzcuaro. What they forgot to mention is that this will be a nuclear plant, probably with two reactors, which means two massive concrete cylinders, higher than the statue of General Morelos on Janitzio."

Now a buzz rippled through the crowd. *Higher than the statue! A nuclear plant?*

Rico, the hothead of the group, couldn't contain himself any longer and stepped up to the mic, taking over from Rafael. "Building a nuclear plant on the shores of Lake Pátzcuaro would not only destroy the lake and with it the local ecosystem, it would also threaten the fishing industry, which is already in jeopardy due to overfishing and understocking. The fragile lake would be compromised by the amount of water it would require to cool a reactor core, not to mention the wonderful sight of the massive concrete cylinders dominating the landscape." Rico could have argued for hours with innuendoes and imagery, but to win any credibility they had to stick to the facts and speak in terms that the *campesinos* could understand.

"What about the benefit to the local economy?" someone shouted from the back.

Paula grabbed the microphone. "The jobs they promised are construction jobs that will be filled by migrant construction workers, housed most likely in compounds near the site. The only economic benefit from all this activity would be for some local businesses, mostly bars and gambling and fun houses. Your towns will become thoroughfares, and your roads will be destroyed by the heavy-duty industrial traffic. The impact on Pátzcuaro and the towns around the lake, all of which are dependent on tourism, would be severe and final. A nuclear plant would change the whole lake region forever and destroy the town and the local culture that has existed since the days of Don Vasco de Quiroga."

To invoke the patron saint of the region carried some weight, and had been carefully considered by NNN. They felt that Don Vasco, with his commitment to and concern for the region and its people 500 years before, would have been right behind them even today.

The crowd was now abuzz, humming and rumbling like a volcano about to erupt, and everybody argued and shouted at once.

Rafael held up both his hands, motioning the agitated crowd to listen and focus. "There are so many reasons to not build a nuke plant and use the water of Lake Pátzcuaro for cooling the reactors. And you all know that earthquakes are frequent amongst our volcanoes. If a quake happened under the plant, it would be a nuclear disaster! Think about that, my friends!"

Rafael was on fire now, and so was the crowd, but his monologue was interrupted by a commotion at the front entrance. Suddenly, the doors burst open, and in came the unmistakable shouting and yelling of el Loco. The panicked audience pressed for the exit, where they were herded through a phalanx of uniformed police. The scared attendees, many of them ordinary farmers and workers, were shoved and threatened with worse. El Loco, his lieutenant and several cops pushed through the crowd to the front and roughly handcuffed Rafael, Enrique and Paula. They dragged them the length of the library, out into the open, and shoved them into the back of the waiting police van.

Carmen Landenberg tried to intervene but was unceremoniously shoved aside by el Loco's lieutenant. The three teachers were driven, with all the sirens blaring, to the police station, where they were dumped into separate jail cells and left to ponder their fate.

Afternoon faded into evening, and suddenly the night loomed long, dark and lonely for the three activists. Peering through the semidarkness, illuminated by the pale streetlights just visible through a high, narrow window, Rafael surveyed his primitive cell for the umpteenth time, but it didn't improve as time went on. It contained a bare wooden bunk, a bucket for a toilet and a heavy steel door with a hatch at face level. He waited and stewed. Was this all worth it? Jail now and what next? Did they really have any chance against the almighty government?

Doubts crept into Rafael's consciousness — doubts about their mission, which had seemed so pure and right mere hours ago, doubts about what to do with his life, which seemed to be a continuous pattern of loss and estrangement, first from his parents, then from his one and only love, culminating in his choice to join the political fringe and his separation from the mainstream of society. *Am I now a complete outcast, a freak, a radical, a lunatic, branded forever?* In the murky, humid solitude of his cell, Rafael saw himself not as a Don Quixote or a Che Guevara but as a failure in all his endeavours.

He curled up on the plank and fell into an uneasy slumber, from which he was rudely shaken. Rafael opened his eyes and stared into the swarthy face of el Loco's lieutenant, who roughly pulled him upright. The lieutenant shoved him into the hallway and down past the other cells, from which his two co-conspirators were also being freed. All three were led into the adjacent office, where Carmen Landenberg was flanked by her lawyer and el Loco, who was uncharacteristically silent but glaring menacingly at the three young friends. "Take them home," el Loco growled, and they meekly followed Carmen into the deliciously cool early morning air.

"First, you all need a shower and a change of clothes," Carmen said, sternly forestalling any questions or explanations. "We will meet later at the school and discuss the present state of affairs."

The three dishevelled revolutionaries thanked Carmen and her lawyer profusely, and boarded the waiting taxi to take them back to their lodgings.

In the bright light of day, Rafael's mind turned from self-doubt and despair to righteous anger. Enrique felt similar waves of heroic feelings wash over him. Like Rafael, he'd found his resolve considerably shaken by the sobering finality of his jail cell, and now he and Rafael needed to transform their midnight doubts into daylight convictions.

"Next time, I'll make the speech," Enrique said, giving Rafael an elbow in the ribs. "You went all preachy and crazy."

"Oh yeah?" Rafael bristled. "Who's the crazy one here? I just got carried away. Anyway, you can make all the public speeches from now on. I think I'll go dumb next time I have to stand in front of a crowd."

"I know, I'm the one with the rock-star charisma," Enrique said, half-jokingly, pounding his chest with his fist. "But it's your golden voice they want to hear."

"You two act like a couple of kids caught smoking in the washroom. This is serious stuff. There is no going back now," Paula said.

Although Paula had also been assailed by doubts in the darkness of her confinement, her thoughts were of a more pragmatic kind, wondering if they had gone about things the right way, or if they should change tactics and go public by way of written exposés and make better use of the media. But who would publish their provocations? They also needed to record their movements and run NNN like a legitimate organization, with a recording secretary and proper minutes.

They all cleaned up and assembled in their kitchen/conference room. Carmen's quiet and dignified manner set the tone and steered the assembly into calm waters by first complimenting the three protagonists.

"Your information meeting was a success and is the talk of the town, and you should be proud of what you did. The police had no legal right to arrest you — it was strictly political expediency," she told them as soon they were seated. "I have also found out from a reliable source that our movement, I'm talking about the NNN, needs to be subverted and stopped. This does not only include police action; they will try to discredit you personally, with false accusations and even threats to your families. *El Sol* will run an article today, with no mention of the proposed nuke plant, tarnishing NNN with a broad radical brush, insinuating links with terrorist groups and the Communist League. Be prepared to defend yourselves against any kind of wild and fantastic accusations."

Paula voiced her newfound resolve to carry on the fight, but as a proper, above-board organization: "Come in from the cold, surface from the underground," she paraphrased dramatically.

"You're right, Paula," Carmen said. "And we also have to break out of the local mould and carry our message out of Pátzcuaro."

Rafael mentioned that two lodge guests from Canada had offered their support and had promised to write to some influential friends back home about their cause.

"We can use all the help we can muster," Carmen said.

Only Rico remained unusually quiet. The incarceration had scared him and made him angry and vengeful, but he knew he had to keep these feelings of rage to himself. His time would come, of that he was sure.

Rafael later informed Karen and Jason of what had been talked about. The two Canadians considered their friends heroes for having gone to jail.

"It's not all that glamorous," Rafael assured them.

Within a couple of days, the public focus shifted from NNN to more important matters and to the all-essential local traditions surrounding the Day of the Dead, just a few days away. This gave the young activists some breathing room to plan their strategy.

Every November 1st and 2nd the Festival of All Saints and the *Noche de Muertos*, the Night of the Dead, is celebrated across Mexico, but in particular in Pátzcuaro. Masses are held in every church and chapel, and street theatre culminates in the all-night vigils at the graves of ancestors. Paula suggested to their new Canadian friends that they all should pay a nocturnal visit to the ruins at Tzintzuntzan (from the Purépecha word for "place of hummingbirds") for the vigil at the tombs and the presentation of *Don Juan Tenorio*, a traditional play about love and death.

"What could be better?" Karen exclaimed.

After the sun had set, all five piled into Enrique's battered station wagon and drove the thirty miles to the centuries-old *yácatas* (pyramids) in Tzintzuntzan, the legendary capital of the old Purépecha empire. A night like no other unfolded, with strange medieval dances performed by torchlight, by dancers clad in frightful masks of skulls and ferocious deities, accompanied by hypnotic drum beats. The audience consisted to a large degree of Purépechas, who sat in large groups or families on blankets spread on the ground, picnicking and enjoying the sombre festivities, while their kids clambered around the ruins. It was a strangely festive atmosphere, ancient in its origin, with a mixture of pagan and Christian elements, but all fascinatingly new to the two young Canadians. They drove home in silence, all of them entranced in their own way by the strange display of folklore and superstition.

Rafael, Enrique and Paula, with the help of Carmen and their new Canadian friends, planned their first public demonstration in Morelia's Plaza de Armas for the second week of November. Carmen warned the young activists that the police would be there in full force and that word had come down from the Mexican authorities to quash any public forum or demonstration.

Undeterred, NNN went ahead with their plans and preparations, hoping that a large turnout would defuse any heavy-handed police presence. They wanted to make sure their message was heard this time, all the way to the Mexican Utility Commission and the Government of Michoacan and Pátzcuaro.

"This, my friends, is a matter of survival now," Paula said, "and we must be prepared to accept whatever personal sacrifices or consequences will arise: character assassination, defamation, even jail. This has now gone beyond an information campaign to a political fight, and we all have to be 100 percent committed." That Paula's dramatic call to arms would be prophetic, nobody could know at the time, but they all solemnly nodded their heads in agreement, and Rico proposed a toast: "To NNN and a nuke-free Pátzcuaro. *¡Salud!*"

Chapter 8
Carmen

The Landenberg textile mill in Thalwil, on Lake Zurich in Switzerland, was part of the town's economic backbone for over a hundred and fifty years, and at its height employed close to three hundred people in the war years, mostly women. They were engaged in the patriotic task of weaving the heavy cloth for uniforms for the proud Swiss Army, doing their part in defending the tiny alpine nation against the evil forces of war: Hitler to the north and Mussolini to the south. A patriotic duty in lieu of better pay. After the war was over, the mill underwent some drastic changes in the name of restructuring and modernization, laying off two-thirds of its loyal workforce in exchange for more efficient automatic machines that took over the work of hands and feet.

The new modern looms were controlled by the forerunners of computers: hole punch cards. These cards, which were folded together like an accordion, had patterns of holes stamped into them. The cards were then pulled over a metal cylinder studded with spring-loaded pegs that fit into the holes. This determined the patterns and the colours of the fabric to be woven, mostly cottons and silk. But they refused to adapt to the newly developed synthetic fabrics like rayon and polyester, which was part of their downfall.

The Landenbergs lived in an old stone mansion overlooking Lake Zurich. They had servants and were considered upper crust, even amongst the fiercely democratic Swiss, who despised aristocracy and class distinctions. When Carmen was just twelve years old, she was already helping out in her family's business, doing odd jobs and following her dad around the vast, noisy factory.

But in the 60s, the Asian tigers crawled out from underneath the heavy yoke of ancient theocratic dynasties and leaped into the modern industrial revolution, putting their masses to work for a fraction of the wages of Europeans or Americans. This spelled the beginning of the end for manufacturing in work-intensive industries like textiles. The Landenberg mill held on by the sheer determination of its owners and workers, always teetering on the verge of oblivion. The mill changed tack and produced high-quality linens and exquisite silks for a few years, but even those sectors were eventually shifted to the third world, mostly China and India, helped along by clever new-age businessmen whose social consciences extended about as far as their own families and bankers.

The Landenbergs had run their textile empire for over two centuries, but the world had changed. Carmen took over the declining family enterprise, but after struggling for several more years, she was forced to close the doors for good. It was a sad day when she had to lay off all the workers and chain the gates.

One tragedy was followed by another: Her dad died of a heart attack, which left Carmen to look after her widowed mother, who succumbed to cancer soon after.

Carmen, twenty-eight years old, single and without parents, rudderless and cast adrift, floated about like a ghost in search of a place of her own, not tethered to her past. For months she travelled, eventually through Mexico, where she found a lovely, very affordable flat in Guadalajara. She stayed for close to a year, learning Spanish and becoming a sort of modern Mexican herself. She travelled to Monterey and Vera Cruz, all the way to Merida, visited the mysterious Mayan ruins of Chetumal and Tulum and even travelled up into the highlands of Chiapas. She stopped in Oaxaca, spent time in Mexico City and then eventually found herself in the heartland of Mexico, Michoacan and its capital, Morelia. She liked it in this colonial city, far away from Thalwil and her roots.

One fine fall day she took a day trip to the picturesque, unspoiled town of Pátzcuaro. From the moment she walked into the large square, surrounded by ancient beech trees and the central statue of Don Vasco de Quiroga standing in the large circular fountain, she knew her odyssey was over.

Carmen fell in love with Pátzcuaro's colonial architecture and its location — two thousand metres above sea level, nestled between volcanoes and wooded hills along the shores of a large lake of the same name. She decided to move her life to this town in the centre of Mexico. She liked the temperate climate and the fact that it had sub-alpine flora, which reminded her a little of her homeland. She also liked the fact that the population was still made up in large part of Indigenous people, the descendants of the once mighty Purépecha.

Because the Purépecha culture lacks a written language, its origin and history remain somewhat shrouded in mystery. Their stories, legends, customs, and even their dialects, are passed down through oral tradition from one generation to the next. There are several theories about the origin of this ancient culture: One claims this race derived from a branch of the Aztecs, while another relates them to the Incas, saying they arrived in this region from Peru via the river Santiago in Nayarit and the present state of Jalisco.

The modern word for the local people, Tarascans, is a corruption of the word *tarascue*, which in the Purépecha dialect means "brother-in-law." Both the Purépecha and the Spaniards adopted this term as a result of the relationships of the Spaniards with the women of the region, and now it is used to designate the descendants of the old Purépecha empire.

During the fourteenth and fifteenth centuries, the Purépecha people formed a powerful and prosperous civilization whose influence spread far and wide. Much attention has been paid to Cortés and to the Aztecs, but it is often ignored that the Purépechas had already discovered iron and that they were the only people the Aztecs or Mexicans were unable to conquer and subjugate, until they were allied with the Spaniards. Even then, 30,000 Aztec warriors were taken prisoner by the Purépecha in the battle of Taximaroa (Hidalgo) against the armies of Cristóbal de Olid, a cruel Spanish captain. He finally defeated Tanganxhúan II, one of the last Purépecha emperors, giving each prisoner the choice between being sacrificed or enslaved.

Pátzcuaro was founded in 1324 by the king Curatame and reconstructed in 1372 by his descendant, Tariacuri. After suffering through atrocious wars at the hands of brutal Spanish conquistadors like Cristóbal de Olid, and later by the bloodthirsty Nuño de Guzmán, the region was eventually saved by the visionary Spanish lawyer and bishop Don Vasco de Quiroga.

With her sizable inheritance, Carmen bought a colonial two-storey, three-bedroom house in the *centro histórico*, with a balcony overlooking the Plaza Vasco de Quiroga. A heavy wooden door led into a private courtyard with antique mosaics on the walls, a slate walkway and a multi-tiered fountain surrounded by exotic plants. From the second storey a wrought-iron balustraded balcony afforded an exquisite view over the busy plaza below. Here in her chosen exile, just thirty years old, she found herself merely alone, whereas back in Switzerland she would have been lonely.

Carmen settled in well and soon made friends amongst the locals, especially with one dashing young police officer, Jorge Bonavista. Swarthy, virile, moustachioed and flamboyant, he was her polar opposite, which made him exotic and sexy. Only a couple of years older than Carmen, born and raised in a prominent family in Morelia, he had chosen a career in policing after having failed the bar exam twice. He was equally intrigued and beguiled by the sophisticated European woman, and the two of them entered into a liaison that was doomed from the onset, mostly due to Jorge's appetite for women. But despite all kinds of alarms going off in her mind, Carmen gave her heart and soul away.

Jorge Bonavista had no intention of ever marrying Carmen, but he did take full advantage of her complete surrender. Their intense and sensual relationship lasted for close to a year, when Carmen broached the subject of a possible longer and more traditional commitment. Jorge was truly horrified. Under no circumstances would he ever be able to marry outside his social class, and certainly never a foreigner. Jorge proudly mentioned that he was in fact engaged to a young *señorita* from a wealthy Morelian family.

Carmen listened to her lover's words without hearing them. It took all her inner strength to appear composed and not lose face or break into humiliating tears. She came out of her trance when Jorge casually mentioned that of course that didn't mean they had to break off their relationship. Furious inside, and chastising herself for having been such a blind, naive fool, she retained her dignity and composure until the door closed behind Jorge. For weeks after, Carmen berated herself. *How could I have been so naive and gullible, so disconnected from reality? I should have known better.* Deep down she had always known this liaison would not stand the test of time, yet she had fooled herself into believing her infatuation would transform into mutual love.

But instead of sweet honey, the fountain of love left behind only tarred misery. She felt betrayed, humiliated and alone as an abandoned child. She had nobody left in this world, nobody who understood her or even offered a shoulder to cry on or a hand to hold.

Carmen felt like one of those lovely monarch butterflies who has lost its way and fluttered about without direction. She stopped eating and locked herself inside her adobe walls, and her mind. Her world became monochromatic, and the vibrant colours of Pátzcuaro faded into dullness. She spent hours in front of her mirror combing her long auburn hair, until one day she took a pair of scissors and cut it all off, purging herself of her beauty.

Imelda, her Purépecha servant, kept looking in on her despairing mistress. She brought her teas and homemade concoctions, as much to feed her as to ease her aching soul and broken heart. Without Imelda, Carmen would surely have succumbed to her misery.

Shocked by her mistress's sudden attack on her hair, Imelda pulled back the heavy curtains and tore open the windows, letting the sunlight and fresh spring air flood the gloomy rooms. She dragged Carmen onto the balcony to witness the lively rites of spring in the plaza below. Young lovers were walking hand in hand through the throng of street vendors hawking pottery and carvings; music was blaring from tinny speakers; the smells of fried chicken and spicy tacos in the sidewalk eateries wafted up to the balcony; and for the first time in months, a small window opened in Carmen's soul and let in some sunshine. Slowly her eyes once again focused on the world outside instead of gazing inward. For the first time in a long while she felt alive and hungry, and a sense of well-being washed over her damaged soul.

"Look," Imelda insisted, "the sun is out and spring is here!"

Carmen's senses awakened once more to the vistas, smells and sounds of her surroundings. She tasted food again with newfound vitality, and slowly but doggedly she embraced her reality, determined to be the mistress of her own world. She clambered up out of the pit of self-pity and kept the curtains pulled back. A new and fresh wind started to blow through Casa Miro, Carmen's residence, much to the relief of Imelda and all who came to know and love the eccentric Swiss senora. Even Jorge Bonavista, who had been very worried about the mental state of his former lover, was relieved by her recovery.

Carmen forgave herself in time, but there was nothing to forgive Jorge, who was always who he was. He had a natural Mexican machismo, was true to tradition and had clear ambitions. He never promised her something he could not give. In the years to come, Jorge was promoted to captain and then to chief of police, and he became a convenient but reluctant ally to Carmen, who shamelessly used him when it came to circumventing red tape and Mexican bureaucracy.

One day while sitting on her balcony wondering whether to open a restaurant or an antique store, Carmen noticed Imelda fussing about with her threadbare blue and black pin-striped shawl, which was always draped around her tiny shoulders. Carmen asked Imelda's permission to feel the cloth.

"*Permisse?*" she said to the bewildered woman, who had a worried look. Carmen rubbed the cloth between her thumb and forefinger and asked, "Who made this?" Carmen noticed the frown on Imelda's face and laughed a pearly, deep-throated laugh she hadn't laughed in many months. This attack of merriment did nothing to dispel Imelda's doubts about her mistress's mental state — not until Carmen put her arm affectionately around the small woman's shoulders and explained that she was interested in the cloth because she knew all about textiles and fabrics.

Imelda told her the shawls were made locally, by backyard weavers. That day Carmen visited the small local cloth factories and came across some primitive hand-worked looms, unchanged since the time of Don Vasco de Quiroga. She decided to open her own factory, and wasted no time in having her two remaining looms hauled out of storage in Switzerland and shipped to Pátzcuaro.

Under her expert tutelage and supervision, they were reassembled and installed in a warehouse space she had rented on the outskirts of town. She then had to find a supplier of wool and cotton, and installed a dye room and a sewing and cutting room, equipped with Swiss Bernina machines she had also imported. A year after she had first conceived the idea, her two looms were weaving cloth of a much better quality than the locals could produce on their antiquated machines. She used the traditional local colour patterns and added some of her own designs. She employed and trained half a dozen weavers, four women and two men, as well as two dyers and two seamstresses, and over the ensuing couple of years built a solid market for her cotton and wool weaves. Rather than expand her small factory, she concentrated on an excellent product. Her Swiss-quality linens in strong Mexican colours were highly sought after and fetched a good price.

Carmen Landenberg swore off permanent relationships but did entertain herself with the odd lover she found amongst the adventurers and travellers that moved through Pátzcuaro. She focused her energy, compassion and good business sense on helping those less fortunate than herself, organizing and funding a preschool and a daycare centre, first only for her workers, most of whom had multiple children, but then expanding to include kids whose parents could never afford to send their offspring outside their humble neighbourhoods.

Carmen hired *abuelas* as teachers, who used their nurturing skills, honed on a lifelong procession of children and grandchildren, for the good of the community. If anybody asked about her origins and inspiration, she would dismiss her own past and point instead to the statue of Don Vasco de Quiroga, saying he was the past that mattered and it was his utopian example that inspired her own life. This, coupled with her Swiss upbringing, her skills, her compassion and her money, made her a well-respected and deeply loved citizen of Pátzcuaro.

• • •

Carmen had heard about Rafael, Enrique and Paula opening up the language school and later a backpacker's lodge. She liked the idea of young new blood in the community. Through them she heard about the proposed nuclear plant, and the prospect horrified her. She didn't need to hear the details to understand how devastating such a plant would be.

On the Sunday after their first makeshift rally, the somewhat demoralized activists sat around the courtyard at the school, trying to figure out what their next options were, when they received a surprise visit from an unsuspected quarter. Carmen Landenberg, the longtime Swiss expatriate and owner of a local textile shop (also the rumoured former mistress of el Capitán) stood at the door. She was tall and regal, her dark hair parted and shoulder length, with streaks of grey that suited her. "I'm here to help. *Estoy aquí para ayudar,*" she said in perfect Spanish, with just a slight musical accent.

Carmen's support of NNN, albeit clandestine in the beginning, lent the fledgling movement a lot of credibility. She also offered

her services to the school, as a teacher for the Germ
students, which legitimized and somewhat cloaked h
visits. Thus, she joined the faculty at ELL, a fact the scho
advertised.

Nobody had to tell Carmen that a project as big as a nuclear
generating plant meant a lot of government money was making the
rounds of local officials and bureaucrats, and that with that much
money at stake, things could easily get out of hand and become
dangerous. At first, keeping a low profile seemed the best way for
her to support NNN, and she helped them with advice and some
money, and became a kind of team mother to the group, a role she
deemed necessary and was comfortable with. She kept the three
young activists focused and within the realms of the possible, and
was a much bigger part of the fledgling movement than anybody
would have guessed.

I may have phimosis. 4 months
of no pull back on prepuce has
made what used to be a silly joke
into a problem reality. Scary.

Chapter 9
Morelia

Organizing a demonstration in Morelia, the state capital, was a bit more challenging than holding an information meeting in Pátzcuaro. Obtaining official permission seemed futile, because a refusal was guaranteed. Political demonstrations, unless they were in support of the PRI, were notoriously undermined, if not outright prohibited.

"There is always deception," Rafael suggested. "Maybe we can hold a public education forum at the university. We could get a permit for that."

In response he got raised eyebrows and shaking heads. "No, no, no!" Paula said adamantly. Everybody got the pun and laughed. They had assembled around the large oval table in the kitchen/conference room at the school. For the benefit of their new recruits, Karen and Jason, who were now committed to the movement, they all spoke English.

"We need to get the message out," Carmen emphasized. "We need to take out a big ad in *El Sol*. Don't worry about the cost. And we have to pick a date. From what I know, the bandstand in the Plaza de Armas is not used during the week. We can simply announce the rally will be held there any day of the week we choose."

The group settled on a day. They all were in favour of a big advertisement. Carmen, with Karen and Rafael's help, composed the layout and text, both in English and Spanish:

> The Comisión Federal de Electricidad plans to build a nuke plant on the shores of the fragile and pristine Lago de Pátzcuaro. NO NUKE NO, a coalition of national and international supporters, will hold an information rally on the Plaza de Armas on Thursday, November 31.

As a graphic background they chose the cone of a cooling tower looming over the island of Janitzio, with General Morelos's fist pointing towards the NNN logo. It looked very dramatic.

Over the next two weeks, the ELL and the Pátzcuaro Travellers Lodge became a frenzied workshop. As the group painted banners and coloured posters, they noisily debated how best to get everybody's attention. They wrote a manifesto containing their core message, which would be in a pamphlet they would hand out. Enrique wanted it to be radical, full of expletives, calling for a general uprising of the people of Pátzcuaro, Michoacán, the whole of Mexico. Rafael and Paula favoured a more toned-down, factual approach, which Rico considered a waste of time.

"The more forceful the message, the more dramatic the impact!" He slapped his hand on the table.

"We need to push information, not some radical political agenda," Rafael argued.

Paula agreed. "We have to appeal to people's common sense, and not come across like commie radicals."

"We have to demand honest and straightforward information from the governments and the Utility Commission," Carmen pointed out. "We have to hold them to a higher standard than just the usual political backroom deals, because a project of this size will affect the land and its people, not just for one political term but for generations to come."

They all agreed and even Rico climbed down from his soapbox, although reluctantly. He had to admit, at least for now, that the factual, informed approach was the best road to respect and acceptance amongst the ordinary people.

They drank *cervezas* and hammered out a Spanish version of the manifesto. Then Carmen, Karen and Jason worked on the English translation. They planned a double-sided pamphlet, one side Spanish, the other side with the English text.

Manifesto of NO NUKE NO

We, the people of Pátzcuaro, Michoacán, do not want the Comisión Federal de Electricidad to build a 700 mw nuclear generating plant on the shores of Lake Pátzcuaro. Lake Pátzcuaro is a shallow lake supporting a fragile ecology, dependent on fishing and yearly flooding of lakeshore farmland. Construction of a nuclear generating plant on the shores of the lake and using its water for cooling the two reactors would be an environmental catastrophe for the region and would destroy the lake, the landscape and our way of life. The interests of the people, their land and their environment come before the interests of the Comisión Federal de Electricidad! We urge the people of Pátzcuaro, Michoacán, Mexico, and the free world to stand up and fight against a Nuclear Power Plant on Lake Pátzcuaro. NO NUKE NO!

Jason suggested sending the manifesto off to different newspapers in Mexico, and also in Canada and the US. "You never know, maybe somebody will print it," he said, tongue in cheek. Karen took on the task with gusto and mailed the manifesto off to over a dozen large newspapers in Mexico. It was a long shot but worth the effort.

Paula also tried numerous times to get an official position from the government or the Comisión Federal de Electricidad, but all she managed to obtain were either telephone hang-ups or outright denials, or at best a patronizing response just short of a hostile threat, along the lines of "these are matters of security not open for public discussion."

Enrique contacted an old friend, still employed in broadcasting but working for a mainstream station. "You're playing with fire, amigo," his old college friend said.

"Yeah, well, I like it hot," Enrique replied tersely, disgusted with the gutless attitude. He hung up the phone. "Everybody wants to be a fucking boy scout. We are a nation of sheep worshipping a mythology of conquests and defeats, praying to a pantheon of wolf leaders. Zapata and Hidalgo would cry in shame at our spinelessness."

"Don't be so melodramatic," Paula said, but then kissed him square on the mouth. She really did love him and knew his passion and outrage to be genuine. He just needed to be cooled down once in a while, but they all needed Enrique's driving force. He was the motor that drove the machine, just as long as he didn't overheat and blow up.

Carmen offered to go ahead to Morelia and be the vanguard. She had some clients to look up as well. She thought it would be prudent to subtly put out the issue. "I'll mention the possibility of a nuclear plant on Lake Pátzcuaro in casual conversation with some of the businesspeople I know and see how it plays. It will give us a sense of what people think. I'll be staying at the Virrey de Mendoza."

They had 1,000 copies of the manifesto printed by a local print shop sympathetic to their cause, and also placed an ad in *El Sol*.

A couple of days later the other five active members of NNN squeezed into Paula's old Land Rover, along with two boxes of manifestos, and tied all their baggage to the roof rack. They passed through the ancient town of Tzintzuntzan, once the seat of the Purépecha kings, towards Quiroga and on to Morelia. Over a dozen other ELL students and tourists staying at the lodge also promised to make the trek to the big city in support. Paula arranged lodgings with an aunt of hers, who remained blissfully unaware that she had opened the doors of her old colonial house to a bunch of "radicals," the soon to be infamous NNN. *Mi casa es su casa* took on a whole new meaning for Tía Linda over the next few weeks. Rafael had contacted Señora Álvarez, his old professor's sister, affectionately called Tía Ana, whom he had stayed with during his student years at UNAM. She received Rafael with open arms and wholly supported their cause.

On their first day in the big city, they all fanned out to drum up support for their rally. Paula and Karen followed a list of backpacker lodges and hotels, while Rafael and Jason made the rounds of the university and language schools.

For Rafael, wandering through the grounds and buildings of UNAM brought back intense memories of Gabriela. He realized it had been a while since he'd thought of her, but when he did, her spectre was as vivid as ever. He smelled calla lily, which she liked so much; in his head he heard the sad notes of "La Paloma Negra," their favourite song. The familiarity of the buildings and grounds haunted him. Although it had been three years since their parting, he still smarted from the aftershocks. This had made it difficult to be open for other romantic encounters, for which there had been no lack of opportunity. Rafael was a good-looking young man, with a full head of wavy black hair that covered his ears and a Che Guevara beard, and of course he had his enchanting voice. He wasn't a monk, but all his affairs had been short-lived, and according to Paula, "You're just like one of your famous butterflies: beautiful but fragile, afraid to get burned or rained on. But you can't stay out of the weather, *amigo*. It's part of the world we live in."

Enrique chose the task of knocking on the doors of Morelia's radio and TV stations, hoping that his personal appeal would bear some fruit. All the activists were armed with stacks of manifestos, printed on bright yellow paper, which also announced the forthcoming rally in the Plaza de Armas.

"Some of these will end up in the wrong hands," Paula had said to Karen.

"That's a risk we have to take," Karen said, as though she were already a seasoned activist. "If we get enough people out, the police will think twice before doing something drastic."

"Mexican police don't care much about public relations," Paula said "I bet you the police are already aware of the protest and preparing for a confrontation."

The five activists started the evening off at a café under the Portales, on the north side of Madero Avenue, drinking *cervezas*, Rico and Rafael singing along with the jukebox. They seemed to know every song. Jason and Karen loved the atmosphere, and although their Spanish was slowly improving, they didn't understand any of the lyrics. Paula assured them they were all about love, loss and death. They left late in the evening, almost forgetting their reason for being in the big city.

Desperate for funds and realizing they were long beyond their intended stay in Mexico, Jason finally screwed up enough courage to call his mother. He asked her for a loan and explained the importance of their prolonged trip. "We're involved with a great group of people, and we're also enrolled in a Spanish school, Mom." He sounded apologetic and somewhat lame, considering that he hadn't called home since they left.

His mother, thrilled to hear from her son, could never turn down her only boy. That Jason would use the funds for education made it even easier to send some money. Karen silently swore to repay her someday and said as much to Jason, but he just waved her concerns aside. "Don't worry, it's not going to impact her life. If you can't ask your parents for help, who else is there? It's not like we're wasting the money. She's supporting a good cause. If we can help to stop the nuke plant, her money will be an investment in a better future."

The fact remained that they were broke and really did need the extra cash. What they would do when that ran out, Karen didn't even want to think about. Their lives had taken an altogether different turn from what had started out as a simple getaway holiday.

• • •

Around the time Rafael, Enrique and Paula founded the Escuela de Lengua Latina and the Pátzcuaro Travellers Lodge, a young graduate by the name of Gabriela María Ramírez started a job as a reporter at *El Sol*, the largest daily in Morelia. At first her projects were confined to a social column about which film star or politician happened to be in town that particular week, and sometimes these assignments turned into interviews, making the job a bit more interesting for her.

El Sol was the more conservative of the two dailies (*La Voz* being the other one), and as such, marched in lockstep with the PRI. Corruption and nepotism, from the president down to the local clerk and traffic cop, were standard fare for the Mexican system, and hardly an eyebrow was raised by the tame scandals Gabriela reported in the gossip pages of *El Sol*.

Although Gabriela's personal philosophy tended to swing slightly more left than the paper's stalwart editors liked, she was hired not only for her stellar academic credentials but also for her family connections. If she had known her dad made some impromptu phone calls on her behalf, she would have been very upset and probably would have turned down the job.

Being one of only two female reporters — the other one was Carmel Sánchez, daughter of the editor — she proved herself invaluable in a short time. Gabriela had ambitions other than covering the rich and famous, and within a year she got her wish. She was moved from her socialite column to political commentary. Her insight and fair treatment of contemporary issues added to the paper's integrity, and her style strayed more often than not from the paper's right-leaning philosophy and ownership. Her boss and editor, Ricardo Sánchez — a married man with a roving eye — liked the spunky young woman, and let Gabriela get away with it. In the end it was all about circulation, and Gabriela's slant on the civic elections and the race for governor of Michoacán added a lot of colour to the otherwise dull and preordained election process. With her candid outspokenness, Gabriela earned the respect of her readers and, in turn, of her superiors.

In the middle of November, her boss showed her the large ad Carmen had taken out in their newspaper and the accompanying pamphlet with the manifesto, both in obvious protest of a proposed nuke plant on Lake Pátzcuaro.

Gabriela scanned the manifesto and the ad with keen interest and then looked straight at her boss. "I've heard the rumours about a nuke plant on Lago de Pátzcuaro for a while now," she said. "A nuke plant there seems rather unusual," she added sceptically. This was the first time she had given the issue any serious thought.

Ricardo, who had big hopes for Gabriela's future as a reporter and columnist, was tilted back in his large leather chair with his hands folded behind his thick neck. He suddenly leaned forward and put his massive arms on the paper-strewn desk in front of him. He had the appearance of a bulldog ready to jump, but Gabriela knew her boss was nothing of the sort. Appearances were deceiving, and Ricardo liked the impression he made on people. It puzzled him, though, that Gabriela had never been intimidated by his tough exterior. What he didn't know was that he reminded her exactly of her own father.

"The issue here is not if it's a good idea or not, Gabriela, but rather why not sooner than later? We as a nation need the energy if we want to compete in this global market, especially since we signed the North American Free Trade Agreement with the US and Canada. Unless we produce our own electricity, we will have to import it from the US, which will drive our manufacturing prices right out of the marketplace. It's either cheap energy or cheap wages. The argument needs to be like this: Thanks to cheap power, more factories can operate at lower costs, which will make room for higher wages."

"I totally agree with you, Ricardo, but this will need careful handling. I'll find out what I can. I am certainly for higher wages," Gabriela said on her way out the door.

Ricardo stared at the closed door for a beat, but then his phone rang.

Gabriela didn't know anything about nuclear power, or any other kind of power generating for that matter, but she knew that a project of this size would result in better economic lives for the majority of the people around the lake. She was worried that NAFTA and the globalization of the manufacturing sector would lead to even cheaper labour in Mexico. That was exactly the kind of thing her father had fought against. Cheaper energy, on the other hand, would mean more economic activity, which would lead to higher wages for Mexicans. She also understood that there would be an ecological sacrifice for Pátzcuaro, but sacrifice was an inevitable part of life, ingrained in the Mexican psyche.

She read the pamphlet and stuffed it into her handbag. She was ready to attend the rally in the Plaza de Armas, not as an adversary but as an observer and reporter. She had no illusions about the political slant her reporting would have to follow. *El Sol* and the PRI were firmly behind the proposal. It was her job to argue the paper's official line, that of her employers, the paper's owners and ultimately her benefactors. In principle, she was in full agreement with that line. Jobs and money for the poorest state in Mexico were a simple necessity, she thought. The people of Michoacan needed the work, and Mexico needed the electricity.

Most people would not support the concept of a nuke plant in their backyard. That much was also clear to Gabriela. When she directly questioned people from all social classes in the days leading up to the rally — teachers, engineers, housewives and artists — about nuke plants in general, and in particular in their home state, the responses were more often emotional rather than intellectual. Yes, we need the energy, but isn't it dangerous? Shouldn't it be somewhere else — maybe on the coast? This was to be expected from a generation that was aware of the accidents at Chernobyl and Three Mile Island. Those were the only two accidents she and most literate people were aware of. What Gabriela looked for instead were intellectual, well-informed arguments, not sound bites or regurgitated, superficial media fodder.

Is nuclear power dangerous? she asked in one of her columns on the subject. Potentially yes, she argued, but so were dams — due to burst open at any time in the future. Coal-fired generators were a blight on the environment, windmills were bird killers and expensive to build, and solar power was in its infancy and extremely expensive to install. On the other hand, renewable energy sources like wind, water and power carried none of the potential threats of nuclear power. There was also the problem of the disposal of burned-out fuel rods, for which nobody really had a permanent solution, but the scientists would figure it out. This was not an issue that ordinary people could solve.

Gabriela researched the topic thoroughly. She learned that currently, in 1994, there were 103 commercial nuclear power plants producing electricity in the United States alone. They were, on average, ten years old, and were licensed to operate for forty years with an option to renew for an additional twenty. The Palo Verde Nuclear Generating Station in Arizona generated more electricity annually than any other US power plant of any kind, including coal, oil, natural gas and hydro. Worldwide, there were thirty countries operating 435 nuclear generating plants. In thirteen countries, thirty-eight new nuclear plants were under construction. Nuclear power had come a long way since December 1951, when an experimental reactor produced the first electric power from the atom, lighting four light bulbs.

The simple fact was that Mexico needed more self-generated energy capacity to drive the new *maciadores* and assembly plants which were springing up everywhere, thanks to the recently signed NAFTA. Without electricity — no machines, no work, no money.

As a journalist, Gabriela knew it was her duty to look at an issue from all sides, but she couldn't help feeling certain pressures. Not only the pressure to keep her job, but also to be taken seriously as a female reporter in a world dominated by male voices. She didn't like to acknowledge it, but there was also the lure of advancement, maybe even an editorial position. On the other hand, opinions had to be relegated in favour of objective reporting. It was complicated.

To hell with those agitators and troublemakers from Pátzcuaro, she thought. *That's what they are, troublemakers!* They didn't see the big picture, only a fraction of it: their own backyard. Electricity-generating plants had to be built in somebody's backyard.

Yes, she would cover the story and stay focused on the factual rather than the emotional, while remaining open and critical. She wouldn't pay heed to her nagging inner voice that wondered if she was selling out, making her a traitor to her idealistic youthful convictions.

She argued vehemently with herself, she had been naive then, in love. She didn't want to remember that period. She needed a clear mind, to stay level-headed and sober. She reread NNN's manifesto, printed on bright yellow paper. She was annoyed with herself for wavering, even for just a split second. Pátzcuaro seemed an unfortunate place for a nuke plant, but there was that huge lake and low population density. Also, the location couldn't be more central in Mexico.

• • •

Just moments after the gang left the Portales, a young couple seated themselves at a small table in a café, just a few feet away from where Rafael and his friends had let go of some of their pent-up tensions. The radiant young Mexican woman, diminutive yet eye-catching, like an exotic bird, wore her long black hair pinned behind her ears and held in place with a silver and turquoise clasp that matched her dangly earrings. Her escort, a gringo with mousy blond hair that hadn't seen a barber in a month, and with a scraggly moustache and a bit of a paunch, looked out of place. Even though he was a head taller than his companion, he faded beside her. Several male heads turned in Gabriela's direction like compass needles drawn to the North Pole, while the women suddenly checked themselves in their pocket mirrors or refreshed their lips.

Bernard counted himself lucky to be in such charming company. It was all due to an unfortunate accident, but hey, that was life: a string of accidents, unpredictable and unrelated, and yet the very essence of existence. A cornucopia of intersections and crossroads, choices and decisions, luck and aptitude. He looked into her large brown eyes. *Volcanoes*, he thought, *full of fire and passion smoldering deep down*. He knew he felt something more than just gratitude towards the serious young Mexican woman. *Am I in love?* he asked himself, not for the first time.

Bernard had arrived in Morelia a couple of days earlier and checked himself into the Hotel Casino, which overlooked the cathedral on Portal Hidalgo. It was a basic hotel, somewhat reminiscent of the '30s and Humphrey Bogart, but well priced and clean. They let him park his camper in a secure parking lot at no cost. His cast had been removed in Guadalajara and although he still had a small limp, he was back in the saddle. He had decided to take Gabriela up on her invitation and look her up in Morelia. He didn't fool himself about the real reason for going to Morelia. It had nothing to do with culture or art.

Gabriela was surprised by Bernard's call and the fact that he just happened to show up in Morelia. She agreed to have dinner with him. She had, after all, been involved in nurturing him back to health and had gotten to know him a little bit. She still felt a tinge of guilt about his accident, although it was certainly not her fault that one of her dad's trucks had run over the Canadian. Gabriela also felt somewhat lost and lonely in the big city, despite being invited to galas and parties as the newspaper's former gossip columnist. But that was work, and she wasn't interested in the people at those events, trying to separate her personal from her professional life.

Despite appearances, her personal life was rather dull, she sometimes thought, since she spent most of her waking hours either at the paper, which was always a beehive of activity, or working at home in her small but comfortable apartment. So when Bernard called her, she accepted his invite and actually looked forward to a bit of social activity outside her usual circle of acquaintances. She was, after all, a young woman in her prime, with feelings and, yes, she had to admit to herself, desires.

Gabriela had picked up snippets and anecdotes from Bernard's former life in Canada while he was convalescing at her family's home, but nothing to give her a picture she could understand. She knew he had been a teacher and involved in some sort of court case, but it was all very vague, and he obviously didn't want to talk about himself or his past. She had never met anybody like him; he just drifted around Mexico, rudderless and seemingly without a past or, for that matter, a future.

They ordered a bottle of *vino tinto* and *coctél de camarones*, and Gabriela asked Bernard outright what had happened to him, not the accident but before, back in Canada. Bernard took a deep breath and searched Gabriela's eyes to see if she was just curious or if she really wanted to know. He took a deep swallow of the tart wine and began slowly and haltingly, not really knowing where to start his story. At birth? When he married? Graduation? He started at the end, the crossroad of his existence. "When I finally ran away, it was almost too late," he said. "In fact it was too late to save my reputation and much too late to turn the clock back."

Bernard's tale of his former life flowed from him like blood from an open wound. Gabriela didn't interrupt, and Bernard took full advantage of the opportunity. His surroundings became a backdrop, the balmy Morelia evening a night on stage. This was his chance to tell his story as he wanted to believe it — himself being wronged, his world shattered by external forces outside his control, like he was a marionette in some cruel puppet show.

Chapter 10
Bernard

In the small Ontario town north of Toronto where he worked as a history and English teacher and lived in a childless, loveless marriage, Bernard was a marked man, a fate worse than jail. He'd been on his way home from work when he spotted Jennifer Robbins on the side of the road with her thumb out. She could have been one of his students; maybe that's why he pulled over and picked her up. He thought she'd missed the school bus.

"Where are you headed to?" Bernard asked, rolling down the window of his Ford Taurus.

"Which way are you going?" asked the young woman, tilting her head to the side and putting one hand on her hip. Bernard took in her tight pink T-shirt and her tight white shorts, about two sizes too small. She carried a small white purse that matched her shorts and sandals. She didn't look like a schoolgirl, he thought. When she climbed into the car, Bernard was already sorry he stopped, but it was too late. There was no turning back.

"I'm on my way home. Can I drop you somewhere en route?" Bernard asked, licking his dry lips. She smiled at him, in what he thought was a lascivious grin.

"You'd like to do me, wouldn't you?"

Bernard sat up straight, shocked and taken aback, not believing what he'd just heard. "What are you talking about?" he said.

"If you don't give me a hundred bucks I'll go to the police and charge you with sexual harassment."

Despite the air-conditioning, Bernard broke out into a sweat. The traffic was heavy and hectic. He timed a yellow light wrong and then tried to race through the red, when a pickup truck T-boned his Taurus. His car spun around, careened across the intersection and slammed into a metal lamppost. When the car came to rest, it looked like it had been squeezed out of a tube: the front half was still its normal width, but the back half had been pinched to half its former size.

Bernard was saved by his seat belt, but when, dazed and in shock, he tried to open the door, he was unable to. He had completely forgotten about his passenger until he heard her moaning. Next, he heard the approaching wail of sirens, and then he felt dozens of eyes boring into him from the crowd that had suddenly gathered around the scene of the accident.

Jennifer had not worn her seat belt. She had hit her head against the passenger window before being slammed against the dash, where she broke three ribs and collapsed a lung, along with suffering a severe concussion. Bernard had broken a collarbone from the seat belt impact.

Two days later Jennifer's parents filed charges of molestation and sexual harassment against Bernard, a teacher.

From that moment on he could suddenly count his friends and supporters on one finger: himself. Neither Candice, his wife, who was horrified by the dreadful spectacle, nor any of her family, nor his colleagues would stand by his side. His protestations that nothing had happened, that he'd picked her up hitchhiking — naively, yes — were drowned out by a united chorus of righteous contempt.

In the eyes of the local media, as well as the townspeople, Bernard turned into a monster overnight, and neither his unblemished record nor his professional credentials, nor the fact that he recounted his side of the story under oath, made any difference. He never again spoke to Jennifer personally, and nobody challenged her version of events, which completely contradicted Bernard's. Even though Jennifer couldn't explain why she'd been hitchhiking, and even though she'd been bragging the day before that she could make a hundred bucks in an hour, and even though the charges were dismissed, Bernard's ability to resume his teaching career, in a small town where gossip trumped facts, was doubtful.

Candice had filed for divorce even before the trial started, and she had no intention of altering her decision after he was let off. She worried more about her own reputation than she did about Bernard.

Cruising south at 30,000 feet with a couple of beers coursing through his blood, Bernard didn't miss any of his former life, and the further away his past retreated, the more he felt he'd made the right choice by leaving it all behind. Nobody missed him; he hadn't left a big hole that nobody could fill. It was more like he'd just gotten out of the way so other people could get on with their lives.

Life before "the Jennifer incident" seemed like a dream, and the car crash had woken him up from a long, long sleep. But that was over now. Bernard had simply walked away from his former life. What had it amounted to up to that point? Nothing much. Maybe that's why it felt so effortless to leave it all behind.

After forcing Candice to buy him out, and then selling everything he owned, Bernard had the unique opportunity to do something different with his future, to steer a completely new course. He cashed in his pension, emptied his bank account, cancelled their joint cards and accounts and applied for a new personal credit card. At thirty-two years old, life was just beginning for Bernard Fowler.

I'm a free man! became Bernard's mantra, and he caught himself repeating it in his mind again and again. To emphasize his commitment to a lifestyle change — which he insisted to himself was synonymous with a personality change — Bernard made some world-shaking decisions. *I'll grow my hair and a moustache, and I'll never wear another tie as long as I live.* When they landed in LA, he felt a bit like James Bond on vacation, stepping into the warm blue day, feeling no pain. He checked into the Hotel Erwin, right on Pacific Boulevard in Venice Beach, and enjoyed his newfound anonymity, cruising the beach, checking out the girls. His sex life had been practically nonexistent for the past couple of years.

Bernard needed a home on wheels. From an ad posted on a message board in the lobby, he contacted the owner of a 1984 Chevy Sierra truck with heavy-duty springs and a Greenline camper on the back, and for five thousand dollars in cash the truck changed hands. The next day, Bernard checked out, bought six-months' worth of Mexican insurance and headed south. Behind the steering wheel of his new road-home, Bernard felt exhilarated. Although he had only been gone from Toronto for a few days, it felt like light years.

He crossed the border at Tijuana and drove down to Ensenada, his first overnight camp in his new home. He continued driving down Baja California, camping and taking his time. The endless desert fascinated him, and he loved the dry heat. He drove with the windows open, road music at full volume. Self-contained and flush with pesos, he contemplated the future, which stretched out in front of him like a big new sandbox yet to be played in. Bernard passed through San Ignacio, a genuine oasis full of date palms that had been planted by the Jesuits a few hundred years ago and were still bearing fruit. At night he felt secure in the cocoon of his road-home and content with the cheap price of food and Pemex petrol. He listened to local radio stations to get a feel for the Spanish language and studied some tapes and books he'd bought.

Up till now, Bernard had been able to describe his whole life in a couple of boring paragraphs that nobody would be interested in, except for the past six months, when he was dragged through hell. That sordid episode, which had started and ended with a proclamation of innocence, encapsulated what people remembered about him and what Bernard wanted to forget about. Both his parents were gone. His father died when Bernard was still unborn, and his mom died of liver cancer, mostly due to alcohol. He had no siblings, and only some distant cousins whom he hardly knew. He decided he would delete all the boring and bothersome parts of his former life and highlight the parts that made him interesting, like the fact that he was a somewhat literary man who knew his authors and classics and, he had to admit, had secret ambitions of being a writer himself. Maybe it was time to add that fact to his new persona. *I'm on a literary sabbatical, researching the background for a book about . . . Escape from Boredom* or *Flight from Mediocrity* or *Turning the Page*, to borrow a phrase from his hero, Jack London. That sounded a lot more interesting than running away from a ruined middle-class existence.

On the ferry from Cabo San Lucas to Mazatlán, Bernard settled himself on the aft deck with some other gringo travellers and backpackers, clustered around a couple of guitar players, smoking reefers and drinking tequila. Bernard ended up talking to a burly blond guy around his own age. The guy introduced himself with a gravelly voice as Randall, "from a small Oregon town called Sublimity," he said.

"You're kidding. What kind of a name is that?"

"When the Germans first settled there, they thought the land was sublime, an empty fertile valley nestled in the foothills of the Cascades. When it came time to get a zip code, they just named the place Sublimity. About two thousand souls live there now. I moved to Seattle and then up to Hollywood North, Vancouver, Canada."

Randall turned out to be an old Mexico traveller. "As a cameraman I can take blocks of time off and travel if I please. For the past couple of years I was married to an actress, but that turned out to be a mistake, and now, free again, I'm heading south with the sunshine."

Bernard told him very little about himself, basically that he was from Toronto on a kind of sabbatical, working on a book.

"Oh yeah? You're a writer?" Randall asked.

"Kind of," Bernard replied vaguely. "Working on a couple of history projects, looking for some inspiration."

Randall told Bernard about a special place in the mountains of Michoacan called Pátzcuaro, situated on a large lake of the same name. "It's magical, man, with a large Indigenous population, the Purépecha, still there in them hills. They hold the best Indio market in Mexico in that town, and the main square is surrounded by lazy cafés and romantic restaurants."

"Sounds fantastic," Bernard replied. He made himself a mental note. *Pátzcuaro.*

"It's not the same Mexico as the beach Mexico," Randall said, "and it's also not the same as any other part of Mexico. San Miguel has its artsy American ambiance, while San Cristobal is the city of the white doves and the Zapatistas, but Patzcuaro is the birthplace of real Mexican folk art."

Bernard's eyes saw the world around him as if it had been freshly washed. His mind felt lighter, with none of the brooding, distracting heaviness from the months before, no self-doubts, not much guilt. He felt positively alive, and when he checked himself in the mirror, he saw a different man. He still had a worried look in his eyes, eyes that always wandered, seldom focused or made contact. Now he tried to look straight ahead. His reddish skin, burned from a few days in the Baja sun, the scruffy three-day beard and bleached hair made him look healthier than the pasty, pale Bernard of yesterday, who had disappeared into his surroundings and always needed to be groomed for his job. *If Candice could see me now.* Bernard grinned at his reflection and shook his head in wonderment, liking the feel of his bouncy hair, grown unchecked past his ears. He looked down at his gut, which still bore witness to a former life of too much junk food, and he resolved to start exercising. He wanted to see his toes when he looked down, not the bulge of his stomach.

The boat docked late the next morning, and Bernard meandered down the coast, through little towns with dozens of shrimp sellers lining both sides of the street, holding out plastic bags full of shrimp to the passing motorists. Bernard drove into San Blás, circled the small plaza once, and then parked in front of an elaborate wrought-iron gate, behind which perched the prettiest little church in all of Mexico. In the square, squatting local vendors offered intricate hand-painted pottery glazed with primary colours, one after the other, all offering the same wares. *How does that work?* Bernard asked himself. *What kind of an economic model is that?*

He found overnight parking in a hotel parking lot, and for a small fee they let him use the facilities. The hotel had a bar attached to it, The Buccaneer, where he found himself amongst tourists and travellers — not a local in sight, apart from the waitress. He talked with strangers who were oddly familiar, though there was an exotic feel in the air. Loud Mexican music blared from the jukebox, and the tequila flowed like wine, when in walked none other than Randall. They ended up celebrating like old friends. The sun was just peeking over the jungle-infested hills when the first rooster crowed and Bernard crawled into his camper for a restless, humid few hours of sleep. He could not get comfortable, and decided to hit the road again.

Bernard stayed a couple of nights in Sayulita, a popular surf beach, but gave Vallarta a miss, heading instead further down, along the coastal highway, with stops in Melaque and Barra de Navidad. He continued along the serpentine road with its spectacular views, to Manzanillo. He stopped at several small seaside pueblos and camped on the beaches.

About a hundred miles south of Manzanillo, Bernard impulsively turned at one of those graphic road signs that indicated a beach. He followed a dusty dirt road past a cluster of huts and a small store and drove through a grove of palm trees, from which he magically emerged onto a pristine, picture-postcard bay with a granular terracotta- coloured beach. A few *palapas* clustered around a stone building that advertised itself with a Tres Equis sign as a place to obtain a cold beer.

Bernard had driven into paradise. Only two other campers were parked on the beach. Jesús (a common name in Mexico, but one that always surprised) and his wife Rosa ran the little makeshift restaurant/cantina and served up the most succulent *camarones* with an endless supply of cold beers, always served with a wedge of lime.

As night fell they watched the fishing boats come in from the open water. The fishermen waited out in the bay for the perfect wave, which would coast them into shore and sweep them right up the beach, clear of the water, where they safely parked the boats overnight. Bernard strung a hammock and, with a beer in hand, contemplated the vast turquoise expanse of the Pacific. *This is surely the apex of my existence*, Bernard told himself, fully immersed in the moment when the orange fireball slowly dipped into the ocean, leaving behind a phantasmagorical display of pinks and oranges streaked across the evening sky.

"I've never seen a place like this, except maybe on a postcard," Bernard said to Jesús and Rosa, who smiled at the lone gringo and opened another beer for him.

Every evening when the boats returned from the sea, a couple of panel trucks with large lettering on the side proclaiming RAMÍREZ FRUTOS DE MAR would arrive to pick up the day's catch. Apart from these trucks, there was little activity on the beach, except for the few raggedy local *muchachos* playing soccer.

About a week after he'd arrived at Bucerias, the name of the beach town, Bernard figured it was time to move on, but since he had no schedule, nowhere to be and nobody waiting for him anywhere, his time was his own. *Just a few more days*, he said to himself. *Maybe this is the time and place to start writing. Maybe this is happiness.* But deep down he knew that happiness was just a figment of the imagination, belonging to fiction and poetry. *Happiness is for pigs and wishes are for children* had been one of his favourite sayings whenever the subject came up in his former life. Nevertheless, at this very moment, he felt content and at peace with himself for the first time in months, or was it years?

That evening as dusk fell, Bernard walked to the store to purchase some staples. Lost in thought, still not accustomed to the hazards of Mexican traffic, he wandered into the road. A panel truck travelling in a reddish cloud of dust was coming at him. The gaping mouth of the driver yelling something was the last conscious image Bernard took with him before the lights inside his head blacked out.

• • •

"You pretty well know the rest," Bernard said, finishing his glass of wine in one gulp. Gabriela nodded gravely, remembering when she first encountered Bernard lying in bed at her parental home in Punta del Sol, still in a coma, with bandages on his head and his leg in a cast, suspended in mid-air by a rope and a pulley. He hardly seemed like the same person sitting across from her.

Gabriela drank her wine and looked at Bernard, not like a friend or a possible lover, but more like an alien, some kind of being from another planet. His story was a tale of woe and misery, of running away and drifting without spirit or meaning, a life so different from her own. She could never run away from her own life, although there were times she wanted to so badly, especially after her brother's death. She had known Bernard now for a few months, ever since the accident, but this was the first time he had openly talked about his past.

A long silence ensued. Bernard wondered if he had upset Gabriela. Maybe telling his story hadn't been a great idea. After all, he'd wanted a clean break from his past, to reinvent himself as another person, disconnect, maybe even get some sympathy. Instead he had brought his past into the present, where it seemed to be doing no good. *I should have just made up a story, a life. I'm the writer, aren't I?*

Gabriela didn't know how to respond to Bernard's story and thought it prudent to say as little as possible. "*Gracias*, Bernard," was all she said. She felt kind of sorry for this man, who seemed lost, but at the same time she couldn't entirely believe he was as blameless as he made himself out to be. Bernard as the innocent victim of a vicious defamation campaign didn't quite ring true. Maybe he'd left something out. Maybe it was just a lusty look, maybe it was something he did at school, a remark, a gesture. All Gabriela knew was that there was no reaction without action. Even in his accident in Bucerias, Bernard was not wholly without blame. She'd heard the stories of the witnesses. He'd wandered into the truck as much as the truck had driven into him.

Gabriela felt sad and strangely detached. It was late, and most of the guests had left long ago by the time she and Bernard finally got up to go. Bernard was empty of words now and devoid of emotions. He felt lightheaded and curiously elated. They got into a cab and Bernard asked for the Hotel Casino. They didn't say anything, but when Bernard took her by the hand and led her out of the cab, into the nostalgic lobby of the hotel and up to his room, she didn't resist.

It was three in the morning. Neither one had slept a wink after their desperate and almost detached lovemaking. Gabriela had found no joy in Bernard's fierce embrace, but she had desperately wanted a release of her pent-up emotions and desires.

"I have to go home," she said, dressing herself in the semi-darkness. The streetlights were casting a pale light into the spacious room. Bernard was just a dark form on the bed, disembodied and a stranger still.

"Let's meet tomorrow evening," he suggested.

"I'll be busy filing a report on the NNN demonstration," Gabriela said, slipping into her shoes.

"I'll call you," he said lamely.

"Be careful," Gabriela said, closing the door behind her.

Bernard lay awake, his feelings a mess. Maybe he'd underestimated the effect his story would have on her. Maybe his lovemaking could have been gentler. He'd practically assaulted her, his need was so great. He cursed himself and rolled over onto his stomach, desperate for sleep and solace. A couple of hours ago he'd been king of the world; now he felt lost and blue. *Happiness is for pigs* was his last thought before he drifted off into a restless slumber.

Chapter 11
Randall

When Randal awoke with a pounding headache in his hotel room in San Blas he felt disoriented and he couldn't find his new pal Bernard. It had been a rough night, but fun — way too much tequila and nothing but a hangover to show for it. *Bernard must have moved on*, Randall concluded and decided to spend some time in and around San Blas, photographing the wild birds living in the estuary of the Rio Grande de Santiago. A couple of days later he pointed his Jeep Wrangler south towards Puerto Vallarta, where he stayed for a few days, but he didn't care for the tourist traps at every corner and the hordes of gringos on their ten-day-long vacations.

He decided to head east, up into the terra alta of Mexico. After a long day on the road, he drove into the chaotic maze of city traffic and straight into the centre of Guadalajara, where he checked into the San Francisco Hotel, a large, rambling colonial pile with two courtyards and generous, high-ceilinged rooms.

Guadalajara pulsated with culture and life around the Plaza de la Liberación. There was music everywhere, and also the seductive smells of numerous street stalls selling goat's head soup, viscera tacos and tortas. From Orozco's murals in the orphanage to the architecture of the Teatro Degollado, Randall found himself thoroughly entertained in the city of roses, and decided to stay put for a while. He also made some local contacts in the film industry, and because he knew the camera gear, he was able to pick up a couple of days as a camera operator. It felt good to be working again. He loved the feel of the camera, and the lens was his third eye.

Over breakfast at the hotel, he met a quixotic, gangly character in a white linen suit. "Hi, I'm Parker from Vancouver. I overheard you talking to a couple of local guys the other morning."

"Randall Cox, from Oregon, but I worked in Vancouver for the past couple of years. Camera operator on a family TV series."

"*The Beachcombers* in Gibsons?"

"Yeah, how do you know?"

"Everybody knows *The Beachcombers* in Canada. I'm a journalist at large," Parker said.

Despite their age difference, the two expats had much in common as far as relationships and rocky careers went, but they didn't talk a lot, since they only met occasionally at breakfast. Randall was a busy guy and Parker preferred to keep to himself. As fate would have it, their paths would soon intersect again and confront both of them with choices that would change their lives.

One fine day in early November, after the Día de los Muertos, Randall came across a bright yellow poster by a group called NNN, advertising an information rally just a few days away, at the Plaza de Armas in Morelia. The poster denounced the construction of a nuke plant on Lake Patzcuaro. *This sounds like an invitation*, Randall thought. A couple of days later he cancelled his apartment, packed up his gear and moved on. *Watch everything, expect nothing, accept what is and do your best*, Randall mumbled to himself. His old mantra had lost none of its immediacy and meaning, guiding Randall along a one-way road towards Morelia, Pátzcuaro and trouble.

Chapter 12
Parker

Anybody meeting Parker for the first time couldn't help but notice his gangly, disjointed physique, like a skeleton in an ill-fitting suit. Parker appeared tall and lanky and wore his stringy flaxen hair combed back behind his ears. His long arms ended in large white hands, which dangled beside his lean, bony body like two pendulums. His feet were those of a clown, shoe size 14, and his legs extended long and skinny, with knobby knees like those of a giraffe. His voice came from a low and hollow place deep inside his chest, as if from a bad loudspeaker.

But it was his looming, angular face, leathery and sunburnt, that was his most striking feature — long, with high cheekbones, imbued with a permanent sardonic look, as if he was constantly surprised by the world around him. His deep-set grey eyes, betraying intelligence and passion, and his large mouth full of prominent, yellow teeth made him look more like a horse than a man. When

Parker smiled, he did it with just one side of his mouth, while the other side was permanently occupied by a cigarette, or these days by a cigar, mostly unlit. In the old days Parker smoked three packs of non-filters a day. "I'm trying to cut down," he would say to everyone offering him a light or a match.

Oddly enough, women often found him attractive. They tended to mother him and felt he needed their protection in this harsh world. Due to his odd physical presence, no matter how hard he tried, he could never fade into the wallpaper or be just a bystander.

In his time Parker had tended bars, driven taxis and airport limos, sold real estate, and worked construction. He eventually found his niche in chaotic newsrooms; for the past two decades, he'd been a journalist in Vancouver.

Success, with its trappings of fortune and fame, eluded him, but he did earn the respect of his peers and his readership. He became known for always telling the truth, no matter how much it hurt. Parker was above all a humanist, and his humorous cynicism hid a generous and compassionate nature. He abhorred religion in all its forms, believing it to be the root of all the evil in the world. "Agnostics and atheists are, for the most part, peaceful and tolerant people and do not kill their fellow men for their differing beliefs. It is the religious zealots like the Ayatollah Khomeini who, with their fanatic beliefs, turn into mass murderers in the name of their exclusive god," he wrote in response to Salman Rushdie's fatwa in 1988. Parker received no small amount of hate mail, and even death threats. "None from secular agnostics," he pointed out.

For the past ten years he had held an editorial position at Vancouver's *Weekend Magazine*, a trendy mag addressing the urbanite, caffeinated, hair-styled, sports-car-owning singles crowd. Parker thrived by pushing the truth and poking fun at the purveyors of high morals, like politicians and business tycoons. Nobody in the public arena was safe from his piercing rhetoric, cringing from his sharp and penetrating pen, and he collected quite a large cult following. His new column started out as "Parker's Pulpit" but soon became 'Bitterman's Gripe,' feared and dreaded by all who were feeding at the public trough.

Parker kept the lawyers with defamation suits at bay for a few years, being backed all the way by the publisher, until the magazine was sold off. That's when a different wind started to blow. Parker took a golden handshake and walked away from his career and commitments at fifty-five with a small pension, still smoking, still drinking and still kicking.

Out of a job and twice divorced, he had choices to make. He could stay put and work on one of the many books he had started over the years but then disgustedly abandoned, always finding an excuse not to finish them. He could theoretically look for another job. Then there was his third choice: He could pick himself up and travel.

Once he did some research and made up his mind, it didn't take him long to turn his plans into action. He bought himself a white linen suit to go with the Panama hat he knew was waiting for him in Mexico. He sublet his apartment to Sandra, a young waitress at the Shamrock, an Irish pub and his favourite downtown watering hole. A little bit of insurance there, in case things didn't work out.

He stepped onto the plane in Vancouver in mid-September, almost exactly a year to the day before the Comisión Federal de Electricidad applied for water rights to Lake Pátzcuaro for the cooling of their nuclear fission reactor core.

• • •

Guadalajara was Parker's first stop in Mexico. He wanted to see the city of roses and tequila. He moved into the reasonably priced Hotel San Francisco and spent the next few days wandering the city and getting acclimatized. He bought himself a Panama hat to go with his white suit and cut a singular figure, striding through the old city like a friendly giant.

Parker had to admit to himself that he was, after all, just an ordinary tourist, no matter which way he looked at it. He hated the concept of the map-carrying, picture-snapping gawker. But he had to check out the city and the sites at least once, rubbing shoulders with all the other turistas.

It took him a few weeks to get the feel of Mexico and learn some rudimentary Spanish. After some research, and talking to quite a few seasoned travellers, he decided it was time to move on to his new destination of choice. He liked the climate of the terra alta, the high plateau of central Mexico, but he found Guadalajara too busy and neglected, and too big a city. He decided on Morelia. From the airport, Parker took a taxi directly to the hotel Virrey de Mendoza on Avenue Madero in the very heart of downtown Morelia. He booked a junior suite with a balcony for two months, for the same price he had paid for his apartment in Vancouver, except here he had all the amenities of a fine hotel, the Virrey de Mendoza being considered the grand old dame of Morelia buildings.

The time-warp grandeur of the hotel, the exotic surroundings, the massive cathedral right next door, the wide Madero Avenue and the generous plazas and parks made Parker feel like he had walked into a pre-war movie set. He made up for his lamentable lack of Spanish with his natural charm and air of a man of the world. He quickly became a fixture in the old hotel, especially the bar, and he settled into an easy routine of early mornings and late nights. Sleep was something Parker had never been good at — six hours at the most — because he always feared he would miss something.

He took an early breakfast and then ventured out for a regular morning constitutional, walking between the murals by Alfredo Zalce and many grand public buildings along the mile-long limestone aqueduct that frames the city's east side. Every day he read the English-language papers, usually sitting on a bench in one of the many parks, and he always found people to watch and sometimes talk to, which would take up most of the afternoons.

In the middle of October an unusual guest checked into the Virrey de Mendoza — an attractive middle-aged woman with shoulder-length auburn hair. She had an oval face and hazel eyes that quietly scanned her surroundings. She was obviously no native to Mexico, but she moved with the confidence of someone at home here. Parker guessed her nationality to be central European from her bearing and mannerism, always respectfully thanking the staff in perfect Spanish with a genuine smile. She politely nodded across the restaurant at Parker when his curious eyes came to rest on her. Through the bartender, Pedro, he found out her name was Carmen Landenberg, a longtime Swiss expatriate and Mexican resident. He learned she owned a small textile factory and shop in Patzcuaro, a town not far from Morelia.

A week after she arrived, Parker also observed several young people, Mexicans and a couple of gringos. They frequented the hotel courtyard and met with Carmen, which he found an odd combination of acquaintances. Parker grew curious, and the following morning he took a seat close to them, pretending to read his newspaper.

Carmen and her friends went over some papers, flyers and newspapers, but they spoke quietly and he couldn't pick up their conversation.

After the group left, he couldn't hold his curiosity any longer and went over to Carmen. "I hope you don't find me impertinent," he said, "but I'm a curious man, and I've been observing your involvement with these young people, who are obviously very excited about something. I can't help but wonder how it is that you all know each other."

Carmen looked up at the tall, lanky man. She removed her glasses, letting them dangle on a neck-string, and after a short pause she pointed to the empty chair next to her. "Why don't you join me? I'm Carmen Landenberg, resident of Pátzcuaro these past fifteen years, and I can assure you we're not plotting to overthrow the government," she said with a wry smile.

Her frank manner impressed Parker, who laughed at her comment and accepted her offer, lowering himself into the comfortable armchair.

"And why are you so curious, Mr. . . . ?"

"Parker, just Parker. It's in my journalist blood to be curious. I can't help myself. I've spent most of my life observing people and their actions. I can't seem to stop just because I've decided to retire to Mexico."

"It's quite simple, really," Carmen said, handing Parker a flyer with the NNN manifesto. This is what those young people are all about, and since I wholly agree with their cause, I'm helping them out."

Parker quickly scanned the pamphlet. This was certainly interesting. He was intrigued as much by Carmen's charm as by the cause she supported. "Maybe I can help," he offered on the spot, surprising himself. "I could write about this and forward it to my old employer. Maybe he'll even send me a small cheque for a good inside piece."

Carmen noticed Parker's large hands, palms up in a welcoming gesture. *They look like bookends*, she thought. She decided, equally spontaneously, to trust this man.

"We can use all the help we can get," she said. "Let me fill you in."

Chapter 13

Confrontation

The big day dawned sunny and balmy, like most days throughout the year in Morelia. "Rich man's weather," Jason said as he stepped into the small courtyard of Paula's aunt's house. Rafael had to laugh at the irony of it. *At least the poor campesinos have decent weather,* he thought. Jason had promised Rafael to show him snow and frozen lakes someday. "I'll take you skating," Jason had said. Rafael just shook his head. He couldn't imagine it.

They had picked 6:00 p.m. for the rally, and the hours of the day stretched before them. Karen, not good at sitting around, went over the plan: "After lunch Jason and I will hand out copies of the manifesto in front of the tourist office in the Plaza de Armas, next to the cathedral. Enrique and Paula can set up at the bandstand. Rafael gets to go to his old alma mater and drum up some support."

Jason was all fired up, and both Canadians were convinced they were about to make a difference in the big world. The risk of danger only added spice. As they sat in the courtyard, Karen reminded Jason of the route back to Linda Alvarez's house. After Paula had confessed to her aunt what they were actually doing, Linda had opened wide the doors of her large old house. She loved the energy and vitality these young people brought to her home, which hadn't seen this kind of activity since Paula was a little girl. She loved that they cared so much about their cause.

"You do the talking," Rafael said to Rico. Rafael was still smarting from his last public experience at the *biblioteca* in Pátzcuaro, where he had seemed to switch personalities in mid-sentence, almost as if he were drugged. He'd never felt so out of place.

"But you can't sound like a preacher, Rico," Paula said. She had doubts about Enrique's being the cooler head of the two. "You must sound more like a teacher, less like a preacher. Facts, not innuendos and promises. Speak from the heart."

Enrique looked somewhat annoyed. He hated being criticized, but he also knew she was right. "What about passion, what about conviction?" he asked.

"It's all about emotional control," Paula said. "Keep cool and talk slow and clear. It's information we need to impart, not fire and brimstone. We want to convince, not convert."

"Slow and clear. Yeah, easy for you to say." Enrique shook out his shiny black shoulder-length hair and retied it into a ponytail.

The sarcasm didn't escape Paula, who laughed and raised her boyfriend's chin with one hand, while with the other she pulled him towards her pursed lips. "I love you, Rico," she said.

"Maybe we'll be on TV tonight," Jason quipped.

"Great, you can send a copy of the tape to your dad," Paula joked.

"We did inform all the TV stations and the newspapers. Somebody will be there to cover the event." Jason said.

"Let's hope so," Paula agreed, but she was quietly worried that maybe they were into this over their heads.

Rafael fidgeted nervously with his cutlery during lunch, pensive and absentminded, while Enrique kept drumming his fingers on the metal table, driving everybody else nuts. Karen kept checking lists and consulting maps, while Jason dug into his food with gusto, the only one with an unspoiled appetite.

Paula had been scanning the local papers. "Look at this," she said, and she put *El Sol* on the table. Rafael seized the paper and his heart skipped a beat as he read the full name of the columnist: Gabriela Ramírez.

Paula looked at him quizzically, wondering what had upset her friend. Maybe she had seen something that wasn't there, but his sharp intake of breath and the puzzled expression on his face betrayed an unusual emotion. The moment passed and Rafael continued reading, casting furtive glances at Paula like he had been caught doing something wrong. Rafael had never told anybody the name of his one big, mysterious love, the one he had ached for when he first joined Enrique and Paula in Oaxaca, now over two years ago.

He took the paper and moved closer to the window, as much for better light as to get away from observing eyes. As he read Gabriela's words, Rafael felt feverish and sick to his stomach. He heard the world around him as if from afar, disembodied, the voices muffled as if behind a curtain, disconnected words floating past him. He clutched the edge of the table and tried to control his breathing. *Gabriela is working for the other side!* He couldn't believe it. His memory of their miserable last moments came back to him, and he felt he must have done something very wrong, something that drove her away from him, not only physically, but also on an astral plane — the realm of timeless lovers and kindred souls. He had never truly believed that they had lost each other. Somewhere deep down, he had always nursed a faint hope of resurrection for their love, convinced somehow that they were destined for each other, though maybe not in this life. After reading this article, an icy calm swept over him, and he felt starkly sober and numb, like he'd been woken up from a deep sleep. His meal had gone cold and his drink remained untouched.

Paula was warily observing her friend, wondering what had upset him, but then reality took over and they all focused on the tasks ahead.

• • •

A balmy breeze rustled the leaves in the large beech trees surrounding the Plaza de Armas, where people were crisscrossing in an abstract pattern like a modern ballet. Bernard read the manifesto while having his shoes shined. It sounded like a worthy cause, but he lacked any insight into the matter. No, he wouldn't want a nuke plant in his backyard either, but on the other hand, the power for his fridge and TV had to come from somewhere. And he knew how Gabriela felt about it. He felt the might of right to be on her side.

He still felt sick thinking of Gabriela's exodus the night before. He hated to imagine how she saw him. Insensitive? Needy? Fat? He wanted to change that view of himself, not only in her eyes but in his own. He felt like such a loser, and it made him mad. Mad at himself, mostly. The cards he had been dealt by fate were not fair. He wasn't a bad guy, just a bit shallow and egoistic — but then, who wasn't? He'd been dealt a useless joker when he'd needed an ace. He wanted to impress Gabriela, but instead he had only embarrassed her and himself. He had taken advantage of her, and now she was avoiding him. He owed her, and he was going to make it up to her.

He tossed the shoe shiner a couple of pesos and wandered closer to the gazebo, where a couple of young people were dragging speakers and mics up to the bandstand. As he sat on a bench, observing from a distance, he recognized a certain rough blonde mop of hair. It was Randall, the cameraman. He remembered their inebriated promise to meet in Patzcuaro.

He got up and went over to him. "Hey, amigo, remember me?"

Randall turned around and stared at Bernard. "Hey! Last seen in San Blas. The Canadian. We talked about this place. You were gone in the morning."

"Yeah, I couldn't sleep and needed to move on. Lots has happened since, including being run over by a truck." Bernard pointed at the manifesto in his hand. "Know anything about this?"

Randall laughed. "I was just about to talk to these guys. I have my camera with me. Thought I could get some action on tape. C'mon."

Bernard saw his opportunity and followed Randall up to the bandstand. Randall introduced himself as a camera operator from Canada. "I got a betacam here and was wondering if I could film. Or maybe even get an interview from one of you."

Rafael and Enrique looked at each other. "That would be great," Rafael said, and introduced himself and Enrique.

Enrique excitedly pumped hands with the two guys, already seeing himself blazing across the world's TV screens. "Film everything you can."

"Excellent," Randall said. "Let's meet somewhere when this is over."

"We'll be at the Hotel Virrey Mendoza later tonight." Rafael returned to his cables and mic stands. Karen and Jason were busy hanging a yellow banner with the NNN logo prominently displayed in large black letters. Paula was nowhere to be seen.

After the two guys left to get their gear, Rafael had sudden misgivings about committing on the spot to an offer from two strangers. *Who were those guys anyway? Were they spies or sympathizers, enemies or friends?* On the other hand, the idea of getting this on film was a good one. Why hadn't they thought of that themselves?

Bernard was feeling a bit out of place, looking like someone who had just lost his dog.

"Bernie, stay with me," Randall said. "You can watch my back. I'll have my eye on the camera while you have yours on the crowd, and you can carry my battery pack and camera bag. That way I don't have to worry about someone coming up from behind. You're now my assistant."

Bernard was happy to have something to do, even though he had no idea what that meant. All he knew was that he had found himself in the middle of the very event Gabriela was in town to cover.

Gabriela arrived at the Plaza de Armas around 5:30 p.m. She brought along Diego, who carried a mic and recorder. She planned to listen to the speeches and observe the crowd. She didn't want to make personal contact with any of the agitators just yet. That could come later, probably the next day. Of course she intended to be professional and get NNN's side of the story. But she knew well enough what the newspaper expected of her.

"Let's go over there by the news stand," she said to Diego. "We'll get a front-row view from there."

Traffic in the Plaza de Armas was changing. The crowd was swelling. More and more people, mostly young males, stopped and lingered at the fringes, like they were waiting for something. Quite a few of these held bright yellow handouts. There was activity on the bandstand itself, and several young people with placards held aloft were fanning out across the plaza. Reggae music started playing from speakers on the gazebo. That alone was enough to gather a crowd. So far, Gabriela could see no presence of any police or security forces. "Maybe this is going to be a perfectly peaceful information rally," she said to Diego. "Like in Europe or America."

Diego stared at her. "You've gotta be kidding me. This is Mexico!"

Paula was making the rounds with banners and placards, asking people if they supported their cause and if so, would they hold one? She was very adept at shaming people into complying. She had that straightforward charm, coupled with an honest, childlike manner. It took a strong person to deny her, looking into those big brown eyes. She passed Gabriela and Diego by the news stand and.

Despite orders not to make contact until it was over, Gabriela could not pass up the chance to introduce herself. "Hi, I'm Gabriela Ramirez from *El Sol*, here to cover the event. Maybe you have read my column?"

Paula was surprised at how small and young Gabriela was. "Yes, indeed, I have read some of your opinion pieces. Would you like a banner?"

"Oh. No, thank you," stammered Gabriela.

Paula laughed. "I didn't think so."

"I know Pátzcuaro well," Gabriela said. "I spent some time there a few years back, in my student days."

"In that case, you must know that a nuke plant on that shallow lake would destroy the fragile ecosystem and a whole way of life, especially for the Indigenous people."

"What about the jobs this plant would bring, the prosperity for many of those Indigenous people, not to mention the energy Mexico as a country so desperately needs? You like your TV, your microwave, your fridge, don't you?" Gabriela argued.

"Sacrifice is a part of life. And this fight is not for me, it's for the future of the land of the Purépecha." Paula abruptly turned away. Diego had recorded the whole exchange.

Gabriela cursed herself for getting drawn into an argument. She felt she liked Paula and wanted to agree with her, but she was frustrated with her for turning away. There was another side to the story. There was always another side of the coin. This was what she told herself, and she reminded herself of her journalist creed: *to be above judgment, without bias and give equal consideration to all sides.* It would be hard to apply that mantra to her present position.

"Redemption Song" was playing from the bandstand, Bob Marley's voice familiar and comforting — but not today. A painful wave of sadness flooded Gabriela as Bob Marley called out about how he fought in his generation, triumphantly.

After the song ended, a tall, bearded young man with a ponytail walked up to the microphone, testing the PA system. Nasty feedback made the people gathered plug their ears. There was commotion on stage as they fixed the sound.

"*Buenos tardes, amigos!*" Enrique said. A few people answered his greeting.

"We asked you to come here and listen to a story of David and Goliath. You all know the story. Goliath is the Mexican Utility Commission and we, the people of NNN and the ordinary people of Michoacán, are David." Enrique looked around the growing crowd, speckled with banners and placards waving up and down.

"We want to bring awareness to the people of Patzcuaro, Morelia, all of Michoacán, Mexico, and the rest of world. The Mexican Utility Commission is proposing to build a thermonuclear reactor on the shores of Lake Pátzcuaro, with a cooling tower taller than the statue of General Morelos on the island of Janitzio. We formed NNN to oppose this mad scheme, and we say that a nuclear power plant on Lake Patzcuaro is not an option. It would destroy the lake, the surrounding farmland and a way of life which has existed here since Don Vasco de Quiroga!" Enrique grew more confident with every word. "Do you want to see a nuclear power plant in Patzcuaro?"

The crowd knew the answer: a resounding "NO!" echoed across the Plaza de Armas. Another noise was starting to build above the crowd. The wail of police sirens could be heard approaching.

Enrique kept going. "Do you hear that noise? That's Goliath approaching. But we have a good and true cause. This is not about political change but about the preservation of a sacred land and a fragile lake and ecosystem: The land of the Purépecha, the land of our fathers, our children and our mothers. We will not let greed and power destroy a way of life. We want you to write and phone your governor and mayors, your newspapers and television stations. We want you to help us stop this mad scheme."

Randall stood right before the gazebo with his lens aimed straight up at Enrique, who he thought bore a slight resemblance to that other charismatic speaker, Che Guevara. Bernard stood poised behind Randall, doing an effective job of keeping Randall's back clear.

The sirens of the approaching police armada coming up Madeira Avenue threatened to drown out Enrique's passionate words. "No Nukes No, NO NUKES NO!" he intoned, and the crowd joined him in a chorus, while the police fanned out on the edge of the plaza.

Randall panned the camera slowly over the heads of the crowd and caught the helmeted men in black uniforms, armed with shields and batons. He steadied his lens on them as they forced their way towards the gazebo. From on top of one of the cop cars, a loudspeaker urged the crowd to disperse peacefully.

Enrique kept on speaking. "We want to welcome the police. We are not a violent group, we're not here to incite a riot, we're here to inform and gather support for an issue that is clearly in the interest of the people! We want you, the police of Morelia, to join us in the fight for what is right! Respect the opinion of the citizens," he urged.

Randall had clambered onto a bench, which gave him a great panoramic vantage point. Right in front of Randall, a group of officers were indiscriminately forcing a path through the crowd with their batons. The leading officer whacked people across their bodies. He cracked his baton over the head of a tall blonde man standing in his way. The man dropped to his knees, and with his camera, Randall captured blood bursting over the blonde hair. A young woman with her black hair in a ponytail, obviously the guy's girlfriend, began screaming at the cops in English that sounded like she was from Australia or New Zealand, as her boyfriend cradled his head in agony while staggering towards the outer fringes of the park. Blood was squeezing between his fingers.

Randall focused on this action while Bernard shoved at other demonstrators who tried to gain access to Randall's bench. Then Randall panned his camera back to the gazebo, where the first of the cops had breached the tight cordon of NNN supporters. One cop raced up the steps and yanked the mic out of Enrique's hand, while two others dragged Enrique away.

Within seconds, over half a dozen riot police had control of the bandstand, surrounding Paula, Enrique, Rafael and Karen. Jason tried to make a break for it, shouting in English at the cops, calling them fascist pigs and Gestapo Nazis, until a billy club smashed into his head. His knees buckled and he sprawled like a limp doll onto the floor. Karen screamed, clawing at the two cops who restrained her. Randall captured it all on tape.

The crowd closest to the bandstand was yelling and shouting at the cops, who formed a cordon around the plaza perimeter and promised, through a megaphone, free passage for anyone wanting to leave peacefully. Many took that option and quietly filed out of the plaza, including Randall, who had put the camera into its case and was walking quickly towards the cordon of cops, urging Bernard to come along. "Remember, we're just tourists, caught in the middle, *turistas*, that's all."

"Got it," Bernard replied, his heart racing.

Gabriela felt like she had been cut off from reality. All around her people were screaming and shouting and bodies were in motion, but she couldn't feel any of it. Rafael had appeared before her, up on the stage behind Enrique. She had recognized him immediately, and he was more handsome than she remembered. Her knees had gone soft and she could hardly stand.

"Are you all right?" Diego was asking her, his hand on her shoulder. People jostled them, trying to get away. Her mouth was dry and she couldn't form any meaningful words. Diego had been recording sound, but Gabriela had been unable to do her job and give a running commentary. She was too upset by seeing Rafael. She'd heard Karen screaming but couldn't see past the cops guarding the steps up to the bandstand. Instead she was watching as the cops tackled Rafael and dragged him and the others away. She also saw Paula being shoved into a paddy wagon.

Her attention shifted to the screaming young gringa with red curls, yelling at the cops in English as they dragged an unconscious gringo between them. A minute later they were all whisked away in a blare of sirens and rotating lights. The crowd dispersed. All that was left were discarded placards, leaflets floating along the ground and the trampled and destroyed PA system.

"I recorded everything," Diego was saying. "All of that anarchist talk. I got it all."

Gabriela staggered to a bench and sat down. There had been nothing wrong with Enrique's speech. It was an appeal to common sense, an outcry for help for a just cause. Rafael, in the midst of it all, was like a vision from the past: older, yes, with a beard and longer hair, but unmistakably her love. Memories she had kept suppressed for so long were flooding back.

Gabriela walked out of the Plaza de Armas feeling weak, bewildered and confused.

• • •

Carmen Landenberg had spent the day at the hotel, keeping away from the young activists and the rally. She remained like the team mother — there when needed but staying out of the game. Having just made Parker's acquaintance the day before, she'd made a plan to meet him for dinner in the hotel, along with the other revolutionaries, after the rally.

Parker, on the other hand, had gone to the Plaza de Armas and witnessed the whole debacle from a safe distance. He saw the police shoving Rafael, Enrique and Paula into a paddy wagon while a couple of other cops dragged Jason and the screaming Karen into a separate vehicle, speeding off amidst a blare of sirens and blue and white flashing lights. Parker was just about to leave when he spotted two young people huddled on the ground at the base of one of the large beech trees surrounding the plaza. He went to them and found the woman panicking and the man bleeding profusely from the side of his head. His ear had been cut open. Parker found a taxi and got them to a clinic, where a doctor patched the young man up. The young couple were from Ireland and New Zealand — Luke and Vena.

The Mexican doctor didn't ask any questions and waived any offer of payment. As Parker escorted them back to their hostel, they talked about the brutality they had witnessed.

"Those cops are out of control!" Vena said. "It was a peaceful protest."

"Come to the Mendoza tomorrow morning for breakfast," Parker said. "I'll introduce you to the members of NNN, the group that organized today's event."

When Parker returned to the hotel, he found Carmen in the lounge, anxiously waiting for news. He quickly filled her in on the evening's action as best he could. He also lauded Enrique's speech, but tried to play down the reactionary behaviour of the riot police in order not to worry her any more than she already was. Carmen instinctively feared something had gone horribly wrong.

At that point Carmen and Parker were joined by the other two westerners in the bar, who introduced themselves as Randall and Bernard.

"Hey," Randall said. "I saw you at the rally. We've just come from there. I've got it all on film." Randall patted his camera case.

Randall told Parker and Carmen what he and Bernard had witnessed, confirming Carmen's worst fears. Bernard just nodded mutely, agreeing with Randall, but in his mind he was silently rejoicing. *I have just fallen into the heart of NNN by sheer fluke. Gabriela will be thrilled.* He was sure of that.

"It sounds like Jason got hurt," Carmen said, worried.

"Yeah, the only people I saw getting beaten by the cops were gringos," said Randall.

"That's going to make some fine press," Parker said.

"All the locals knew to get out of the cops' way."

"Who else got hurt?" Carmen asked.

"A young man from Ireland," said Parker. "He's here with his Kiwi girlfriend. I guess he was in the wrong place when the police ploughed their way to the bandstand. I think he's gonna be okay. I invited them for breakfast tomorrow morning."

It was past 10:00 p.m. when an agitated Paula, Enrique and Rafael filed into the hotel lounge, looking ragged and tired. All three had been released, after being fingerprinted and warned that next time they were going to go to jail. They had no clue about Karen and Jason's whereabouts.

"I saw Jason being hit over the head and dragged away," Rafael said. He felt sick about the whole thing. "We couldn't help him. We were in handcuffs."

Paula sat with her head held high, her hands clenched together. Rico put his arm around her. Neither one said anything. They hadn't expected the police to come down on them so fast and so hard. "Never underestimate the brutality of the police," Paula murmured. "Never again."

"They stormed the bandstand and we were immediately surrounded," Rafael said. "Just like that, they forced us into the paddy wagon. I've got bruises all over my body, but they made us all sign release forms stating that we had been treated fairly and held in protective custody because of the threatening mob. We had to sign. What else could we do?"

"We need to find Jason and Karen," Carmen said. She asked for the phone and started dialling. She knew just who to call in order to get some swift answers.

Chapter 14
Aftermath

Bright sunlight poured into the high-ceilinged, closet-sized room when Vena pushed the old shutters open. She and Luke had met only three weeks before, in Puerto Vallarta at the Hotel Roger on a rainy afternoon, watching old movies. And now she was sitting by Luke's bed, worried about him and thinking of her home in the land of the long white cloud, so peaceful and so far away.

Luke winced, recoiling from the sudden stab of sunlight, and clenched his eyes shut. He felt his bandaged ear with his hand and foggily started to recall the events of the previous day. They had been handed a pamphlet by a young Mexican woman — something about a nuke plant — and, curious, they had agreed to join the rally. He remembered how the cops indiscriminately and brutally crashed into the peaceful demonstration for no good reason.

"I should have kept my mouth shut," he said, "and not yelled at them." His agitated shouting had resulted in a billy club glancing off the side of his head. He felt sick and suffered from a blinding headache, but he had insisted he was okay, despite the doctor telling him he probably had a mild concussion. Vena affectionately stroked his forehead.

"I'll be all right," Luke said. "I'm supposed to be a Jedi."

"A Jedi, like in *Star Wars*." Vena laughed, despite the seriousness of the situation.

"Yeah, my mom named me after Luke Skywalker, if you can believe it. I think she saw the whole trilogy twenty times."

"Where's your lightsaber?" Vena joked.

"You're my lightsaber," Luke said, taking Vena's hand in his.

Vena gave Luke an affectionate hug.

"It's too bright in here," Luke said, putting his hand over his eyes. Vena closed the shutters again, enveloping the small room in a cave-like gloom.

When Parker had dropped the young couple off at their hostel the night before, he had suggested they come over to the Virrey the next morning for a meeting with everybody else. Vena looked at Luke and decided he was in no shape to attend anything that required attention and participation. "You stay here and rest, Luke. I'll go and find out what happened," She said. He didn't object.

Vena fetched him some coffee, water, fresh fruit and tortillas, before taking a cab to the Virrey. The bellhop pointed her to the opulent lounge, where she spotted Parker sitting beside a sophisticated middle-aged woman and three young Mexicans. Parker saw Vena standing at the entrance, waved her over and introduced her all around. Vena explained that Luke needed rest and that he had a minor concussion and a bloody ear. "I hope I'm not intruding," she said, noticing the sombre mood of the gathering.

"Your friend is lucky to get away with a bandage," Carmen quietly said. "Our Canadian friend Jason was not so fortunate."

Vena sat down, feeling somewhat out of her league. She felt like she had been cast into some dime-novel spy thriller.

"He's still in hospital, in critical condition with an open head wound," Carmen explained. "We're just hoping he's going to pull though. At first the police wouldn't even tell his girlfriend which hospital they took him to. But Karen alerted the Canadian embassy and they were finally able to break the impasse. Jason's dad is a politician of some kind. Both his parents are flying here as we speak."

Enrique shook his head. "I can't believe this happened. The fucking cops. This time they've gone too far."

"They obviously had orders to come down hard on us," Paula said. "We can take this as a sign that we present a real threat."

"I've called the chief of police and demanded an official apology, but that doesn't do anything for Jason," Carmen said.

Randall, with Bernard in tow, joined the solemn group, holding up a cassette. "I've got most of it on film, and I've already made a couple of copies. I'll distribute it to the local media, and maybe Parker here can send it to his people in Vancouver."

"Excellent!" Parker said. "I'm writing a dispatch to my former editor this morning. I'm sure they'll print it. A copy will also go to the Canadian Consul General in Mexico City. This time the police have hit the wrong people over the head. I would like our new friend here, Vena, to give us an official statement as well." Vena nodded numbly.

"But what we don't want to do is focus on the violence," Paula said. "It will overshadow our cause. We need to keep our issue up front. That's what the government and the police are fighting, not us personally but our cause."

"She's right, the fucking cops will not stop us," Enrique declared. "We'll hold another rally in Patzcuaro, but this time we invite the media ahead of time."

Rafael, who seemed unusually quiet and distracted, had not said a word, his head buried in a newspaper.

"I've read her article," Paula said, pointing to Gabriela's headline.

DAVID VS. GOLIATH!
The police smash peaceful demonstration
in Plaza de Armas.

It went on to quote parts of Enrique's speech and to describe the heavy-handed response of the police. The article did not judge, but one could read between the lines that Gabriela Ramirez was not happy with the outcome.

"It's the best NNN could expect from *El Sol*," Paula said.

"Let's meet here again this afternoon," said Carmen. "I'm going to track down Karen. Parker and Randall, get that story out to your people. Rico, Paula and Rafael might want to think about what NNN's next move should be. If you plan to hold a rally in Patzcuaro, you'll have to plan it well."

"How can I help?" Vena asked.

"Maybe you can go back to your hostel," Parker suggested, "and find out if any of the other foreigners there are talking about NNN and the demonstration. And take care of your friend for now."

The group disbanded and arranged to meet again at 5:00 p.m.

Bernard, the quiet witness to this gathering, walked out to the lobby to look for a phone.

• • •

Bernard's call surprised and unsettled Gabriela. She thanked him for the information — the names of the people involved, their plans to hold another rally in Pátzcuaro, the fact that one of the NNN members was a Canadian, presently in a coma somewhere in a hospital in Morelia, whose father was a Canadian politician on his way to Morelia. But his information didn't endear him to her. Instead it had the opposite effect. She understood that he only wanted to please her.

Most of the information, Gabriela could have acquired from other sources, but she didn't say that to Bernard. The one thing she was glad to learn was that the group was planning to go back to Pátzcuaro.

"Can you meet me for dinner?" Bernard asked.

"I have to leave town," she lied. "I have to go cover a different story." It wasn't totally a lie. Though she had no assignment to go to Patzcuaro, that was where she planned to go. "Be in touch," she said. She hated herself for her two-faced behaviour. It was not in her nature to string someone along, but she did want his information.

Bernard had no real interest in NNN's cause, but he liked being part of the intrigue that surrounded the scene. He also liked Randall, who, with his brusque, in-your-face manner and self-assured personality, was the polar opposite of Bernard, who hung along the periphery, feigning ignorance rather than admitting insecurity.

He felt his past sneak into his subconscious — the way he'd fled his town rather than hold his head high and let everybody know it was he who was wronged. Disappearing could've easily been interpreted as an admission of guilt.

He caught a glimpse of himself in the lobby mirror, his thinning hair, worn too long to cover the bald spot, his sagging cheeks. Despite his tan, he looked tired, and the paunch straining against his T-shirt didn't help. *I need to exercise, get in shape*, he told his reflection once again.

Gabriela was the only person Bernard had confided in since his flight to "freedom," and even then he had painted a one-sided picture of his former life and fall from grace. But instead of eliciting compassion and sympathy, he had put her off. He would have been better served by inventing some new past. *What the hell was I thinking? Nobody would know the real story, and what does it matter anyway. I'm a new man with a new future. Why not a new past too?*

The second phone call Gabriela received at work that morning unsettled her much more than Bernard's call. She recognized the smooth voice right away, and all the intervening years of separation collapsed in an instant. She tried to be cordial and detached, but her hands were shaking and her heart was drumming in her chest like a hummingbird.

Rafael had rehearsed the call in his mind over and over, but all that resolve melted away the instant he heard her voice. He tried to sound businesslike, in control, but his voice was strained. "I read your article this morning. I thought it was good. I mean, I guess you tried to be fair, but of course you're working for *El Sol*."

"You mean for the enemy?" Gabriela interrupted, instantly sorry for the brusque tone of her voice.

"I guess you could say that," Rafael stammered. He was silent a moment and then blurted, "How are you, Gabriela?"

Gabriela could hardly speak. "I'm fine," she whispered. "How are you, Rafael?"

"I'm okay. Teaching Spanish in Patzcuaro, and running a travel lodge for the students." After a beat, he added, "And this. You know, NNN."

"I'm surprised you're back in Patzcuaro," Gabriela said. "I thought you went to Oaxaca. How did you end up back there?"

"It's a long story. Maybe someday I can tell you."

"I would like that," Gabriela said, tears welling up, which jerked her back to reality. "Why are you calling me?" she asked, trying to steer the conversation away from the personal and back to the issue at hand.

"Only for business," he stammered, caught off guard by her change of subject. "I was wondering if you wanted to talk to us, maybe see the story from our side. You know, like an interview of the enemy, or something like that."

"Even if I agreed with your cause, Rafael, and I'm not saying I do, even if I wrote a piece supporting NNN, *El Sol* would never publish it," Gabriela said, trying to defend her position. "You know, Rafael, there are some valid arguments supporting a power plant in the centre of the country. Mexico needs the electricity, and it has to come from somewhere. It has to be generated in somebody's backyard, and people never like it, no matter where that is, or by what means it comes into their homes to power their fridges, TVs and microwaves — coal, hydro or nuclear. If we import the electricity from the US, people feel exploited, and most people want to be self-sufficient, which means we have to produce the power here in Mexico. I know you say that your cause defends the Indigenous people, their way of life, but what about defending them against exploitation from abroad?"

Rafael didn't respond, and Gabriela thought she had lost the connection. "Rafael, are you still there?"

"Yes, I'm still here." But he went quiet.

"What's the matter?" she asked.

"I can't argue with you over the phone."

Gabriela grew quiet too. She felt the distance between them, and yet in a strange way it felt like they were continuing a familiar conversation, like the "black and white" project from their student days. Not knowing what to say, she asked Rafael about the Canadian who'd gotten hurt. "I hear he's in hospital in a coma and his parents are on their way to Morelia?"

"How do you know about that already?" Rafael asked, surprised.

She swallowed. "I'm a reporter. I have my sources," she said lamely, already feeling guilty about having used Bernard's information.

"Well, I don't know anything new," Rafael said, a little wary. "Maybe you can find out and let us know."

"I can try."

"I wish we could sit down face to face," Rafael said honestly. "Maybe in Pátzcuaro."

Gabriela's throat tightened. "I would like that," she said.

She hung up, leaned back in her office chair and closed her eyes. She had avoided thinking about Rafael for so long, convincing herself that the past was the past and that she'd had no choice but to honour her family. In time she had gotten over the loss and heartache, fiercely telling herself that she had done the right thing. Being a young, educated, good-looking woman from a well-to-do family, she had attracted plenty of suitors, but none had resulted in any kind of romantic relationship. The night before last, when her physical needs clouded her judgement and she gave in to Bernard, she had been left only with a cold feeling of emptiness, and now that, out of the blue, she had reconnected with Rafael, she felt both sad and guilty.

Rafael's voice had awakened something deep inside her, had stirred old embers back to life, making her feel warm inside; yet she shivered and pulled her shawl around her shoulders. She lost track of the passage of time, oblivious to her surroundings, until Carmel, her colleague, poked her head in the door to ask about her follow-up story.

Gabriela sat up in her chair and, not missing a beat, said, "We need to find out where they took that Canadian boy who got hit over the head by the police at yesterday's demonstration."

● ● ●

Karen sobbed without tears, biting her knuckle, staring at the inert body of her boyfriend, covered by a white sheet from neck to toe. His head was bandaged and his eyes were closed. Drip lines fed clear liquids into his arm and electrodes monitored his vital signs. The undulating wave with its incessant *beep, beep, beep* was reassuring and frightening at the same time.

Nurses who spoke no English came and went at irregular intervals, checking the machine and the plastic IV bag and then leaving with hardly a glance at either the patient or his desolate girlfriend. They were busy, efficient and probably under orders not to communicate. Karen felt alone, lost and, for the first time in a long time, homesick. Homesick for her language, her mom's lasagne and her dad's jokes. She missed Toronto, with its insane traffic, the 401, Harbourfront, High Park and the beach, the exotic smells of Kensington Market, the Peruvian flute player on Yonge Street, the *ding-ding* of the street cars, and even the gleaming gold, glass and steel towers of Bay Street.

Karen couldn't get her head around what had happened the last few weeks, and she wanted to go home. Instead, she stared at the peeling battleship-green paint of the hospital walls and listened to the distant yet constant noise of the busy city: honking cars, screeching tires, people yelling, mariachi music blaring from a dozen different speakers. It all bypassed the still form on the bed in front of her. *Beep, beep, beep . . . Drip, drip, drip.*

It had been so hard to call Jason's mother and tell her what had happened over the phone. Karen was talking into a plastic appendage, not to a real person, waiting forever for a connection which was tenuous at best. Jason's mother, upset, had put his father on the line. He didn't ask a lot of questions, recognizing the emergency.

They were on their way to Morelia, and though Karen longed for them to arrive, she also couldn't help feeling guilty.

She had called Carmen at the hotel and filled her in. This seemed far too high a price to pay for supporting NNN. They hadn't signed up for this, to become martyrs, to end up in hospital or worse. Tilting at windmills, that's what it was. The Mexican authorities would not be pushed around by a bunch of hot-headed activists. They made that clear last evening, and it was ironic that the only two people hurt were foreigners. Carmen had told her about Luke, the Irish guy. Karen buried her head in her hands and fervently pleaded with a god she never knew, crying out to a higher power she desperately wanted to exist and to intervene on behalf of Jason's recovery. She wasn't religious, but she was praying for a miracle.

Jason's parents arrived at the hospital the following morning by taxi, straight from the airport, still in their Canadian sweaters and coats. They stared down at their son's bandaged and bruised head like he was someone else. Jason's mom wanted to know everything to do with her son's medical condition, while his dad raged against those who had done this to Jason. Both felt helpless and desperately powerless. They were in a strange country, in a substandard hospital, although the attending medical staff were doing everything in their power. To airlift Jason in his present condition was impossible. They sat with Karen all day and into the night, and talked and cried and hoped. Karen went out and bought some roadside tacos and pops, which lay untouched by Jason's bedside.

All three were jolted from their chairs by the awful silence when the heart monitor stopped beeping and the world ended for Jason.

Chapter 15
Fallout

Karen's voice sounded eerily calm, like that of a robot, when she called Carmen with the terrible news. Shortly after, she was escorted from Jason's room, in shock, unable to process the finality of Jason's death. All their dreams evaporated, all their wishes denied, all their ambitions annulled. Their own dance school together — gone. A house in the country — just a dream. Kids, maybe one or two — never. More travels, the future, all the tomorrows together — vanished. Karen couldn't fathom the future without Jason. Who would make her laugh late at night in bed after they made love? Who would hold her when she felt down, who would cook her breakfast? Egg whites on brown toast with the crusts cut off. Jason had invented this treat just for her. The drugs finally numbed her racing mind and dropped her into a deep, dreamless sleep.

Carmen also felt numb. This had not been in the script. Dying for the cause was never part of their bargain. It plunged their whole campaign into a different realm. From a strictly political struggle, it was now a fight for survival.

Carmen called everybody for an emergency meeting in the dark lobby of the Virrey, where she imparted the sombre news. The members of NNN sat stunned. This was a shock that nobody had been prepared for. There was confusion, then incredible sadness and grief, and also anger at the police, the system and death itself. How could this have happened? Enrique got up, no longer able to sit, and began pacing, his hands in his hair. He shouted about the police. Rafael and Paula just sat and stared. The guilt they felt for dragging the Canadians into their cause was palpable. Nobody knew what to say or do.

"Everybody get some rest and we'll meet here before dinner time," Carmen said. "At the moment there is nothing we can do. Parker and I will contact the media, and we'll also be in touch with Karen, and Jason's parents."

Bernard found out from Randall what had happened, and wasted no time in calling Gabriela with the grisly news. She called the chief of police, who told her which hospital Jason had been sequestered in, and confirmed his death by going straight to Jason's floor and confronting the clerk and then the nurses. She rushed her hastily written report to press without her editor's approval, just in time for the morning edition.

The news of Jason's senseless death at the hands of the brutal police spread throughout Mexico and around the world. The fact that Jason's father happened to be an MP in Canada made it an international incident. This was not the kind of publicity NNN had solicited, but overnight the small grass-roots organization was elevated in status, which brought powerful groups like Greenpeace and Earthwatch onto their side.

Of course, the politicians and the police refused any responsibility and claimed Jason had stumbled and hit his head on the curb — unfortunate, but in no way the fault of the police, who'd had to stop the demonstration getting out of hand. They produced several witnesses who collaborated this story, until Randall's video footage flashed across the screens of millions of viewers in

Mexico and around the globe, a complete embarrassment to the police. Eventually the mayor of Morelia and even the governor of Michoacán were forced to make apologies for the "unfortunate accident," as they euphemized the slaying.

Now the voices of the official Mexican opposition — the PAN, the PRD and other fringe groups like the Zapatistas — jumped into the breach opened up by NNN and denounced the thugs in uniform, going for the head of "the dictatorial and corrupt masters at the helm of the PRI." This amounted to a lot of blustering and some media exposure, but the effect remained largely inconsequential, because Mexican politicians didn't give a damn about the voice of the people. They did, however, dance on the strings of their foreign puppeteers in Washington, D.C.

Questions were raised in Parliament back in Ottawa about Jason Neumann's role in NNN. The Mexican ambassador had branded NNN an "eco-terrorist" group on the fringes of legality. No evidence was brought forward to support that claim. The world's press was clear about one thing: a young Canadian activist had become a martyr for the anti-nuke movement, albeit without his consent. In Canada, reporters suddenly wanted to know all about the CANDU reactors — how many, when and to whom they were being sold.

The controversy over nuclear power was rekindled by Jason's involuntary sacrifice. The incendiary, emotional debate raged between those who hailed nuclear power as an environmentally friendly source of electricity and those who predicted catastrophic consequences in case of failure and everlasting problems with production and storage of radioactive materials. They championed other modes of power generation still in their infancy like, solar, tidal and wind.

Randall's footage of the demonstration received popular airplay for the next couple of days. Over and over, the clubbing of Jason was replayed, and the rest of Randall's footage was cleverly cut and edited to show that there was plenty of intended violence. The resulting dramatic clip lasted only thirty seconds, but it was enough to make any viewer cringe. This was how Vena's parents saw their daughter on New Zealand TV, her arm around her boyfriend with his bandaged head, proudly flashing the victory sign at the camera at the end of the reel.

Parker's article, a typically passionate account, was published not only by his former Vancouver paper but also in the *Globe and Mail*, the *Montreal Gazette* and the *Winnipeg Free Press*. He completely exonerated NNN, touting them as the social conscience of Michoacán and blithely calling the handling of the demonstration by the police *brutal, unprovoked and in the tradition of jackbooted, club-wielding thugs serving their political masters rather than protecting the citizens of a modern democracy.*

All of a sudden the members of NNN, as well as its supporters like Parker and Randall, were in the international limelight. Even Carmen Landenberg didn't escape the glare of the media lens and was prominently displayed in the Patzcuaro print media together with her friends. Her involvement lent NNN much-needed social legitimacy and credibility among ordinary folks who had never heard of NNN or their cause.

The fact that the organization existed solely to stop the construction of a nuclear power plant on Lake Patzcuaro was now buried under the weight of Jason's death at the hands of the riot police and the avalanche of political spin and outfall from that event. It was that very predicament that bothered Enrique, Rafael and Paula the most, while their foreign supporters like Luke and Vena, and especially Karen, were trapped in their own personal dramas. Even Carmen had to dodge persistent rumour-spinners in the Mexican boulevard press, some of whom tried to portray her as the brain behind the movement, the foreign influence who denied the Mexicans what the Swiss had all along; Switzerland had more nuclear power plants than Mexico.

The three core members, along with Carmen, took a taxi back to Patzcuaro — to evade the public on bus or train — while Parker remained in Morelia "to keep my finger on the pulse here."

The three friends found themselves alone at last, sitting in the kitchen in the Patzcuaro travel lodge and arguing about the future of NNN and their personal involvement. Only two days had passed since Jason's death, and they found themselves in a whole new world.

The fact that groups like Greenpeace wanted to support NNN felt like both a blessing and a curse. Not only would the Mexican authorities not look kindly upon the involvement of such a notorious international activist organization, they would try everything to discredit and disallow them along with NNN. Protecting Lake Patzcuaro and the region was becoming part of a much bigger campaign, and as such, in danger of slipping out of the control of its founders.

"This could derail the whole process," Paula said. "We should make these guys from Greenpeace know that their support might just as easily backfire and put the Mexican government in a position of 'might is right.'"

"Having the Canadian government involved can do no good either," Enrique said. "Their own nuclear energy commission is behind supplying CANDU reactors to the Mexican Utility Commission. We know whose side they're on."

Rafael disagreed. "Their politicians are demanding answers from the Mexican government about their police. They are going to have to be more careful with us. We can take advantage of all this attention and turn it to our advantage. And we owe it to Jason to do that. We need to think this through and make the best of this mad carnival, while keeping our eyes on the goal: the preservation of the lake and the way of life in and around Patzcuaro. We need to ask ourselves: What would Don Vasco de Quiroga do?"

"Nice line, Rafael, but what *would* Don Vasco do?" Paula asked.

"Of course he would stand with NNN and the people of Pátzcuaro," Enrique cried. "He would tell us to plan the next demonstration on the site of the proposed plant and to invite the world. He'd tell us to get going now. We will use the spirit of Don Vasco de Quiroga to guide us."

All three felt inspired by Rafael's suggestive question and Rico's passionate answer, and it made them feel a whole lot better about themselves, giving them a much-needed fix of motivation and confidence, as well as a philosophical and spiritual direction for their continued attempt to thwart the mighty Mexican Utility Commission.

Self-doubts assailed Carmen in the gloomy twilight of her bedroom, where she lay with her eyes wide open and staring at the dark ceiling. Was this cause just a diversion, or did she really believe they could win the lopsided fight? *Even more importantly*, she wondered, *is my heart really in this fight, or am I just a fashionable environmentalist?* She questioned her own motivation, her sincerity, her commitment, her involvement. *They are so much younger. Maybe this isn't my battle.*

She finally drifted into a fitful sleep and woke the next morning with no new resolve. *I'm drifting like a cloud who doesn't know if it should rain or disperse. I'm a goddamed marshmallow when I should be a rock!*

The next day Carmen joined her three young friends at the lodge and was surprised by their sudden activity and newfound vigour.

"We know now how to move forward," Paula said. "We're bringing Don Vasco de Quiroga on side." She gave Carmen a big, bright smile. Carmen had slept badly, but when she saw Paula full of new confidence, a weight lifted. She knew where she belonged. *This is a good cause. This is the right thing to do. This is not a fad, a cause célèbre, this is what I believe in my heart, and this is where I will fight, on the side of right, and it is where I belong, right here, right now.*

Carmen gave Paula a big, long hug and whispered, "Thank you."

Surprised and touched, Paula asked, "Is everything all right, Carmen?"

"For the first time in days I feel that what we're doing isn't wrong. I now know we will win."

• • •

Back in Morelia, Randall and Bernard did a few sporadic interviews around the city, Randall with the camera on his shoulder, Bernard guarding his back and carrying the extra lenses and batteries. There was no shortage of opinions, from the university campus to the plaza in front of the fantastic double-spired Morelos Cathedral, and even back in the Plaza de Armas. The opinions were unanimous: Nobody liked the way the police handled the demonstration, and people were even less impressed with the government's subsequent lies on the matter.

On the issue of a nuke plant on Lake Pátzcuaro, the locals were divided. They saw jobs and prosperity for a perpetually poor part of the country, while the more educated were strongly against the project: "Certainly not on Lake Patzcuaro!" The tourists who knew about the issue were wholly on the side of NNN and dead against the way the Mexican authorities had handled the issue.

Bernard carried and set up the equipment and took care of the sound recording, changing and labelling cassettes and even helping Randall with editing and transferring from film to VCR at the university's film department. Randall and Bernard met with Parker, who kept in touch with Carmen. This direct pipeline to the core group in Pátzcuaro supplied Bernard with fodder. He called Gabriela every day with the latest, but he had yet to get another date with her.

Vena, with NNN's official sanction, gave interviews to her dad, who was a reporter, and thereby to the New Zealand media, along with Luke. They also used this platform to highlight the struggle of NNN against the almighty Mexican Utility Commission and the government. This resonated well in the land of the long white cloud. The Kiwis, with the help of Greenpeace, had banned all nuclear activity in their own country, to the chagrin of the US and even the French. The 1985 killing of Ferdinand Pereira, a Greenpeace photographer on board the *Rainbow Warrior* in Auckland Harbour at the hands of the French secret police had been condemned worldwide.

Paula addressed the question on everybody's mind: "Should we hold the rally before or after Christmas? During *Navidad* in Mexico nobody wants to think or talk about politics. On the other hand, if we wait too long, our campaign will lose momentum and the fire will turn to ashes that may be hard to reignite." Paula's metaphor struck home. Timing was everything.

Rafael agreed. "We need to capitalize on the present momentum and bring the ordinary people to our side. We have to organize another rally."

"Rafael is right. Christmas is eight weeks away and people's attention will shift away from us," Paula said. "Maybe we can organize the next rally around families. This is, after all, an issue that affects everybody, especially the children, who will inherit the future."

"Let's have kids and *piñatas*," Enrique said, keen on the idea.

"Yeah, I believe that could work," Rafael agreed. "It's a bit risky, since it could be perceived as manipulative, but I think it could be a success."

"We should hold the rally at the proposed building site," Enrique suggested.

"We'll never get the permission, and then we're trespassing. Besides, the logistics are too complicated. No power, water, washrooms, et cetera. And how will people get there?" Paula asked.

The next day Carmen had good news. "I've talked to my friend Arturo Pimentel Ramos, who owns and operates the Villa Pátzcuaro Campground and Motel."

"We know Arturo," Paula said. "We stayed with him when we arrived."

"He says there is plenty of room to fit a few hundred people. As you probably know, Arturo is also a respected historian, one of the keepers of Pátzcuaro's soul and an adamant defender of Vasco de Quiroga's legacy and way of life. He's happy to support us and has offered his land for our purposes."

"That's fantastic," said Paula. "If they want to stop us, they'll have to confront us on private property and be up against some very respected people."

"Let's invite everybody," Rafael suggested, "including the clergy and the politicians. Maybe we can turn the whole rally into a celebration for everybody, young and old, families, friends and tourists. It needs to be for the people, by the people, in order to have any relevance. The Utility Commission and the Mexican government want to paint us into a corner, isolate us as a fringe movement. Let's show the world that this is not an issue pushed by an "ecoterrorist group" but by the ordinary people of Pátzcuaro. NNN is the people for the people, in the spirit of Don Vasco de Quiroga. That way, the police won't be able to crush the event."

"Now you're talking," said Paula, giving her friend a curious look. That was Rafael's longest speech in days. Something was different about him. He seemed more energetic and cheerful, like he'd changed batteries.

Everybody loved the concept, and they talked long into the night, laying the groundwork for the big day.

"I'll talk to the chief of police about it, to forestall any unforeseen problems. We should also let Parker and Randall know. They can be our Morelia office," Carmen suggested.

"Ask Randall if he wants to film everything," Enrique suggested. "I'm sure he'll jump at the chance."

They agreed on December first for a possible date, a Saturday, over three weeks before Christmas. "That will give us five weeks to put it all together."

"Let's do it," cried Rico, "and give everybody the perfect Christmas present: The preservation of Lake Pátzcuaro."

Chapter 16

Regroup

El Sol and its star reporter Gabriela Ramírez seemed to have had the jump on everybody else, to have known the movements and inner workings of NNN long ahead of other news outlets. She wrote that a new rally was planned in Pátzcuaro, and also mentioned that Luke, the Irish boy, had written a song. She even quoted excerpts from an article in the *Auckland Star*, written by Vena's dad.

"Where's she hearing all this?" Enrique grumbled, as the group busied themselves around the kitchen during the morning breakfast. "She just knows way too much and way too soon." He pushed the paper at his friends. Paula and Rafael read the column.

Rafael had never confided in his friends about his involvement with Gabriela Ramírez. Their relationship, which had ended, ironically, in Pátzcuaro, remained his secret. He didn't know why he'd never talked about it, but the more time passed, the less inclined he'd felt to bring it up, even with his closest friends.

But now that she had returned like some fiery comet orbiting very close, he felt petrified and elated. One part of him just wanted to run towards her, while another part told him to hold off. He was trying to pretend he had moved on and was no longer in love. *She was never meant for me*, he argued with himself. *She is bitter fruit, and if I fall for her again without her reciprocating, it will be my death.* I need to stay strong and keep my distance. But the fact was, her presence impaired his feelings, compromised his mind and made his heat beat faster.

Gabriela had said she'd come up to Pátzcuaro, but Rafael didn't even want to think about that. How would he react if he met her face to face? He couldn't possibly behave like it was just business. He could try to act normal, whatever that meant. He stood and looked at himself in the old mirror in the bathroom. Yeah, he looked older, and he had a dark beard that he hadn't had when she knew him. His hair was also longer, covering his ears. He looked the rebel, the outlaw, rough and wild — nothing that would endear him to her family, he mused, and then chastised himself for even thinking along those lines. He decided to get a haircut, maybe shave that beard as well, appear more like a young lawyer or teacher rather than a bum or revolutionary. He turned left, then right, checking out his visage, trying to see himself through Gabriela's eyes.

"What are you doing?" asked Enrique, walking by the open bathroom door.

"Nothing," replied Rafael self-consciously. "Maybe I'll get a haircut tomorrow."

Enrique just shook his head. Crazy talk. Maybe the stress of the past few days was getting to his friend. It was all a bit much, much more than any of them had imagined. The whole NNN seemed to have taken on a life of its own, and rather than them controlling it, it was starting to control them.

In one way it felt like déjà vu from their last days at Radio Libre, when the establishment had conspired against them and smashed their radio station, except this time the stakes were much higher. NNN found itself squeezed into the same counter-establishment corner by the Mexican government, and the tabloid press painted them as outlaws and subversives. At this point, more than anything else, they needed the trust of the ordinary people; they had to show their cause was genuine and everybody's cause, not just a way to fight the government and grab attention. Maybe Rafael was on to something — they needed to look respectable, whatever that meant. *Get rid of my beard and hair? Hell, no! That's crazy talk.*

On top of all the NNN activity, this particular time of year also happened to be the busiest season at the ELL, and students flocked to the language centre for courses and drop-in lessons. All three friends were teaching classes during the day and working on NNN's business after hours, sometimes long into the night, talking until they were out of words. It was a busy life and stimulating in many ways, but it left little time for fun.

Carmen had called on her old nemesis, el Capitán, and asked him for a meeting, which he reluctantly agreed to.

"My Carmelita," Jorge greeted her, kissing her cheek like a proper gentleman and leading her into his palatial office, furnished with garish antiques.

Carmen sat down in a large leather chair. Across an acre of desk, el Capitán leaned back, clasping his hands behind his thick neck, and observed his old flame from behind unmoving, ink-black eyes. She had aged well, he had to admit — better than his wife, who had gone rounder and closer to the ground after four children and a lifetime diet of beans and tortillas. He folded his hands and despite his hunch, asked what occasion had honoured him with her visit.

Carmen also observed her former lover, who still looked attractive, with his trimmed moustache and greying eyebrows and sideburns on his swarthy Mexican face. But she had come armed with the knowledge that she was glad their affair had ended when it did, giving her the freedom to grow and the independence to choose her own life.

She sighed and looked him straight in the eyes. "You look well, Jorge. How are the wife and kids?"

"Thank you for asking. We are all well. What brings you here after all these years, Carmelita?"

The term of endearment put her off a little, but she smiled. "I have one simple favour to ask of you, Jorge. It is this: Don't fight the common people."

El Capitán raised a bushy eyebrow and folded his hands over his small paunch.

Carmen told him of NNN's plan to hold a family-oriented celebration at the Villa Pátzcuaro Campground and to use the occasion to showcase their cause with information, interspersed with music, dance and children's activities. "We'll invite food vendors and have a market area. This is a celebration, not a political rally — a family affair — and we want to show the best of what Patzcuaro has to offer, a way of life that is worth preserving." She added, "There will be no need for police presence, out of the ordinary."

Jorge lit a cigarillo, leaned forward over his desk and blew a smoke ring straight up, towards the high ceiling. "My marching orders come from higher up, but I can let you know this much. I don't have the manpower, nor any desire to launch an action similar to what the police did in Morelia. We will concentrate on the flow of traffic."

"Thank you, Jorge," Carmen said.

"*De nada*, Carmelita. But just one more thing. There is a meeting in Veracruz next week. I am invited, and so is the chief of police from Morelia, some important people from the Comisión Federal de Electricidad, and some hombres from the *federales*. There is the small matter of the coin having two sides."

"Of course the coin has two sides. But if you like, you can let the other side know they are all invited to our event. As are you, Jorge." Carmen stood. "And you can bring your children." She closed the massive wooden doors behind her.

El Capitán looked out the tall window at the magenta jacaranda tree in full bloom, and slowly blew some smoke towards the ceiling. He sighed.

Carmen told Paula and Enrique right away what Jorge Bonavista had said. Rafael was apparently off getting his hair cut.

"That means they're worried and are taking us seriously," Paula said.

"It could also spell trouble. What if the *federales* decide to come on their own? They don't have to ask el Capitán," Rico said.

"You have a point. That gives us even more incentive to make this a family day. They're not going to bring out the army against their own kids. Not in front of the media," Carmen pointed out.

"I hope you're right. Better let Parker and Randall know."

Carmen called Parker, who in turn told Randall, and moments later, Bernard left another message on Gabriela's answering machine.

Randall eagerly agreed to film the whole event. Thanks to the footage from the Morelia demonstration, which had been broadcast across North America, he had earned some newfound credibility and also some money.

He immediately called a couple of producers he had worked for and pitched the concept of a documentary about NNN and their fight for the preservation of their unique environment. He received the backing he was looking for, along with the promise to distribute the finished product. This was the break he had been chasing all his professional life.

Randall was teaching Bernard the fine the art of filmmaking, i.e., carrying equipment, plugging in mics and batteries, listening to your boss: don't question, just do it, hurry up and wait. Bernard was a willing student, and it provided the perfect cover for his clandestine activities, of which Randall was not aware.

Randall also schmoozed himself into the film department at UNAM for post-production services, with promises of worldwide exposure, invaluable creative experience and future fame and fortune.

Randall Cox was about to do what everybody in the film industry secretly dreamed off: make his own film. He couldn't believe his luck, to have walked into the hottest political controversy in all of Mexico, and possibly North America, by sheer fluke. Forgotten were his marital troubles, his losses and bad karma; his finances were in better shape as well, and the future looked promising. As Randall focused on this new job, it seemed like years dropped off him. He laughed more, worry lines in his face receded and his dark eyes shone brighter.

Even Bernard noticed the subtle transformation of his new friend, full of dynamic energy. He was jealous. He wished he could feel like that, but despite his own attempt at reinventing himself, he felt no different. The same old demons still haunted him into the night, the same flabby gut, the same sullen face staring back from the mirror.

Bernard enjoyed being behind the camera with Randall, but unlike his mentor, Bernard had no ambitions for the long-term future. His mind was fixated on Gabriela, and he desperately wanted to please her, hoping to be rewarded. It didn't enter his mind that his betrayal made him more pathetic in her eyes, even though she took advantage of his information, while kicking herself for doing it.

One way to resolve her dilemma was to go up to Pátzcuaro. But she was scared to face Rafael. Seeing him at the rally had destabilized her. She didn't know what would happen if they stood in front of each other. When Bernard told her about Randall's documentary and his own role in the making of it, as well as the Day of Celebration, she filed this information away for later use. Publishing it would have meant free publicity for NNN. Instead she told her boss she wanted to cover NNN on the ground in Pátzcuaro. Emilio grunted, but he didn't know how to refuse the smart, wilful woman.

On the day she intended to go to Pátzcuaro, an early morning phone call jolted Gabriela's life into another dimension. The news was bad. Rodolfo, her father, had suffered a massive heart attack at the family home in Punta de San Juan. Isabel, Gabriela's mom, found her husband slumped over his desk in his study. Rodolfo Eduardo Ramírez was dead at the young age of fifty-eight, ripped from his life at a time when he had been contemplating partial retirement, handing the business over to his nephew Francisco, who was his brother's son and a long-time partner in the family business.

Gabriela boarded a flight to Manzanillo, where she was picked up by her two younger sisters, Theresa and Amanda. The three siblings had drifted apart over the years, but they were now united in grief. Isabel, their *mamacita*, the quiet rock of the family, had all her girls at home again. If only it could have been for a happier occasion.

Parker held court in the lobby at the Virrey de Mendoza, where he'd become a regular fixture. Where the Escuela de Lengua Latina in Pátzcuaro was NNN's headquarters, the hotel lobby became the international media centre. Parker, the official spokesperson, received journalists from the US, Canada, Europe, and as far away as New Zealand, and handed out his well-organized information in a manner that kept the cause of NNN, if not on the front pages, at least in the papers. Of the Mexican journalists, only Gabriela Ramírez at *El Sol* seemed to have her own information source, to the puzzlement of the group. Parker badly wanted to meet her and find out where she got the goods on NNN almost before they knew themselves.

Paula, Enrique, Rafael and Carmen put the word out in Pátzcuaro and received a lot of support from the locals, who generally didn't trust big government or big business. In order to finance the event, they decided after some heated debate to hook up with Greenpeace, who offered their help in setting the whole thing up.

Within a couple of days, Madison Bailey from Vancouver, Canada, showed up in Patzcuaro. She looked more like a schoolteacher than a member of a radical movement. Straight auburn hair and bangs framed her pale oval face. She wore green-rimmed glasses to match her green eyes and dressed casually in khaki and jeans with running shoes. Madison spoke perfect Spanish. "My mom is from Cuba," she said. When Paula gave her a questioning look, she explained, "I was born in Miami, but then we moved to Canada in the seventies. My dad didn't want to go to Vietnam." It seemed that she came by her activist tendencies honestly.

Madison came armed with a laptop computer. "It's an Apple PowerBook165c; it even has a colour screen." She proudly showed the portable computer to her new friends, who were equally proud of their IBM PS/1, which had a 10-MHz Intel processor and a 1-MB memory.

Madison's computer was loaded with stats galore about the proliferation and location of nuclear power plants, and even projections for the future. Besides money, she also brought production management skills to the table. She helped the group draw up a proper agenda, timetable, cost breakdown and list of technical requirements. Madison had a mandate, which was also Greenpeace's mission statement. "Greenpeace exists because this fragile earth deserves a voice. It needs solutions. It needs change. It needs action," she explained to the members of NNN, sitting around the kitchen table.

They didn't have a lot of time.

Chapter 17

Positioning

It was Madison's idea to promote the NNN rally at Patzcuaro as a "Day of the Living," not to counteract the Day of the Dead but instead to highlight and promote a way of life as it existed now, while at the same time preserving the future without a nuke plant on the shores of Lake Patzcuaro.

"What is this Day of the Dead all about? Sounds kind of morbid to me," Karen said, starting to tear up.

Carmen put a protective arm around her and tried to explain. "El día de los Muertos is a holiday celebrated throughout Mexico, but its heart is in and around Pátzcuaro. The holiday focuses on gatherings of family and friends to pray for and remember those who have died. The celebration occurs on the first and second of November, in connection with the Catholic holiday of All Saints' Day and All Souls' Day."

Paula added, "Traditions include building private altars honouring the deceased, which hold sugar skulls, marigolds, and the favourite foods and beverages of the departed, and visiting graves with these as gifts. Scholars trace the origins of the modern holiday to Indigenous observances dating back thousands of years, and to an Aztec festival dedicated to a goddess called Mictecacihuatl."

"Today tourists outnumber the local mourners, who honour their kin's departed souls in an all-night celebration that includes plays and music, food and lots of fireworks," Rico said. "Whole families gather early in the day on the old ruins in Tzintzuntzan in order to save a good spot for the night's entertainment. Accommodation is impossible to find, and the restaurants, plazas and artisan shops are all teeming with people, including our Pátzcuaro Travellers Lodge."

"You must have seen the bizarre skeleton dolls for sale in the shops around town. It all plays into this cult of the dead, which today is mostly a tourist attraction," Carmen explained for the sake of Karen, Madison, Luke and Vena. "These delicate *catrinas* — clay or papier-mâché dolls with grinning skulls, dressed in gaudy, raffish clothes like from a nightclub in hell — are coveted collector's items. They have their origin in the Revolution, where the macabre joke was that the dead look more glamorous than the living. Masks and paintings and all manner of carved and moulded artifacts pay homage to this bizarre cult, all the while celebrating the ephemeral world we live in."

"Bizarre indeed," said Karen, shaking her head. "But I think Jason would have gotten a kick out of this custom."

"To el Día de los Muertos," toasted Rico.

"To the day of the living," countered Madison.

They had a poster designed — there were no shortage of artists in Pátzcuaro — and a stack of flyers printed and shipped, most of them to their friends in Morelia.

Karen, Luke and Vena had become close friends in the wake of Jason's death. The two girls became inseparable, and Luke sometimes felt like the fifth wheel, often keeping to himself, playing his guitar, while the girls were out canvassing the people of Morelia, petitioning government officials, rallying support in cafés and the university, and plastering Morelia with posters announcing NNN's *Día de Celebración para toda la familia.*

Theo Neuman, Jason's dad, now back in Canada, supplied some valuable information through Karen. He felt that Jason would have been pleased. Apparently, two CANDU reactors were on order by the Comisión Federal de Electricidad, with delivery slated for 1996, two years hence. There was no mention of where they were supposed to be installed. Karen also supplied some technical data on these reactors: CANDU stood for Canada deuterium uranium. It was a Canadian-designed pressurized reactor that used heavy water (deuterium oxide) for moderator and coolant, and natural uranium for fuel. The two reactors would need a large body of available water for cooling purposes.

Karen passed this information to Carmen, who passed it on to the group. It didn't make them feel any better.

Through his teenage years, Luke had played guitar in a neo-punk band called the Warps, which had achieved some minor fame within Dublin's music scene. Now in Patzcuaro, Luke rediscovered his muse. He spent a lot of time with his guitar and worked with Rafael on a few songs. One song in particular was inspired by recent events and had a catchy refrain. They called it "Radio Active":

Come to the land of butterflies and volcanoes
You'll find the soul of the Purépecha
but Lake Patzcuaro is boiling
and we're all singing:
Shining radio active
Burning radio active
Turning radio active
[repeat]
And everybody cries:
We are all Don Vasco's children
living off the lake and land
shaping, carving, painting, weaving
and we're all singing:
[refrain x 2]
Join us in this magic place
in the heart of old Mexico
Together we can stop them

Let's all keep singing:
[refrain x 3]
Burning, burning, burning

Luke and Rafael played the song for the girls later that day. Everybody clapped and swayed. They recorded it on a small portable cassette player, with both Luke and Rafael on guitar and alternating voice, while Paula and Vena provided backup vocals. NNN had their theme song, albeit in English, but Rafael and Carmen were able to come up with a Spanish translation.

Since Rico, Paula and Rafael were also busy teaching and running the school, Luke and Vena offered to travel to Morelia to talk to Parker and Randall about some of the logistics and propaganda. Luke also wanted to scout out how they could record their song.

"No stories in *El Sol*," Enrique observed one night, throwing the newspaper on the table where he, Paula and Rafael sat together. "It used to be that I didn't like Gabriela Ramírez's stories about us. Now I'm thinking that any press is good press. She hasn't written anything for a week."

Rafael stroked the rough stubble on his shaven chin. It was painful for him to and pretend all was normal. He resigned himself to the fact that just like a fiery comet, she had passed him by. She wasn't coming to Pátzcuaro. She was disappearing from his life again, probably this time for good. He felt sad.

• • •

During that week of frenzied activity, Gabriela remained at her mother's side. They talked, cried and answered phone calls, greeting an endless string of visitors. The day of the funeral emerged from the humid darkness like most mornings in Punta de San Juan, hot and clear. The small seaside village emptied out, leaving behind only the very old and the very young. Everyone else joined the solemn black procession behind the draped coffin, as it wound its way up the hill like a long black serpent. It arrived at the old

Spanish church with one bell ringing its farewell to one of the town's favourite sons. Rodolfo was laid to rest amongst his kin in the hallowed ground of the small cemetery overlooking the azure bay glittering below.

Rodolfo Eduardo Ramírez had been a beloved and feared man. Loved by his employees and the fishermen of the Michoacan coast, feared by the competitors and punters who wanted to muscle in on the Ramirez empire. He set high standards and expected no less from those who worked for him. He was a fair man, but hard on himself and those around him, including his family. Once his granite mind was made up, neither God nor the devil could change it. Rodolfo died a very wealthy man. In life, he was generous to the hard-working village folk and those in genuine need, but unforgiving of his enemies. Gabriela's papa was not an easy man to love, and an impossible one to ignore.

Tradition dictated that Gabriela, being the oldest and still single, would take care of her mother. There was no shortage of funds, and Gabriela wouldn't have to work another day in her life. But Isabella, although devastated by the sudden death of her husband, also understood that her oldest daughter had a life and a career of her own, and she did not hold her to her traditional duty. Instead, she urged her daughter to return to her job, get on with her life, and if time permitted, she would love to see her more often, now that she was alone.

Isabella, now unencumbered by the larger-than-life presence of her husband, also felt a strange new sense of freedom. Being now the sole and undisputed head of her family, she was suddenly in charge of her own affairs. Although without any formal education, all her adult life she had quietly watched and learned how her husband ruled his business and how he dealt with friends and foes. All the while, she had been in charge of the busy Ramírez household, not openly, but behind the scenes, like a stage manager. Now she could combine the two skills, and within a short time she asserted herself as the undisputed head of the family.

Gabriela could feel her mother's relief at being free for the first time in her life, and she knew her mamasita would be just fine. Also, her two sisters, one of whom still lived at home while the other had married a local boy, would keep their mom company. This made her own choice to return to her life and job a lot easier.

Not much had changed in Morelia, except everybody at the office was surprised to see her, and tiptoed around her, surprised that she was not clad in traditional black but back in her civilian clothes. Her only outward display of mourning was a delicate black woven wristband. The old cliché that life goes on didn't bypass Gabriela, and she picked up where she left off. Her answering machine was full of messages from Bernard, who sent his condolences, a slew of the usual telespam, invites to lunches, solicitations to cover earth-shaking stories, which mostly turned out to be somebody else's view of the centre of their universe. Two messages were different. The first one was from UNAM's language department, inviting her to apply for a teaching position in journalism. The other call came from Rafael, asking if she was still coming to Pátzcuaro.

• • •

In the old port city of Veracruz, at the edge of a large, flat plateau on the Gulf of Mexico, the harbour sits anchored by a massive 500-year-old fortress, San Juan de Ulúa, which used to guard the city against hostile forces and pirates of days gone by. The city centre is a roundabout traffic hub where the six main roads intersect. Veracruz's port is the gateway for many industrial plants and oil refineries, the core of Pemex, Mexico's vast monolithic petroleum empire. One of Veracruz's modern office towers houses the main administrative centre for Mexico's Utility Commission, which included two nuclear generating plants: Laguna Verde 1 and Laguna Verde 2.

On a perfect sunny afternoon in mid-November, several executives of the Utility Commission, el Capitán from Patzcuaro, the chief of police from Morelia, the head of security from the federales in the state, and representatives from the Michoacan governor's office met in a government building boardroom. The sole reason for this high-level meeting was the construction of Patzcuaro

1, the proposed nuclear generating plant on Lake Pátzcuaro, and in particular the annoying opposition of NNN and its sympathizers.

Everybody sat around the large oval table, bare save for pitchers of water and glasses. No briefs, no agenda, no writing tools. At its head sat Manuel Rodriguez, Chairman of the Comisión Federal de Electricidad, a small man with immaculately coifed hair and a pencil moustache. His low, powerful voice contradicted his physical size and demanded immediate attention.

"The last thing we need is to be daily fodder for the world's media. We are a utility commission and in the business of providing electricity for Mexico. We are not politicians, and it is not our job to propagandize or defend our work." He continued, his small delicate hands folded in front of him, his elbows on the polished surface of the mahogany conference table. "Our mandate is to build and deliver electricity, and the only criteria we are interested in are technical. We do consider environmental factors, like the projected impact on the bodies of water used for reactor cooling and the amount of soil and water we displace, as well as the disposal and storage of burned-out fuel. Also, access roads and high power lines are within our jurisdiction. Social and political consequences are not. That, gentlemen, is why you are all here. To assure us that no ragtag organization of hotheads will disrupt our business."

Everybody waited for someone else to speak first. Jorge Bonavista, el Capitán and chief of police in Pátzcuaro, cleared his throat. All eyes were on him.

"Señor Rodríguez, gentlemen, we seem to have a small problem. No Nukes No, or NNN, as the group calls themselves, have drummed up a lot of support amongst the citizens of Pátzcuaro, and I believe in Morelia as well." He gave a perfunctory nod to his colleague from the police in Morelia, who sat unmoving, staring at the picturesque view of the Veracruz harbour without seeing it. El Capitán continued, "As we speak, they are planning a rally — or a festival, as they call it — for the first of December, somewhere in Pátzcuaro. They have invited families and children to this event." This time Jorge Bonavista didn't look at his colleague from Morelia, or anyone else for that matter.

"Señor Capitán, that is exactly the kind of publicity we do not need," Manuel Rodríguez replied in his unemotional voice. "I don't need to tell you that this is a sensitive situation. We are also dealing with the Canadians, who are becoming reluctant partners, thanks to the mess in Morelia." He stared unblinkingly at the chief of police from Morelia, who lowered his gaze. "I don't have to tell you, gentlemen, that this is a delicate matter, one of utmost importance, one that threatens the future of Mexico's economic foundation. Billions of dollars are at stake, and I don't have to paint a picture of the positive economic impact a project of this size would have on the whole region, the province and the country as a whole. We do not take this matter lightly."

"Neither do we, Señor Rodríguez," the governor's representative chimed in. "We take this very seriously and will do everything in our power to dissuade this group from any further subversive action. We will stop this party that el Capitán is speaking of."

"This is vital," Manuel Rodríguez said. "There is the delicate matter of appearances. We understand that Greenpeace is now actively involved."

"Armed force will not dissuade these people from organizing and working against this project," Jorge Bonavista said. "If there is another incident like the one in Morelia, it will only help their cause."

"What about our media?" a member of the Commission asked. "Where are they? The government has to make its case convincingly with the help of our friends in the media. We need to persuade some of those people on which side to stand."

Everybody murmured their assent, and they all agreed to do what they could to counteract NNN.

The sombre meeting was adjourned. "We will all meet again in the New Year if there is any need. *Feliz Navidad*," said Manuel Rodríguez as he rose. He turned his back on the group and left the boardroom.

• • •

Gabriela took a taxi to Pátzcuaro rather than the crowded bus. Riding through the undulating, dry countryside, past Capula and through the snail's-pace traffic of Quiroga, Gabriela's eyes were glazed. The driver tried unsuccessfully to engage her in some kind of conversation to pass the time, but he didn't get past the usual small talk, like the constant scarcity of money or the potholes in the road, which never got fixed. "Maybe they'll fix them when they build that nuke plant," the cabby mentioned wistfully, but he only got a curious look from his passenger.

The past few years dropped away like a dream as the taxi drove into Tzintzuntzan and then followed the lakeshore into Pátzcuaro. The cone-shaped island of Janitzio, with its massive and ludicrous granite statue of General María Morelos at its apex, fist defiantly raised to the sky, sat in the middle of the calm, shallow waters of Lake Pátzcuaro.

What would a nuke plant on its shore really do for the lake, its people and the region? Gabriela asked herself, not for the first time, but this time with the view of the lake to help her out. Yes, there would be an economic boom, work for many people. And then what? She tried to envision the massive concrete cylinder of the cooling tower against the backdrop of the volcanoes, dwarfing the islands in the lake. It was not a pretty picture, but then, progress seldom was. Twelve-lane highways weren't pretty, neither were airports or hydro dams or refineries, but all were necessary evils to facilitate our modern way of life. What about the lake and the people who now live around it? Gabriela had no definitive answer, and struggled between sober intellectual arguments and emotional misgivings.

They drove past the statue of Don Vasco de Quiroga. What would he think of the present controversy? It was a valid question, but Gabriela easily knew the answer. She sighed. Just before she'd left Morelia, she had been called into her boss's office and found herself on the wrong side of a very strange paternalistic talk.

"Gabriela, let's make one thing clear. We do not condone the subversive actions of those punks of NNN, and we will do everything in our power to dissuade our reading public from sympathizing with that lot of anarchists. You do understand what that means, or do I have to write it down for you? Go to Pátzcuaro and deliver what this paper hired you to do."

The whole speech was rather absurd, missing her boss's usual cynical humour, almost as if he was repeating somebody else's words. She looked at her editor blankly and said nothing, but wondered whatever had happened to journalistic values and integrity, fair approaches and objective reporting.

I have a hatchet job to do and I don't like it one bit, Gabriela said to herself. She still hadn't responded to that job offer at the university. She was stalling. She needed to go to Pátzcuaro on a legitimate errand — not to see Rafael. She tried not to think about him. As if there wasn't enough other emotional baggage to clutter up her mind: her dad's sudden death, her dishonest involvement with the Canadian, the looming confrontation up ahead. But she couldn't get Rafael's face, as she'd seen him on the bandstand, out of her mind.

Gabriela booked a room at the hotel Mansion Iturbe on the north side of the Plaza Vasco de Quiroga. She deliberately chose not to stay at Los Escudos, but when she crossed the plaza and looked up at the colonial facade of the old dowager hotel with the café under the arches, the memories from that magic week all those years ago flooded back over her like a wave of warm water. She experienced a sudden, disorienting reality shift, but she yanked herself back to the present. During all the intervening years, she had tried to convince herself their love had been just an infatuation, without substance or lasting effect, but deep down she had known the truth, and now she felt its effect.

But I have work to do, she told herself. No time for emotional turmoil, and not a time to lose focus.

Her phone call reached Rafael during an all-night session around the kitchen table, hammering out details about the forthcoming Day of the Living. He knew instinctively, before he heard a word, who was on the other end of the line.

"Rafael, it's me, Gabriela."

"I know. Where are you?"

"I'm staying at the Mansion Iturbe." There was a long pause. "I would like to interview you," she said. "Will you meet me for breakfast?"

Rafael would have agreed to meet her on the moon, but he kept a calm demeanour despite his racing heart.

Paula looked at her friend and thought he had been acting kind of funny lately, distracted and almost depressed. Kind of like he had been when they first met in Oaxaca. Her intuition told her it had to do with love; just who or where was a mystery.

Rafael was afraid that Paula, who looked at him funny, knew who was calling, although there was no way she could. He felt guilty. He should have informed his partners that Gabriela Ramírez from *El Sol* was seeking an official interview with him, but he procrastinated. I'll tell them later, he promised himself. "Why you?" they would ask, and then I would have to tell them everything, come clean about our former history together and explain and answer questions. Let me first find out what Gabriela wants. Besides, I don't really know what it is I want, except to see Gabriela.

The next morning Rafael walked down to the Plaza Grande, crossed the old square surrounded by massive white-painted elm trees and the twelve original palaces, and entered the restored lobby of the venerable old Mansion Iturbe. He didn't notice Rico on the other side of the square, who had come down to buy the day's papers. Rico noticed Rafael walking, head down, into the hotel. He didn't pay it any heed though, only casually mentioning it to Paula when he got home.

Paula pursed her lips speculatively. "Something is up with Rafael. He's been acting strange lately. And what's with the new clean-cut look? Maybe this has something do with his visit to the hotel. We'll ask Madison to check the guest list there. See if anything interesting comes up."

"Why don't we just ask him?" Rico said.

"Ask him what, exactly? Who his barber is? What he's doing at Mansion Iturbe first thing in the morning? Now that would seem like we don't trust him."

In the courtyard of the old hotel, Rafael spotted Gabriela before she saw him. She was sitting at a table with her profile to him, her hair loose over her shoulders. He stopped for a moment, his heart racing. He felt the urge to back away, to compose himself, but he forced himself forward. He went to her table and looked down at her familiar face, her black wavy hair parted in the middle, one half tucked behind her ear, exactly as he remembered. Gabriela looked up from her notepad, and Rafael noticed the small tape recorder. Strictly business, he thought. That's all she wants. And she's working for the other side. With his heart pounding, he wondered what the hell he'd come here for. He felt like a fool, a child that had been told not to pet the lions at the zoo, not to jump into the deep end of the pool, not to walk home alone in the dark.

"Rafael," she said. "You look nice." Her face grew hot. What a foolish thing to say, she reproached herself.

"How are you?" He sat down across from her.

"Well, I don't know. I guess I'm fine, considering."

Rafael just looked at her, and no words came to him. The waiter came over, and he ordered a coffee.

"I've got what I want, I suppose," she said, trying to sound casual. "A career in journalism, a good job with a respectable newspaper, my own column, a nice apartment. I even have a new job offer I'm considering." Gabriela felt suddenly like she was bragging. She didn't mean to tell Rafael all these things; they just flowed from her naturally. It was not like her to gush in public, but then Rafael wasn't really the public, was he? "But my dad. . . my dad just died two weeks ago." Tears suddenly spilled down her face. She dug in her purse for a tissue.

"I'm so sorry to hear that, Gabriela." Rafael handed her his napkin. He was surprised by her candid emotional outburst; he'd expected distance, control and denial of their former intimacy. It brought him back to the last time they'd been together, and he felt like putting his arms around her. "I know how much you loved your dad, and I'm truly sorry."

"Thank you. I'm sorry. I shouldn't bother you with all this stuff. I don't know what came over me."

"Gabriela, please don't apologize. Remember, I'm your friend. I always will be." Rafael didn't know if he had overstepped her limits, but he couldn't help himself. They'd both gone way off script. The conversation unnerved both of them.

Gabriela wiped her eyes and collected herself. "This was supposed to be an interview." She smiled ruefully.

"I haven't told my friends I'm meeting you. I'm feeling like some kind of traitor. But I wanted to see you." Rafael looked into her eyes. "I never told anybody about us. I mean, they don't know that we have met before."

Now it was Gabriela's turn to be surprised, and she looked at Rafael with renewed affection.

"Me neither. I've never told anybody."

"It's our secret, then."

"How will you explain our acquaintance to your friends?"

"We met at UNAM, shared a couple of classes. It's the truth — at least, part of it."

Gabriela looked at him and suddenly she couldn't help telling him all about her job at *El Sol* and how her heart wasn't in it. "I wanted life to be easy," she said. "I wanted to do what my father felt was right."

Rafael told her about Radio Libre in Oaxaca, how he and Paula and Enrique had moved to Pátzcuaro and founded ELL and the travel lodge, how they'd found out about the proposed nuke plant and consequently embarked on NNN's quest.

"Gabriela, how did you know what's going on almost before we knew ourselves? About Jason, his dad coming from Canada, even when we returned to Pátzcuaro."

"I don't feel good about revealing my sources," Gabriela said evasively, stirring her hot chocolate.

"I think my friends think I'm the source. They definitely will when they find out I know you."

She looked at him. "It's your friend Bernard."

"Who is Bernard?" Rafael was confused for a moment, and then it dawned on him. "You mean that middle-aged guy who hangs around with the filmmaker?"

"I guess that's him." Gabriela said, and then filled Rafael in on how Bernard had been run over by one of her dad's trucks, his broken leg, how they had nursed him back to health and that he had looked her up in Morelia. She omitted their one night together, avoiding Rafael's eyes. "He met Randall, the filmmaker, on his own somehow. I never solicited any information; he just called me, almost daily. I should have told him to stop it, but then again, I felt I had the scoop, and my editor loved it." She looked up at Rafael. "You probably think I'm an opportunist, a user, and you're right. But I feel trapped, Rafael."

Rafael just shook his head. "Your reports didn't do any harm. In fact, they probably helped us out. Maybe your articles made us look like guerrillas and revolutionaries. We aren't, though. We're just concerned teachers and broadcasters. But we do have the support of some very established people." He told her about Carmen Landenberg, the Swiss expatriate businesswoman from Pátzcuaro, and the fact that they had scientific evidence to verify the fragility of the lake, which could not survive cooling a nuclear reactor core.

It was a long breakfast meeting, and neither of them touched their food. Instead, they talked like they each had lived on their own island for the past three years, and indeed they had. It became increasingly obvious to both of them that their old love had never really died, but had only been buried, denied, suppressed deep within themselves.

As their hands rested beside each other on the table, their fingers lightly touched. They both fell silent and just stared into each other's eyes. Their hands moved together, their fingers entwining.

"Rafael, I'm no longer bound by my father's creed."

"I know. And I need to make peace with my own father. Maybe we can do it together."

"I would like that."

"Where does that leave our interview?" Rafael smiled sheepishly.

"Well, for starters you need to come clean with your friends, tell them we know each other from university. No need to keep hiding the past. We didn't do anything wrong. Also, tell them who the informant is. As you said, he didn't do any real damage. Then maybe we can all sit down together and come up with a plan."

Rafael agreed, and they parted reluctantly, with a long, passionate hug that neither wanted to end. Their foreheads touched. Then their lips.

Rafael floated into the ELL's lunchroom, but stopped in his tracks when he saw the solemn faces of his friends. Even Carmen was there, which was unusual in the middle of the day.

"What's the matter? Who died?" he asked flippantly.

"Of all the people to betray us, we never thought it would be you," Paula said.

Rafael looked from one to the other and met nothing but accusing faces. Only now did it sink in that he must look to them like a traitor, and he hastily tried to explain, sounding even more guilty. "No, no!" he cried. "It's not like that, it's not me. I can explain."

"Madison checked the registry at Iturbe while you were talking into her tape recorder. She saw both of you, Rafael."

"Please, please let me explain," he pleaded.

"Even a murderer gets his day in court," Paula grumbled.

"She has a point," Madison intervened.

"Let's have it, then. What's going on?" Rico said.

Halting and confused at first, Rafael started to tell all: how they met at UNAM, their falling in love, their week in Patzcuaro and even their painful parting and the reasons for it. "I know I should have told you I knew her when it first dawned on me that it was her who writes for El Sol, but I didn't know what to do, didn't think it mattered, since we hadn't had any contact until the other day on the phone, when I agreed to do the interview. I wasn't thinking. I just wanted to see her." Rafael fell silent.

Everybody sat quietly, listening to Rafael unburden himself. It slowly dawned on Paula why their friend had been so withdrawn when they first met in Oaxaca, and his story explained a lot.

Rafael repeated, "I didn't know what to do, and I didn't know if she still had feelings like I have. I'm sorry." He looked down, close to tears, his hands buried deep in his pockets, shoulders hunched forward like an old man.

"Why didn't you tell us at the beginning, back in Oaxaca?" Paula asked. Rafael stared at her quietly, his eyes unblinking and far away. She suddenly didn't need him to explain. She realized how difficult it was for Rafael, the fact that he couldn't change where he was born, how he had to give up his love because of class distinctions, forces outside his control. In an instant, her anger at her friend gave way, first to pity, then compassion. She shook her head and got up to give him a heartfelt hug. "I know now, Rafael, and it's okay. No need to be sorry. We need you, my friend."

"Who is it, then, that gave her all this info about us?" Rico wanted to know. "If not you, then who?"

Rafael then told them about Bernard, how he was the guy always on the periphery, together with Randall, privy to all those meetings in Morelia. "All he wanted was to endear himself to Gabriela, using us, NNN."

"He didn't unearth any state secrets. It's not like we're plotting to overthrow the government," Carmen soberly pointed out.

"Still, fuck him, the slimy bastard!" Rico slapped his fist into his other palm. "I'd like to get my hands on him."

"What about Randall?" Madison asked. "Can he be trusted?"

"We don't know, but does it really matter? He's a good filmmaker," Paula said.

"What should we do about Gabriela?" Madison asked. Everybody wanted to answer at once, but then they gave Rafael the floor.

"I think all of us together should give her the interview. She'll be fair."

They all agreed that this indeed was the best course of action. They approved inviting her to the ELL but left it up to Rafael to set up a time. Carmen gave Rafael a reassuring hug and then said goodnight, while Madison excused herself with things to do. Paula and Rico stayed behind and teased Rafael about his secret love life, harassing him until he almost cried for help.

Chapter 18

Changing Sides

Parker called his troops in for an emergency briefing at his office in the lounge of the Virrey de Mendoza. They all arrived within minutes of each other, wondering what the occasion was — Luke, Vena and Randall, with Bernard in tow. After everybody was comfortably seated, Parker put his large hands together and looked at each member of the small group one by one.

"I've had a phone call from Carmen in Pátzcuaro. Apparently, we have an informant in our midst." He shifted his large, lanky frame in Bernard's direction, looking straight at him. "Do you have anything to say, Bernard? Because this is the only chance you get."

Bernard's face burned, and he looked from one to the other for signs of sympathy. There were none, just curiosity mixed with disgust. His mind was furiously racing for an exit strategy, but all he could think of was *Time out, I need time out!* But this wasn't a hockey game.

"I'm not sure what you're talking about," Bernard said, in a lame attempt to gain time.

"You supplied Gabriela Ramirez, the journalist at *El Sol*, with updates and info on the inner workings of our little group. We were all surprised by how quickly that journalist got information without interviewing us. Well, now we know." Parker's deep baritone gave his accusations an added sense of gravitas.

Bernard sat still, stunned into silence.

"Come on, Bernard, is this true, did you really do that?" Randall asked, staring at his supposed friend with disgust.

Bernard squirmed in his seat. All he could do was try to defend himself. "I never told her anything that would hurt the cause of NNN. In fact, I probably helped out by way of increased exposure. Anyway, I knew Gabriela from before. We went out a couple of times. I thought maybe this would help."

Randall was furious, and his temper got the better of him. "Help what? Get into her pants? Is that what this comes down to?"

"Let's just cool down," Parker said. "We don't want the whole hotel to know our business."

"It's not what you told her that matters, it's the fact that you broke people's trust," Vena said angrily. "NNN is a small group. It's not some powerful organization."

"I don't think we need your help anymore," Parker said.

"Bastard," Randall said through clenched teeth.

Bernard slowly got up. He was sweating despite the air conditioning. His whole new world was crumbling in front of him. He walked from the lobby like a zombie.

Nobody said a word until Parker clapped his hands and ordered a round of drinks from the hovering waiter. "No damage done, my friends. It's disappointing and maddening when something like this happens, but hey, the good news is we're moving forward. The big day is on track in less than two weeks, and according to Carmen, we've got the expensive suits in Veracruz rattled. Don't be surprised if somebody approaches you in the next few days with some dubious proposals or threats. Meanwhile, here's to success and a nuke-free Patzcuaro."

At some point in the evening Randall offered Bernard's job as soundman to Luke, and the young Irishman accepted on the spot. More reason to celebrate. Then Luke borrowed a guitar from one of the ever-present mariachis, and with Vera's accompaniment, sang a soaring rendition of "Radio Active," which had the whole lounge clapping and singing the catchy refrain.

Shining radio active
Burning radio active
Turning radio active

Rafael went to get Gabriela, and together they walked back through the narrow streets of Pátzcuaro's *centro histórico*, towards the Pátzcuaro Travellers Lodge and the Escuela de Lengua Latina. As she entered, Gabriela knew that she had crossed the line. The night before, she had made some phone calls and faxed her acceptance of the teaching position to UNAM. This would be her last piece of journalism for *El Sol*, and she wanted to make it a good one.

She had met Paula briefly at the rally in Morelia, and now she found herself surprised by her warm reception, considering they had been virtual enemies until yesterday. Gabriela shook hands with a wary Enrique, who was less welcoming. He didn't quite trust this meeting with the enemy. Carmen and Madison both greeted her with friendly respect, and Rafael just sat there staring at her. Gabriela knew each one's superficial history, in addition to what Rafael had told her, but she was still surprised when she met them face to face by how different they were from the wild-eyed extremist revolutionaries they'd been made out to be by certain people. This made Gabriela cringe inside. Even she had been tainted with stereotypical images and prejudices.

Paula looked like a young businesswoman, dressed in a skirt and jacket, her shoulder-length black hair tied in a ponytail. Only Enrique looked the part, with his Che Guevara looks, scraggly beard and hair over his ears. Madison, the Canadian from Greenpeace International, struck Gabriela as a slightly geeky office intern, while Carmen Landenberg, the enigmatic Swiss expatriate, exuded aristocracy with her natural and dignified air, a product of her upbringing. An unlikely group of dissidents and troublemakers.

It was a Sunday, with no classes scheduled. They proudly led Gabriela on the grand tour of the school and the adjacent travellers lodge, and then congregated in the spacious communal kitchen/ conference room, gathering around the large wooden table. Paula busied herself by the kitchen counter, and soon the aroma of strong Mexican coffee wafted through the air.

Gabriela had come armed with a tape recorder and notepads, which she set in front of her, feeling a bit like an intruder. She figured it was best to be direct. "I guess you all know about Rafael and me now, the fact that we knew each other before, in a different life. I can't believe he never told you, but then, I never told anybody either. It was all rather complicated." She took Rafael's hand.

That confession broke the ice, and they all began to tease Rafael about his secret love life. "We figured he was gay," Enrique said, slapping Rafael on the shoulder. They all laughed, relieved — most of all Rafael, who basked in the moment. Life had never held more promise than in that instant. When the hilarity subsided, everyone became serious once more. There was business to attend to.

"I have to tell you that my mandate from my editor is very straightforward: *Find out what you can about the members of the group, discredit them, misrepresent them if necessary, and expose any dirt under the carpet.*"

"Well, then," Paula said, "you might as well start with your own tantalizing former involvement with one of the founders of NNN."

Gabriela smiled, shrugging her narrow shoulders and tucking her hair behind her ear. "I guess that conflict of interest pretty well blows the whole op, doesn't it? I might as well tell you, this will be my last assignment for *El Sol*; I've accepted a teaching position at UNAM. In other words, don't hold back."

They all started talking at once, until Carmen stopped them and suggested they supply Gabriela with all the facts about the proposed nuke plant. That included their latest secret weapon, which Madison, courtesy of Greenpeace, had brought to the table: a recent dissertation about the current state of Lake Pátzcuaro and its impact on the region, by one Jesús Heredia, an environmental biologist from UNAM. It proved, with graphs and measurements, that the lake was dying due to leaching of fertilizer, prolonged droughts, silting, and raw sewage outfall from the growing communities around the lake. Although Lake Pátzcuaro was a large body of water — in fact, the second largest high-altitude lake in the world — it was very shallow. A nuke plant on its shores would severely impact the already stressed and fragile lake.

"This validates everything we've been saying," Paula said, after skimming through the research paper.

Gabriela added, "We'll need to point out that the negatives of such a huge project would outweigh the positives, which are mostly short-sighted economics: basically, the resulting construction boom, which in itself would leave a dubious legacy in its wake."

"We also have to ask the questions that the Commission cannot truthfully answer without implicating itself," said Paula. "We now have the data to support our arguments about maintaining a way of life and the social fabric of the region in the spirit of Don Vasco." She added, "Never mind the personal histories of the members of NNN. This thing is bigger than all of us together."

They talked and Gabriela recorded and made furious notes. They ordered in a lunch of Tarascan soup and tortas from the neighbouring restaurant. Gabriela felt like she had suddenly woken up from a long dream. How she had missed this kind of genuine activity, the camaraderie, the banter. It reminded her of her university days, especially when she looked across the table at Rafael, who couldn't take his eyes off her.

When the interview was over, Rafael offered to walk her back to her hotel. Hoots and catcalls came from Paula and Rico. Gabriela accepted Rafael's offer gladly, but mischievously pointed out that she had a lot of work to do. She gathered her equipment and stack of papers and promised to show them the draft before she submitted it to her paper, which in itself would be a challenge. She had to get it past her editor and boss without being censored.

The big day was a week away and preparations were in full swing. Volunteers were flocking in. Everyone wanted to help out. Tourists, students and locals were busy building a stage and a kids' playground, and a truck full of palm leaves and poles was brought in to build covered stands for vendors. One problem was the latrines, but it was solved by digging a five-metre-long trench and covering it with planks and dividers and a thatched roof — ten cubicles in all.

But a week before the event, a phone call came from the municipality to Arturo Pimentel, the owner of the campground. The caller, an administrator for the Tourism Board'sbranch in Pátzcuaro, told him that holding a rally on his property would be considered a violation of the Board's guidelines, and his license to operate a campground could be in jeopardy. The same day, a hand-delivered letter outlined a new work project at the Pátzcuaro campground's entrance, to commence immediately, citing sewage and water pipe upgrades.

"I never heard of such a thing!" Arturo said on the phone to Carmen. "For all I know, there are no pipes buried there! All they want to do is cut off the access." Arturo was audibly upset.

"Leave it to me, Arturo," Carmen said.

Carmen called el Capitán, who acted cold and standoffish. "Carmen, you are better off cutting your ties to that anarchist group, or your name and your business might suffer as a consequence. I can only tell you that the *federales* are now involved. The matter is out of my hands."

She hung up on him.

Parker called Patzcuaro and passed on some news he'd heard from Karen in Canada, who'd had a conversation with Jason's dad. Theodore Neumann wanted her to tell NNN to cease their activities if they wanted to honour his son. Karen had argued with Jason's dad on the phone, telling him that to honour Jason would be to fight. In fact, her plan was to go back to Mexico and help NNN.

The following day a call came from NNN's landlord. He informed them that he would be selling the building, and they would have to vacate the Travellers Lodge and the ELL by the new year, which was less than a month away. Their landlord had always been an ardent supporter of the young entrepreneurs, but now he refused to discuss the matter any further.

It was obvious: The group was being pressured from all sides. All they could hope for was enough support from the people of Pátzcuaro. "It's either jump ship or stay and fight," Enrique told Arturo at the campground. "It's up to you."

Madison, busy at work, was able to obtain the names and addresses of the executives at the Comisión Federal de Electricidad, including their chairman, Manuel Rodríguez.

A few days later, Manuel Rodríguez received an invitation to the Día de los Vivos, on Saturday, December 15, at the Villa Pátzcuaro Campground on the shores of Lake Pátzcuaro. *Bring your friends and families for a day of celebration in the spirit of our father Don Vasco de Quiroga.* Enclosed with the invite was a copy of Jesús Heredia's research paper.

Manuel Rodríguez flipped through Heredia's dissertation, and something in it gave him pause. Rodríguez was not an unreasonable man, and he could be persuaded by facts and figures. He had no interest in the social and political consequences of his mandate; that was not his territory of expertise. His job was to produce and deliver electricity. For that, he got paid handsomely. But on the spur of the moment, he called his wife and asked if she and their twelve-year-old daughter Lupita would like to go "up country" for a small holiday. They were delighted with the proposal. He booked three flights to Morelia and had a car and driver waiting for them. The Rodríguez family booked rooms at the prestigious Gran Hotel Patzcuaro.

Manuel paid for the trip out of his own pocket, and he didn't tell the other board members about his trip to Pátzcuaro. All he said was that he would be out of town for the weekend for a family function. He actually looked forward to a weekend in the heart of Michoacán, so different from the urban, industrial lowlands on the hot and humid Gulf of Mexico.

Chapter 19

The Day Before

The word was out. Posters and flyers advertising Día de los Vivos were distributed throughout the lake region and in Morelia. Food and craft vendors were lining up for the opportunity. Students from UNAM were being recruited to volunteer on the day, with promises of free food and "good times for a good cause."

Randall, with his new roadie Luke in tow, canvassed the city and interviewed people on camera. Most of them had heard about NNN's fight against the electrical utility, and most of the interviewees believed the cause was a good one but, on the other hand, felt it was futile. The general consensus was that Mexican authorities and politicians don't listen to the people and would rather use guns than words in settling disputes. A case in point was the Zapatista uprising with Subcomandante Marcos in San Cristóbal.

Karen arrived in Morelia, and Carmen met her at the airport. Karen cried from the emotion of being back with her friends. On the drive to Morelia, she told Carmen that she'd broken off communication with Jason's dad after he told her that he'd been forced to bow to pressure from the Mexican attaché and the Atomic Energy Board, who were not about to lose a lucrative contract for two CANDU reactors. "None of my grandstanding will bring back Jason," he told her "and the economic benefits for both countries, as well as the overreaching political implications, were bigger than any one voice. The best I can do is to stay mum on the issue and abstain from stirring the pot." Stirring the pot was exactly what Karen had in mind when she travelled back to Pátzcuaro.

Back in New Zealand, Vena had grown into a heroine in the media, fighting the good fight of David against Goliath, the nuclear industry. Vena was proud of the fact that New Zealand had been declared a nuclear-free zone, much to the chagrin of the US and France.

Rafael and Luke, with the help of Randall, were able to record their song, as well as a couple of Rafael's own songs, with Luke accompanying on guitar, at the university in Morelia, for the cost of the tapes, a few beers and a promise from Randall of more paid work to come after the Day of the Living in Pátzcuaro. Armed with the precious recording, Rafael and Luke joined the girls, and they all headed back to Pátzcuaro.

Parker accepted a personal invite from Carmen to come to Pátzcuaro and stay at her flat. "I have plenty of room, and I'd be happy for the company," she said. It was an offer he wasn't about to refuse; besides, he had never been to Pátzcuaro and was curious to see the fabled town and the threatened lake. Parker had never been more content, thanks to his mentorship of the young activists — not to mention the titillating new acquaintance of Señorita Carmen. His life had taken on new meaning, and retirement in Mexico had turned out to be one of his better decisions, mostly due to the pure luck of being in the right place at the right time. Proof positive that even old dogs can find new meaning and purpose in life.

Gabriela's boss, Emilio, left urgent messages at her hotel, which she kept ignoring. She knew exactly what he wanted. She had to play this one very carefully if she wanted her last editorial, her *pièce de résistance*, printed, and holding off until the last possible moment was an integral part of her plan.

She stole time away from her writing whenever she could to be with Rafael, whose time was also very limited in those hectic days. Sometimes he came over for breakfast or lunch, and always in the evenings after the day was done, and anytime in between. By now they had given up all doubts and barriers to their passion, and they made love often and with abandon, as if making up for all the lost time. It exhausted and rejuvenated them, and afterwards they would just lie together, laughing and talking, limbs lazily draped around each other, watching the shadows of the sun or the street lights dance across the room. There was so much to fill in, so many dreams and schemes, that they never ran out of words.

They discussed Gabriela's article for the paper at length, as well as the upcoming day of reckoning for NNN and their hopes for success and support. Invariably, the subject changed to their families, their wishes and, always, their future together. The streams of words became rivers, and then lakes and bigger rivers that flowed into the ocean of their resurrected love. They needed to be close to each other, craved each other's caresses, and when they made love, time was infinitely suspended. They wanted nothing more than to retreat to a room and not come out for a week. But that had to wait.

They now walked hand in hand, unperturbed by who might recognize them. They revisited familiar places, like the *biblioteca*, never tiring of Juan O'Gorman's mural. Or they stole a moment, sitting on one of the stone benches in the Plaza Grande. They often ate on the fly at Mariella's food stand, and sometimes they got lost in the labyrinthine *mercado*, where nobody knew or bothered them.

They had traversed a barren landscape and reached their own oasis, leaving obstacles of tradition and social traps behind. They had crossed the chasm of class difference and emerged from years of self-imposed exile. It wasn't a fight against shadows and ghosts, but rather a journey through an invisible maze, neither one of them aware of each other's predicament until they met again at the crossroad of circumstance, which led back to their lost paradise.

They combined their talents and practically co-wrote the editorial for *El Sol*. They argued endlessly about the slant of the article. Rafael favoured a more radical point of view, outright dismissing the argument of jobs and economic necessity, while Gabriela pleaded journalistic integrity and insisted on a more balanced approach. It reminded them of the time when they co-authored the "black and white" debate all those years ago at university.

They consulted Paula and Rico, who approved of the result, which was a fair and objective look at the issue. In other words, the essay turned out completely contrary to the dictum of Gabriela's newspaper and did not at all conform to the tenets of her boss's overlords. Gabriela now genuinely believed her exposé reflected the truth of the issue, the interest of the people and the lake, and the realistic impact of the gigantic project. They were aware that the article only reflected one truth. There were other truths, like the fact that a lot of money was at stake and all the stakeholders would lose their investment in this high-end venture. It was an equally powerful truth, one with a lot more clout, rooted in control and violence, than the simple facts, which were that it would impact the people who depended on the current way of life, who could not see their future past the large impact of a nuke plant in their backyard. It was of paramount importance that Gabriela's article got published uncensored.

Gabriela contacted Emilio and pleaded for time. "It's a complicated issue, and important for the region," she said. "And I really want to do the process justice. I'll send it in tomorrow, I promise. Please just let me do my job." She didn't lie to her boss — she didn't want to; she just didn't tell him the whole truth.

Emilio's Achilles heel was that he could never refuse his star reporter, especially when she treated him like a father, asking if she could stay out longer at the party. *Yes, dear, just be careful. Don't let those boys fool you. Stay away from the tequila.*

The cab dropped Parker off on the northeast corner of the Plaza Grande, in front of a big, iron-clad set of wooden double doors. He rang the bell, and Imelda let him into the inner sanctum of Carmen's house. He first stepped into a tall-ceilinged terracotta-tiled entrance room, which also served as the carport. He noticed the large cast-iron candleholder in the shape of a tree on the sidewall and the heavy ornate black iron chandelier overhead. He then followed Imelda into a rectangular open courtyard with a large fountain at its centre; the space was filled with exotic plants: birds of paradise, orange and lemon trees, bougainvillaea, poinsettia trees and many more tropical plants. These were set in large ornate pots and arranged along intricate garden beds lining both sides of the tiled walkway.

Straight through the courtyard, Imelda led him into the traditional open kitchen, with multi-coloured tiled counters, modern appliances and high-beamed ceilings, adjacent to a large wooden dining suite and a spacious living room featuring an imposing fireplace. On the other side of the kitchen, French doors led into another large courtyard full of plants and stone sculptures, including a striking Chacmool statue, as well as a central avocado tree. From this space, several doors led off into separate bedrooms with en suite bathrooms and fireplaces, all furnished with traditional beds with ornate headboards, and carved dressers. The bathrooms had Talavera tiles and enamelled or copper sinks, each room painted in a different bright colour, with carpets, wall hangings and bedspreads from Carmen's own looms.

"Come on up. I'll give you the rest of the tour while Imelda fixes us a snack," he heard Carmen say. Feeling like a little boy in a fantasy castle, he stopped in wonderment, looking up at Carmen, who was leaning on the ornate balustrade, clad in a full-length lilac gown with an embroidered black cape draped across her narrow shoulders, her long silver hair pinned behind one ear with a lacquer pin. A perfect vision of beauty, in Parker's eyes.

"You look like a proper queen in her castle," he said, awestruck, beholding the lovely figure, who smiled down at him, obviously enjoying his enchantment with her house. Parker walked up the tiled staircase onto the mezzanine, with more doors leading into various rooms. This was obviously Carmen's domain, her personal quarters: sitting room, office, another large bedroom featuring an ornate balcony overlooking the plaza below. "A palace," he cried, his arms outstretched like a giant scarecrow, his large face lit up like a jack o' lantern.

Carmen was proud of her house, her *casa*, on which she had spent a lot of time and energy. "You can pick your room," she offered. "*Mi casa es tu casa.*"

Parker floated rather than walked through the old but modernized colonial house, pointing and exclaiming over and over what a beautiful place this was. He picked the room closest to the kitchen. Carmen laughed. "Wise choice. You'll hear Imelda preparing breakfast every morning at 7:00 a.m., except Saturday and Sundays, her days off."

There were a few items related to Carmen's former life: a Swiss *pendule* (a red enamelled mantel clock); a large ceremonial bell hanging from a wide black brass-decorated leather collar; and a couple of framed pictures — one of a multi-roofed building (presumably the former family textile mill) and one of a lovely turreted villa on the lakeshore, her former family home back in Switzerland.

After they partook of some of Imelda's lovely tapas — small *quesadillas* garnished with fresh avocado, *tomatillos* and *salsa fresca* — Carmen took Parker on a tour of the Plaza Grande and along the many cafés, restaurants and shops lining the sidewalk under the gothic arches surrounding the Plaza Quiroga. Parker instantly fell in love with Patzcuaro as he followed his friend through the cobbled streets, through the old town with its palatial Spanish buildings, feeling oddly rejuvenated by the clean, cool mountain air — or maybe by the closeness of his companion.

The lure of the town and its smells and sounds, views and bustle, also mesmerised Karen, and she felt like she was finally emerging from a grey fog into the sunlight. For the moment, the recent tragedy remained hidden beneath layers of immediate impressions, and she found herself able to live in the moment once more. She bought a beautiful embroidered white shawl from a Purépecha woman, sitting curbside with her wares next to the Plaza Grande. The old *abuela* thanked Karen with a broad smile, which made her ancient face even more wrinkled. From that day on when Karen walked by her, she was greeted with that same all-knowing smile. It gave Karen strength and comfort, and returned a sense of wonderment which had gone out of her life with Jason's death.

Randall, Luke, Vena and Karen had reserved rooms at the Patzcuaro Travellers Lodge, right in the heart of all the activity. Everybody was in high spirits; even Karen had a smile on her face when they all met up for dinner.

Pátzcuaro's charming historical centre and vibrant atmosphere mesmerised the young activists, especially Randall, who had never been there before. Within minutes of their arrival, he was cruising through the town, up the winding, cobbled road to the top of Volcan del Estribo Grande. After climbing a long, steep flight of steps, he stood at the apex and took in the spectacular view overlooking the town and the whole valley below them. The large glassy surface of Lake Patzcuaro, with the island Janitzio at its centre, stretched out before them, ringed by the numerous volcanoes like so many sombreros strewn across the landscape.

"It's magic!" exulted Randall, slowly turning with his camera for a panoramic shot.

The big day loomed less than a week away, and most of the activity at the school revolved around the event. It turned the whole building into a frenzied beehive. There was also a sense of foreboding in the air, as before the launch of a space rocket or the kick-off in a World Cup final. In the days leading up to the big day, musicians, dancers and street performers kept the crowds entertained in the two main plazas. Luke, Rafael and the two female backup singers practised the "Radio Active" song every chance they got. Luke had polished the song, which now had a definite reggae feel with an ascending cord progression during the refrain that could be played as an endless loop, alternating in English and Spanish. "It could go on for hours," Luke said, strumming away, while Vena and Karen rolled their eyes.

"Rockstaaar," Vena said in her nasal Kiwi accent.

On Friday morning Gabriela Ramirez's column appeared for the last time in *El Sol*, the voice of Michoacán. She had filed her report late the night before and faxed it directly to the typesetter, bypassing her editor and boss.

Emilio had reluctantly agreed to Friday's front page and had reserved the space in advance. After some sparring over the phone, they agreed on the headline:

ELECTRIC STORM IN PATZCUARO
'No Nuke No' or 'Go Nuke Go'?

The lead article was already set in print, with two columns of space reserved on the front page. By 10:00 p.m. the meat of her article was still missing, but Gabriela promised to have it in to the typesetter by midnight. "I'm sorry about the delay, but it will be all right, I promise."

Those were Gabriela's last words to her editor. He left the office feeling not quite right about this arrangement. Why was she so late? It was not like her, always on time, always keen to have him read what she wrote, looking for approval. He seldom had to correct her writing, but still, Emilio didn't feel quite comfortable about this odd arrangement, and he slept badly as a result. He was up again with the rooster's first crow, just when the paper hit the streets of Morelia. When he grabbed a copy from a bundle by a news stand and scanned the first page, his heart pounded so hard he thought he would have a heart attack.

He frantically hailed a cab to the office. "I knew it!" he cursed over and over, realizing that it was too late to fix the damage.

Reading Gabriela's article, Emilio had to admit that it was not an outright condemnation, as he had feared, but a fair and balanced assessment of the situation. She started out with Mexico's need for energy, infrastructure and jobs, and how nobody wanted a nuke plant in their backyard, and that on the surface, *el Lago de Pátzcuaro seems like the perfect place to build such a facility. It's in the centre of Mexico, next to a large body of water and in a sparsely populated area.* In counterpoint, she cited *the strong scientific evidence of the lake's fragile condition*, pointing out that the water level was sinking every year and the water quality getting progressively worse, even without the added stress of the voracious water needs for cooling a nuclear reactor.

> The people around Lake Patzcuaro, in particular the Purépecha, were not consulted and do not see the long-term benefits of a massive construction project with its invasive short-term impact. There is also an aesthetic side to consider. One or two concrete cones, taller than General María Morelos's statue on Janitzio Island, and the high power lines, criss-crossing the unblemished landscape like hanging laundry in the presidential dining room, will negatively affect the local tourist industry. The crown jewel of Michoacan is in danger of becoming the crown's toilet, with the future radioactive waste being flushed into el lago de Pátzcuaro.

The positives must outweigh the negatives, she argued, and went on to list them.

> What is more important — the preservation of the fragile lake and a way of life, and maintaining the attractiveness and the social fabric of the lakeside communities, or a ten-year construction boom that will forever alter the land of the Purépecha with the influx of quick money and migrant construction workers, most of them single men?

The article mentioned NNN only briefly, as an environmentally concerned organization based in Patzcuaro with large local and international support. They are fighting the omnipotent Comisión Federal Electricidad for the survival of the lake and a way of life.

Her arguments were as much rooted in science as in social philosophy, a risky stance in Mexico's boardrooms and halls of power.

The wisest move for the Comisión Federal de Electricidad would be to rethink their plans, to go back to the drawing board, to listen to the people and to acknowledge the scientific, social and environmental evidence against their project. Why not build Laguna Verde III near the other two, on the industrial planes surrounding Veracruz?

On the whole, the editorial was a passionate appeal to soberly assess the consequences of the proposed nuke plant, with its need for water, concrete, labour and local resources, and without a plan of where to store the burned-out fuel once the plant was running.

She concluded on a personal note intended to help Emilio postpone his retirement:

This essay does not reflect the views of the owner or editor of *El Sol* but is my own personal conviction, reached after having studied the Commission's proposal and the relating scientific evidence, as well as having interviewed countless people in and around the Patzcuaro lake district. I believe this conclusion to be the right one for Patzcuaro, Michoacan, Mexico, and all the people living in the land of the Purépecha. Signed, Gabriela María Ramírez.

The phones were ringing at *El Sol* the second Emilio González stepped into his office. He relayed all calls to his secretary, who looked at him in desperation. "What should I say, *señor*?"

"Tell them I'm having a heart attack. No, better yet, tell them I'm on holiday. Oh hell, tell them whatever you like, María," he said, slumping into his chair. The only bright spot in this melodrama was that the Friday edition of *El Sol* was sold out by noon, a record, as far as Emilio knew. Thinking of sales, he called for another special edition to be printed. *Might as well make the best of it*, he thought.

Everybody at the Pátzcuaro Travellers Lodge and at the ELL read Gabriela's editorial. But their optimistic mood was somewhat dampened when a large backhoe showed up at the Villa Pátzcuaro entrance and started digging a ditch across the road, practically cutting off access to the grounds. The workers themselves had nothing to say, except that they were just doing their job.

"Let them dig," Arturo said with a wink at Rafael, who was trying to reason with the civic workers. "Let them do what they have to do and leave."

They let the workers finish their ditch and leave as quickly as they had arrived, guarding the trench with a couple of flimsy barricades for safety. As soon as the digging crew were out of sight, Arturo pulled up his small red tractor and dragged some beams and planks across the ditch. Everyone pitched in, and half an hour later they had built themselves a proper bridge. Proudly, they surveyed their handiwork, which was strong enough for cars to pass over. They even built a railing and decorated the whole works with colourful streamers and bunting. It almost looked like a moat with a drawbridge.

As they were finishing, four camouflage-coloured military pickup trucks pulled into Pátzcuaro, manned by black-uniformed *federales* armed with their usual arsenal of semiautomatic rifles, including a machine-gun turret on top of the cab. They parked around the police station and up and down the main road leading into town, close to the Villa Pátzcuaro entrance. This looked serious. When Carmen called on el Capitán, he just said curtly, "They're here for your own protection."

Randall and Luke were on top of a neighbour's roof with a camera on a tripod. They had a panoramic view of the access road and got all the activity on film: the backhoe, the bridge-building and now the arrival of the military vehicles.

Inside the grounds, preparations were also under way. Vendors were setting up their stands, some under the palm-thatched roof; brewery cords with coloured light bulbs were being strung between the stage and the vending booths; and the stage was being decorated, with a large NNN banner across the front. Enrique worked on the PA system, and Paula kept busy stocking NNN's info booth with posters and pictures of the lake, including an artist's rendition of the massive concrete cone of the cooling tower dwarfing Janitzio

Island and the volcanoes in the background. All seemed ready, including security provided by half a dozen locals, who would stay overnight on the grounds. No telling if someone would want to come in to the campground and sabotage their efforts.

Later that evening Gabriela and Rafael slipped away. They walked hand in hand through the town in the cool evening, and sat down on one of the stone benches in Plaza Vasco de Quiroga, underneath an ancient elm tree. "I wonder what he would think of all this," Rafael said wistfully, pointing at the tall statue.

"Of course he would approve," said Gabriela. "After all, that's what he was up against: the clerical and political authorities, who wanted nothing else but to subjugate these people and stick them into the silver mines or let them toil in their fields for the Crown. Holding the Spanish church and conquistadors at bay was no easier than stopping the Electrical Utility Commission."

Rafael nodded and looked at his friend. He felt he could never take his eyes off her, and he knew he could never live without her. "What are we going to do when this is all over?" he asked.

"Carry on, Rafael. You have your teaching job here and I have mine in Morelia. We can spend the weekends together, for now, that is."

"I don't know if I can stand to be apart for a whole week, now that I have found you again."

"I know. I feel the same," she said.

They sat, tightly holding hands, watching the dancing *viejos*, the old men, entertain a group of onlookers: kids on their bikes, their parents behind them, teens and young lovers promenading and criss-crossing the square in a random pattern. It was a scene of quintessential harmony, an atmosphere both pleasant and comforting, as though there were no problems, no tears, and no pain and no suffering in this world.

Chapter 20
Day of The Living

A pink dawn draped over the misty lake, and the long shadows of the surrounding volcanoes retreated to make way for another clear blue day. Roosters crowed, dogs barked and the odd motor started up, shattering the stillness of the early morning.

Rafael had slept badly. He'd tossed and turned in bed, thinking of Gabriela's delicate, shapely body, her large coffee-coloured eyes, his hands stroking her thick wavy hair, his fingers tracing her neck to her shoulders, her upper arms, her breasts, kissing, touching. He rolled over sweating, forcing his thoughts to the day ahead, anything to take his agitated mind off her. Rafael was in love, and his mind was addled and somewhat compromised. What would she think, how would she answer, what would she choose?

In the morning he seemed distracted, but in a nice way. Paula and Rico couldn't get mad at him, even if they did have to prod him out of his daydream, ask him twice or show him again. His friends treated him as they would a disabled boy, with patience and resigned understanding for his impaired state.

El Día de los Vivos happened to fall between El Día de Nuestra Senora de La Salud and Navidad. The first day celebrated a pilgrimage with the usual array of parades, dancing and craft fairs, and also signalled the official start of the Christmas season. Vendors and artists who contributed to the festivities at the Basilica also booked at the Villa Pátzcuaro Campground, hoping for extra commerce; only a few cancelled their prior commitment when they saw the *federales* parked nearby in their military vehicles, looking mostly bored but still maintaining a threatening presence. Most vendors of pottery, weavings and carvings set up their stalls as planned. The threat of violence was not aimed at the Indigenous people selling their wares.

Gabriela weathered the first onslaught of protestations from her editor and co-workers, but there were few from her readership. Those who didn't like her switching sides were the ones whose livelihoods depended on construction projects, including those who hoped for employment should the nuke plant go ahead. She could understand their complaints, and she deflected those of her bosses, knowing she had done the right thing for herself and the Pátzcuaro region. She felt proud to have taken a stand, although she didn't like the accusations of having created and abetted news instead of just reporting. Reporting was never objective, she thought. Yes, she had changed her views, yes, she had tricked her boss, but she had done it all with her conscience at ease. Many readers agreed with her condemnation of the project.

Emilio got through to Gabriela on the phone. He scolded her for how she'd manipulated him and for knowingly going against the paper's mandate.

"I'll be resigning, Emilio," she said.

"What?" he said. "No, that's not what I mean! I don't want you to leave."

"But I am, and it's not because of you or the paper's owners. I've been offered a teaching position at the university. It's what I want to do, and I think I'd be good at it."

There was a pause, and then she heard Emilio chuckle and then laugh. "You sure know how to exit on a high note. Your swan song was your best reporting, not because you tricked your editor and thwarted your bosses, but because you spoke from your heart, and it resonated with the readership. We sold out two complete print runs. I wish you well, Gabriela, and please keep in touch."

Gabriela didn't know yet how to solve some of the existential riddles of how she and Rafael could be together, but she knew that was what she wanted. She could feel her love grow every time she looked at him, touched him, held his hand, felt his breath on her, his scent, his eyes, his devotion. On the morning of the Day of the Living, she looked at herself in the bathroom mirror, absentmindedly tucking her hair behind her ear. She smiled, turned a half-pirouette, looking coyly over her shoulder, thinking of Rafael: "The next dance is for you, my love."

Nobody wanted the Day of the Living to be a success more than Paula and Enrique. Both had worked long into the night on last-minute details. Enrique was worried about the power supply. They had no generator, running all the band equipment and lights off the campground's tenuous power source. "If they had a nuke plant here, you wouldn't have such problems," Paula said and they both laughed.

Carmen had invited everyone to her house for an early breakfast prepared by Imelda. Parker had fallen in love with the stoic Purépecha woman's cooking and the way she ran the household. She tolerated no meddling in her kitchen, no matter how well meaning it was. Parker had been told in no uncertain terms that he would have to drink the coffee she made when she was in charge, and that his offering of help was more of a hindrance than an advantage. He could take a hint, but his fondness for her didn't diminish one bit. Carmen smiled when he told her that Imelda was the real boss in her house and that the two of them were merely Imelda's guests, barely tolerated by Her Highness.

"She is just jealous, Parker, afraid you might take me away to some alien land, where nobody would know how to prepare *mole* or *tortillas*."

"She might be right, Carmen. The thought has crossed my mind."

"Well, maybe you should just stay here. That way we would all be well fed."

Parker looked at Carmen. He hadn't felt like this towards anybody in aeons, not since his twenties, a lifetime ago.

The breakfast meeting was lively and loud, with everybody laughing and talking about the day ahead, psyching themselves into a positive space. Imelda floated through the throng, effusive in her element, functioning at full throttle and efficiency. She loved nothing more than a large family laughing and eating together, and the NNN founders, sympathizers and associates had evolved into a large family with all its dynamics.

Together they had grown into a strong unit, and they felt they had right on their side, not because of a blind belief or a set of pre-ordained answers like a religion, but because they were on the side of ordinary people, on the side of the future and on the side of tomorrow's children. Whatever the outcome of their fight, the legacy would endure beyond their own lives, like the spirit of Don Vasco de Quiroga's message. NNN's doctrine stemmed from the conviction that benevolent foresight and disinterest would benefit everybody and help shape a sustainable future in a common-sense fashion. It was this legacy that would eventually be their monument to posterity.

They all crammed into several minivans en route to the Villa Pátzcuaro Campground. The makeshift wooden bridge was still intact. Half a dozen *federales* trucks were also still parked close by. Randall and Luke took up their camera position on the rooftop. Vendors were already setting up their stands or just spreading out a blanket on the ground, stacking hundreds of cups and mugs into pyramids and displaying all their wares at once. People were starting to drift in, mostly curio seekers, tourists and young people hoping for some kind of excitement. Before noon the place was crawling with people, and the first musicians took the stage.

Paula and Rafael manned the NNN booth and were busy explaining their position and handing out pamphlets and copies of their manifestos. They asked people to sign a petition against the nuke plant on Lake Pátzcuaro, which would be sent to the Comisión Federal de Electricidad. They had started the petition in Morelia and had collected a few hundred signatures to date.

They felt good about the way the event was progressing but apprehensive of what the government had in store for them. They knew they were walking a thin edge with an abyss on both sides. One side led to imprisonment and defamation by the authorities, forfeiting opportunities and travel privileges and losing face, while on the other side loomed the risk of making enemies of the working poor and some local businesses that would feel deprived of lucrative jobs and opportunities if the project was shelved. But if NNN succeeded in winning the hearts and minds of the ordinary people with events like the one today, and if they could get the project cancelled, they would be heroes, and celebrated as visionaries.

"It's one thing to get the nuke plant cancelled, but what kind of jobs can we promise the people instead?" Paula mused.

"Tourism and improved agriculture, maybe even viniculture. Instead of spending billions on a nuclear plant, the government could subsidize farmland reclamation around the lake. They could invest in infrastructure and put people to work fixing and improving their sewer plants instead of flushing it all into the lake. There are lots of ways the lives of the people of this valley could be improved. Building a mega-project is not the long-term answer.

"We know that, the technocrats in the capital know it, but it eludes the people here, who remain poor and resigned. For the young ones, it's either run away to the big cities or join a criminal gang. Subsistence farming and mixing margaritas for the gringos is not the future they aspire to," Paula said, in a sombre mood despite all the festive activities around them.

"Let's get this done and then we'll work on the future," Rafael said to his friend, putting his arms around her shoulders and giving her a reassuring squeeze.

"What are you two up to?" Rico asked, taken aback by their serious faces. "Did the power go out, or did we run out of beer?"

"*No, amigo,*" Rafael replied, "just thinking about the future. Nothing you need to worry about, since you have Paula, here."

"And you will have your hands full with Gabriela," Rico said, grinning. "Let's go test out the sound system."

• • •

Manuel Rodríguez and his family ate breakfast in the solarium at the Gran Hotel Pátzcuaro that morning. The three had taken an instant liking to the picturesque town. Pátzcuaro proved to be a shopper's paradise, and suddenly there were a lot of things the Rodrigues household lacked in furnishings and decor, like lacquerware and copper. Manuel treated his wife and daughter to a boat trip to Janitzio in one of the flat-bottomed launches from the *muelle* (dock). He could clearly see how the muddy lakeshore was creeping into the lake because of the low water table. His wife knew vaguely that her husband's job involved providing electricity to the nation, but she was not aware of the particular project planned for this lake. Manuel chatted amiably with the people hanging around the harbour and got a pretty clear picture of the depleting state of the lake. He kept his findings to himself and enjoyed the rare outing with his family.

As they got close to the island, they saw a show of traditional butterfly-net fishing. The steep walk up to Morelos's statue took about twenty minutes, past tacky souvenir shops and restaurants, all selling the same menu: *chiles rellenos, arroz mexicano* and deep-fried small fish the size of French fries. Manuel tried one of the fish, offered by a colourfully clad young Purépecha woman: pure salt and grease. "*No, gracias,*" he said, dropping a couple of coins into her hand. The panoramic view from the top of the island was spectacular. Manuel borrowed a pair of binoculars from a tourist and surveyed the shore, the shallow mud flats giving way to reeds that went back a long way, until they finally reached terra firma with thin patches of maize growing up a gentle slope. On their way back to the hotel, Manuel remained lost in thought.

• • •

Villa Pátzcuaro Campground had never accommodated so many people. Whole families, with kids and grandparents, mingled with students and young people who had come from Morelia and the surrounding towns. Paula and Rafael collected dozens of signatures and handed out pamphlets, pointing out phone numbers and addresses of politicians and executives of the Comisión Federal de Electricidad. Musicians, mostly acoustic, as well as a couple of roaming mariachi bands, kept the crowd entertained and gave the whole event a festive atmosphere, more like a folk festival than a political rally. The *federales* and the local police stayed outside the campground, hanging around the perimeter, but they didn't interfere or stop anybody.

Nobody noticed the small bespectacled man sauntering with his hands behind his back, following his wife and daughter around the craft stands.

Randall and Luke had come down from their rooftop perch and were now filming the crowd close up, Randall with the camera on his shoulder and Luke behind him, carrying cables, mic and battery packs. They eventually set up near the stage, ready to record Enrique's address.

Rico was nervous, but he had honed his speech and polished it, making it more a lecture than a sermon. Carmen and Parker had also arrived. They wandered around with linked arms like an old married couple, checking out the weaving and embroideries, stopping off at the NNN booth to see how the day was progressing. "Look at all the people," Paula gushed. "Isn't it great!"

It was at this point that Manuel Rodríguez was accosted by Paula, who asked him to sign the petition.

"Sorry, no thank you," he said, trying to move on.

"Dad, what does it say?" asked Isabel, not realizing they had just been put on the spot by the very people who could define her dad's and, by extension, her own future.

"It's nothing, dear," Manuel said, trying to dismiss the question.

"Is it about the big project you are going to build?" she asked innocently while her mom was trying to steer her away from Paula, who found herself suddenly on full alert.

"What big project?" she asked, "are you from the Comisión Federal, sent to spy on us?"

"Yes and no," Manuel said defensively. "But I'm not here in an official capacity. I'm here with my family as a private citizen to enjoy the day."

"I hope you take a good look around," Paula said, trying to be civil, not knowing how to deal with this chance encounter.

Just at that moment there was movement in front of the stage, and Manuel took his wife's arm with one hand and Isabel's hand with the other and led them away from the throng of people surging towards the stage, leaving a perplexed Paula behind.

Enrique introduced himself and gave the reason for the meeting. "*Amigos*, we are gathered here to inform you of the grand plans the Comisión Federal de Electricidad has for you. They want to transform this town, this lake, this way of life, by building a nuclear generating plant on el lago de Pátzcuaro. We know that this will destroy an already fragile lake, but we also know that the lure of a job is a hard one to resist. We only ask you to inform yourself and make up your own mind based on the facts and not on promises and intimidation. We only want the best for everyone's future, and a nuke plant on our shores is not the answer to that. I ask all of you to join us in one voice that says, *No Nuke No, No Nuke No!*"

Enrique's speech provided the only blatantly political element in an otherwise festive family gathering. People listened to his passionate but reasoned outline of why there should never be a nuclear power plant built on Lake Pátzcuaro. In the end, he evoked Don Vasco. "I'm sure you all can imagine whose side he would be on." The crowd cheered and many chimed in with his rally cry.

None of the invited politicians showed up — not the mayor, not any reps from the governor's office. Two opposition candidates running for mayor of Pátzcuaro, one a woman, made a brief appearance, no doubt seeing the potential votes to be gained by supporting NNN's cause.

Rico's speech was followed by Luke and Rafael singing "Radio Active," with Vena and Karen supplying back-up harmony. Luke's engaging stage personality was the polar opposite of the quiet, almost shy young man they all knew. Rafael sang the refrain in Spanish, and his wide-ranging baritone took hold of the crowd and had them all singing and dancing along. When the song ended, Luke invoked the day's mantra once more: "No Nuke No…No Nuke No…," which echoed across the valley. It could be heard by the idling security forces, who looked nervous but lacked orders to intervene.

Rafael parked his guitar and took hold of the mic, and carried the crowd with his kinetic voice, as he appealed for common sense and sober reflection. "Close your eyes and just imagine the impact of a massive nuclear power plant sucking up the waters of Lake Pátzcuaro."

He could have said anything and they would have believed him. As Gabriela listened, mesmerized by Rafael's voice, she was just as drawn in by him as everybody else was, not only because she loved him, but because he had something that could only be called a gift, a talent that set him apart. She had never heard him address a crowd, and she could see how he held them spellbound without any apparent effort on his part. His voice touched something inside everyone.

As night fell, the three-quarter moon and strings of coloured bulbs bathed the Villa Pátzcuaro Campground in festive light. Eventually the vendors gathered their wares, the families rounded up their kids, and by ten o'clock, only the volunteers and members of NNN were left behind. They sat together on the empty stage, looking across the deserted campground and the empty stalls. It felt anticlimactic.

Enrique was almost sad, and he voiced what everybody felt. "What did we accomplish here? Was it just a country festival, and did our message even reach the people? We got much more attention in Morelia."

"Yes, but we don't need violence to make our case," Paula said. And then she told them about her chance meeting with Manuel Rodríguez. "He admitted to being from the Commission, but going incognito, as it were. He didn't seem at all like an ogre, rather small and reserved, with a pretty wife and daughter."

"I sure would have liked to talk to him," Rico said, smacking his hand on his fist, "and give him a piece of my mind. Why didn't you bring him up on stage?"

"First of all, he was a private citizen with his family, Rico. Secondly, he vanished before I could even formulate a strategy to take advantage of the situation, and thirdly I don't think personal confrontation would have been the wise approach."

"Let's hope he took away a different point of view," Gabriela said. "Maybe he saw how unfeasible the whole project is."

"Whatever happened to the federales and the police? Why were they even here?" Enrique asked.

"You wanted to be thrown in jail?" Rafael said. "We can't bemoan the fact that this was a peaceful demonstration."

"That's true," Paula said. "We did what we could, and everybody did a great job. We need a drink. Let's go back to the lodge."

Rafael and Gabriela had other plans. They slipped away, leaving the others to head back to the lodge, where they carried on until early morning.

The Día de los Vivos carried very little weight in the press the next day. The Pátzcuaro media reported it on page two, congratulating NNN on conducting a peaceful event, but didn't even mention the central issue: the spectre of a nuke plant on the lake. The hung-over members of NNN gathered at the campground for the clean-up, which was a depressing job. Rafael and Gabriela arrived a bit later, but they had a good excuse. "We had to answer some questions at the hotel. Some people recognized us."

"*El Sol* didn't mention the event at all, as though it never happened. Neither did the TV stations," Paula remarked. It all seemed very puzzling and a bit disappointing. They were being ignored, and that hurt almost more than being trampled on.

"Maybe it's too close to Christmas?" Enrique said, stuffing a garbage bag.

"No, I don't think so. Look at the turnout — it was a good party," Karen said. "Randall has all of it on film, and with some dramatic editing and cutting, it will make a great doc, especially with Enrique's speech and Luke and Rafael's song."

"Exactly. It was a party, not an education course or a political protest rally. We all had a good time and we did get the message out. If the media now chooses to ignore us, that just means they've been told to ignore the issue," Paula said, trying to get the strings of lights down.

"They're snubbing us. It's a smart tactical move," Gabriela pointed out. "That way nobody needs to do anything. Ignoring the elephant in the room does not make it go away, though."

They were tired and somewhat confused, feeling at an impasse, not knowing how to go forward and continue their activism.

Arturo commended them for hosting a great day and consoled them by pointing out that now people were aware of the issue. "The people who came yesterday will make other people aware. And when the bulldozers move into town, people will fight. The Purépecha are very patient, but they always stand up for their rights."

Chapter 21
Endings

Manuel Rodríguez called the meeting at the Comisión Federal de Electricidad to order. He had in front of him Jesús Heredia's research paper and some aerial pictures of Lake Pátzcuaro, present and past, which he had obtained from the Michoacán government.

"I hope you all read the paper in front of you, and I want you all to look carefully at these pictures of Lake Pátzcuaro. Don't ask me why we have never seen these photos before. We all know the cliché that a picture is worth a thousand words. I myself have just come back from a short family vacation in Pátzcuaro. These photos don't lie."

All the executive members of the Commission gaped at the pictures, which showed the lake as it had been in 1975 and again in 1985. The last photos were from the current year.

"As everybody can see, the lake's water level is slowly but surely receding. As the report here explains, the reasons for this are manifold: soil erosion and silting, prolonged droughts, increased usage, et cetera — but this does not concern us. What does concern us is the fact that the water needed for cooling the reactor core is not available in sufficient quantities anymore. Yes, there is still a lot of water, but the lake is shallow and is fed from underground springs which are also receding; some of them have dried up completely. In other words, gentlemen, this is no longer a good place to build a nuclear power plant."

Stunned silence followed this statement, and then a babble of voices tumbled over each other. Manuel held up his hand and quietly continued. "I know what you are all trying to say. This is an early assessment, and our scientists are going up to Pátzcuaro to appraise the situation on the ground and get back to us with a new feasibility study as soon as possible. As to what we tell the press, or for that matter, the local activist group that has been hounding us — nothing at all. As far as they are concerned, we never planned a plant if we never build one. It is a non-issue. We will revisit this matter once the reports are in. Until then, *feliz* Navidad to you all. Go and enjoy your holidays."

Not everybody around the polished conference table agreed with their CEO, but the timing was difficult. Christmas was less than a week away, and though all of the men may have looked like tough, powerful businessmen, they were all deeply sentimental people and preferred the idea of enjoying their holidays to fretting about work. They stood up from the table and wished their boss *feliz* Navidad *y un buen año nuevo*.

• • •

The language school and the traveller's lodge were both booked to capacity until December 23, when the school closed until the New Year. Paula, Enrique and Rafael spent all their energy keeping the two enterprises afloat. The good news was that their landlord showed up a couple of days after Día de los Vivos and informed them he could extend the lease for another year.

"Really?" Paula said. "Why did you change your mind?"

"Well, the situation has somewhat changed," Carlos said, avoiding eye contact.

"That's fantastic news, the best Christmas present ever," Paula said, somewhat bewildered.

The silence from the Comisión Federal de Electricidad was deafening, and neither *La Voz* nor any of the other papers mentioned anything about the Day of the Living, nor any other news regarding the nuke plant on Lake Pátzcuaro. Carmen tried to find out what was going on by contacting the Governor's office. "As far as we know, there are no plans to build a nuclear facility on the lake." When Carmen wanted to know about the engineering company working on the lakeshore, the office denied any involvement or knowledge. When Carmen called the Mexican Electric Utility in Veracruz, she was put through to Manuel Rodríguez, who told her there had never been a plan to build a nuclear facility on Lake Pátzcuaro. "It was just an option we were looking at, nothing more. *Feliz* Navidad."

"And that is that," Carmen said to the assembled group, who sat silently around the kitchen table.

"I think it's fantastic news," Gabriela proclaimed. "There won't be a nuke plant in Pátzcuaro and we can all relax."

"Does that mean we won?" Rico asked, somewhat confused.

"I think it does," Paula answered. "They decided to abandon the project without any confrontation. Somebody at the Comisión is very cunning. I'm happy to accept the result and declare victory. What do you all say?"

Everybody cheered and talked at once. Only Karen sat quietly with her hands in her lap. "Jason would have been happy to know he backed a winning cause," Carmen said to her young Canadian friend. "You can now go on with your own life, knowing that you have lifelong friends in this town." Karen accepted a long hug from her wise friend and then joined the others for a long night of talk, drink and celebration.

A letter arrived at the school during these in-between days, which Paula brought along to show to everybody. "It's from Bernard," she announced, "the Canadian who worked with Randall. Let me read it you. It's quite touching."

Hello to everyone,
I know how you all despise me for my lack of judgment
and my betrayal, and I wholly apologize for any damage
my behaviour has caused. I want you to know that I have
done my utmost to champion your cause. It's one way to
atone for my transgression. I especially want to apologize
to Randall, and if there is a way I can make good for my
behaviour, please give me a chance. Last but not least,
I want to thank Gabriela for all she's done for me. It is
because of my misplaced feelings for her that I have acted
not in your or her best interest but only in my own. I
hope to learn from this mistake and be a better man for it.
Please don't hate me and thank you for listening.

Bernard Fowler

Nobody spoke for a few beats, until Rico said, "I think he really means it."

"Yeah, he's done all the damage to himself," Paula pointed out, "and he is paying the price. As far as I'm concerned, he is forgiven."

"I can't blame him for falling in love with Gabriela," Rafael said. Everyone laughed. "What about you, Randall?" Rafael asked. "How do you feel about the guy?"

"You know, I never even knew his last name. I liked him okay. He's a smart enough man, just a troubled one. Kind of lost. Yeah, sure, if I run into him I'll let him buy me a drink. No point carrying grudges."

When Rafael told Gabriela about the letter later on that night, she sat down and said nothing for some time. "I have a confession to make, Rafael, and maybe you will hate me for it, but I have to tell you."

Rafael held up his hand to stop her, knowing exactly what she was about to say. "You were free and alone. I have not been a monk, myself. What we have now is whole and complete."

They held each other for a long time, and as Gabriela cried, both understood that they were still healing from their long time apart.

Madison felt Greenpeace's involvement wasn't needed for the time being and that she had done all she could to support NNN. She had become good friends with all of them and promised to keep in touch.

She then joined Randall to head down to the coast, to Zihuatanejo, for the holidays and to catch some sun before returning to Vancouver. She and Randall had been hanging out together like a couple of teenagers on their first date, ever since the Day of the Living. They were an unlikely couple, and both denied that anything was going on, which in itself was proof positive of their tryst. Madison donated her Apple laptop to the school.

"I'll be back in Morelia after the holidays to edit the hours of tape down to ninety minutes. We will have a great movie," Randall promised. "I got some fantastic footage. You'll all be stars." Randall also had a good live recording of Luke's and Rafael's song. "The theme song in the film," he assured them.

Luke and Vena also decided it was time to move on. They were heading down to the Mayan coast and, after New Year's, all the way to New Zealand. Vena's dad had secured them two cheap flights, and Vena promised Luke he would find work there, maybe even in the busy local film industry. He also wanted to record some of his songs as soon as he could afford it.

Karen decided to return to Toronto to her family for Christmas. She was the saddest of them all, since for her this spelled the real end to her and Jason's story. "I'll probably teach dance again, but I'm thinking of going back to university, maybe become a kindergarten teacher. I can always dance."

It was a bittersweet farewell, everyone promising to stay in touch. Each one took a piece of Patzcuaro with them. For Randall it was the vistas and the architecture, for Luke the music, for Vena the camaraderie of the gang and for Karen the powerful memories. Through it all wove the philosophical thread of Don Vasco de Quiroga, which had helped shape the social and ethical convictions of them all.

That left Parker, who had occasionally been invited by Carmen to spend time upstairs, and who was happy to stay on in Pátzcuaro indefinitely, thoroughly enjoying his retirement, although he seemed busier than ever, typing away at his old manual typewriter.

"What on earth are you writing?" Carmen wanted to know.

"It's a collection of stories about complete strangers who find themselves by chance in an exotic place, get involved with each other and engage over a common issue. Their cause, relationships, loves, betrayals and losses."

Carmen looked at her ungainly friend, with his long arms, clumsy hands, ill-fitting clothes, unruly crop of greying brown hair and droopy eyes and long nose. She already loved that man with all his faults. The heart, she thought, is mightier than the brain.

"That sounds like a familiar story," she said laconically. "What's it called?"

"I'm calling it *Mariposa Intersections*. It's just a working title for now."

"I like it, Parker, but maybe you should get one of those laptops like Madison has."

"I wouldn't know what to do with one of those. I'd miss my old Corona. It's been a faithful friend for many years and not dependent on any kind of power, nuclear or hydro."

Carmen laughed. That was another thing she liked about Parker. He knew what he had, what he could do and what he liked — simple and straightforward. No complicated unresolved issues, no power games, no unnatural desires, no extra baggage. Yes, she liked her roommate, and gladly offered to let him to stay on.

"Of course I accept, but you know I'm secretly in love with Imelda."

"That makes two of us."

Rafael looked like he hadn't slept in days, and the simple truth was he hadn't. During the day he taught at the school, and the nights he spent at Gabriela's hotel room. They had rediscovered each other in ways that only young lovers can, and when they were not engaged in wordless activities, they talked — about their families, their future and also what should happen to NNN and how to keep going. They had all invested so much passion, time and commitment into their cause that it was hard to just let go.

Gabriela had arranged to return to Punta de San Juan for Christmas. That left Rafael with some choices to make about what to do during the holidays, but they arranged to meet up in Guadalajara for New Year's Eve. "I know a fabulous hotel there," he said, "and I'll take you to my favourite restaurant for el Año Nuevo, to La Fonda de San Miguel Arcángel."

"Why don't you go back to El Rosario, Rafael?" Gabriela suggested. "I'm sure your father has forgiven you by now, and they would very happy to have their son back."

She was right, and Rafael knew the time had come for him to return to the gateway to the mariposas, to spend time with his family for the first time in five years. Now that he had found his soul mate again, he could return home with confidence, his head held high. He missed his old friends and his village up in the hills above Angangueo.

As he boarded a bus at the very spot where he and Gabriela had once said farewell to each other for good, he promised her that next time she would be with him

As the bus pulled out, Rafael settled back into his seat and let his mind drift over everything that had happened and everything yet to come. He thought of returning to UNAM for postgraduate studies, but mainly to be near Gabriela. She was a wealthy woman now, and she had insisted she'd help him financially, but he didn't want to hear about that. He was thinking about doing something different, something he'd never tried before. He had music in his mind. Songs yet unwritten were coming to him, songs he wanted to sing.

Navidad in Pátzcuaro, as in all of Mexico, is a holiday full of colour, lights, fireworks, exhibitions and concerts, and the anticipation is more spectacular than the holy night itself. With the school closed for two weeks and the lodge booked until the New Year, Paula and Enrique found some time to themselves. They could have left town, but they didn't want to. This was their home now, and what better place to celebrate the festive season than in Pátzcuaro, surely one of the nicest places on earth.

Chapter 22

Beginnings

Rafael's old high school teacher and patron drove him up the mountain from Angangueo, filling him in on the local news and on his family. They happily received their prodigal son back into the fold with open arms. Even his padre welcomed his son back, hugging him tightly, acting as though nothing unusual had ever happened between them.

Arturo proudly showed off his almost-new 4×4 GMC pickup truck, and not a mention was made of the one Rafael had bought for him all those years before. This truck he had paid for himself, with unmentioned help from Rosa, Rafael's older sister, who had replaced Rafael in guiding tourists to the Mariposa Sanctuary. Rosa, unlike Rafael, gave all her earnings to her padre. It had taken some hard work to convince the warden of the sanctuary to let a young woman be a guide, but since he had liked Rafael and he understood Arturo's dilemma, he relented, casting himself as a modern, progressive administrator by hiring a female. After all, he had his eyes on the mayor's office, and he hoped this would help his popularity with the female voters, as indeed it did. Besides Rosa, there were now half a dozen female guides leading the tourists up to the mariposa milagro (the butterfly miracle), high up in the alpine forest of the Transvolcanic Mountains.

Rafael told his family all about his accomplishments in the years since he'd left the confines of this small hamlet. He told them about Gabriela, but never mentioned their years apart, and received old Arturo's blessing upon promising to bring his girlfriend to El Rosario at the very first opportunity. Nobody had ever heard of his involvement with NNN or Radio Libre in Oaxaca. No point telling them now about these past adventures, when there were so many new and exciting endeavours up ahead to talk about.

Arturo invited the neighbours and friends over for a farewell party, and Rafael sang and played the songs everybody knew, and even some of his own songs, to the pleasure of his enraptured sisters and proud mamasita. Even crusty old Arturo and Rafael's two older brothers, who still ran the expanded family farm, applauded his virtuosity.

Rafael left El Rosario for his New Year's Eve rendezvous in Guadalajara with a buoyant bounce in his step, feeling like a young god descending from his mountain.

• • •

Both the language school and the Pátzcuaro Travellers Lodge remained fully booked until March, it being the busy season for tourists in Mexico. Paula and Enrique folded NNN, since there was absolutely no news about the intention of the Comisión Federal de Electricidad with regards to the nuke plant.

"There won't be a nuke plant on Lake Pátzcuaro," Carmen pointed out. "This is exactly what we fought for! I have it from a good source that the project has been cancelled. Unless we hear differently, we have done our work."

At first the two young activists were almost disappointed, but then Carmen pointed out that they could easily transform NNN into an ecological and environmental movement. "The lake still needs our attention." They took Carmen's advice to heart and founded SLP, Salvar el Lago de Pátzcuaro. There was much work, education and lobbying to do in order to save the depleting Lake Pátzcuaro, and both Enrique and Paula immersed themselves enthusiastically into the new venture.

. . .

At the end of February, Rafael took Gabriela up to the sanctuary. They went in the morning, before the sun crept over the mountains and before the tourists arrived. Leading her up the well-trodden path brought back strong memories of his childhood, the time in his life before he even knew how to dream. As they reached the grassy plateau, the first rays of sun began to spill over the distant eastern mountains. They continued on up the trail until they reached a dense grove of pine trees. No theory, no science, no words could explain the wonderment of the monarch butterflies that gather every year at the same time in this ten-acre patch of pine forest high up in the very centre of Mexico.

Black clusters hung like hives from the pines, turning orange as the first butterflies opened their wings to expose themselves to the warmth and light as the morning fog dissipated. Slowly, and then with increasing frequency, the mariposas detached from the clusters and fluttered free. They floated upwards in an ever-growing orange and black cloud, as thousands silently filled the air around them.

"This is the most beautiful thing I have ever seen," Gabriela whispered, holding on to Rafael, who watched the sky fill with burning gold. He beamed with pride, as though these butterflies were his personal gift to his love and the world.

Author's Notes

I t has been over twenty years since the events in this account took place. Not much has changed, least of all our perception of nuclear power. It is still one of the preferred methods of power generation throughout the world. In France, unlike in Germany or the US, nuclear energy is accepted, even popular. France's decision to launch a large nuclear program dates back to 1973 and the events in the Middle East that they refer to as the "oil shock." Over the next twenty years, France installed fifty-six nuclear reactors, satisfying its power needs and even exporting electricity to other European countries. Canada presently has nineteen nuclear reactors, and Mexico still only has two: Laguna Verde I and II[1].

Most of the world's electricity is produced by fossil fuels: 39 percent by coal, 22 percent by natural gas and 5 percent by oil. Hydro produces 17 percent of mankind's energy needs, and nuclear

---

1   http://www.world-nuclear.org/information-library/current-and-future-generation/nuclear-power-in-the-world-today.aspx

power comes in at 11 percent, while geothermal, wind and solar production supply 7 percent of the world's electricity needs[2].

As of November 2016, China has thirty-six nuclear reactors and twenty under construction. The US is the world's largest producer of nuclear power, accounting for over 30 percent. The US has one hundred nuclear reactors (plus four under construction), providing almost 20 percent of its electricity needs; but it still relies heavily on coal-fired generators and natural gas — 33 percent each.

Today there are about 450 nuclear reactors generating electricity and about sixty new nuke plants under construction in fifteen countries.

Nuclear power currently provides around 11 percent of the world's energy needs. It produces vast amounts of energy from small amounts of fuel, without the pollution you get from burning fossil fuels.

On July 29, 2003, a distinguished team of researchers from the Massachusetts Institute of Technology (MIT) and Harvard released what co-chair Dr. John Deutch calls "the most comprehensive interdisciplinary study ever conducted on the future of nuclear energy."[3] The report maintains that "the nuclear option should be retained precisely because it is an important carbon-free source of power."

"Fossil fuel-based electricity is projected to account for more than 40 percent of global greenhouse gas emissions by 2020," said Deutch. "In the U.S., 90 percent of the carbon emissions from electricity generation come from coal-fired generation, even though this accounts for only 52 percent of the electricity produced. Taking nuclear power off the table as a viable alternative will prevent the global community from achieving long-term gains in the control of carbon dioxide emissions." Not much has changed since this report was tabled.

Solar power, which makes up less than one percent of total energy consumption, has grown from 335 to 13,000 megawatts in the US alone and is today the second largest source of new

---

2   http://www.tsp-data-portal.org/Breakdown-of-Electricity-Generation-by-Energy-Source#tspQvChart

3   http://web.mit.edu/nuclearpower/

electricity generation (behind natural gas)[4]. Germany has spent an estimated $222 billion since 2000 on renewable energy subsidies, but emissions have been stuck at roughly 2009 levels and actually rose last year, as coal-fired plants filled a void left by Germany's decision to abandon nuclear power[5].

Nuclear power is still hailed as a "clean fuel," and the deep caves in the Canadian Shield are touted as the perfect storage facility for the burned-out fuel rods. All is well, then — or is it?

As the search for a definitive method for the disposal of nuclear waste (plutonium) drags on, the drawbacks of merely storing the waste are mounting. The mixed oxide fuel method would provide a relatively quick solution but would not completely provide for the waste's disposal. The vitrification method (seal the plutonium in glass and bury it) would also provide a more effective means of dealing with nuclear waste than simple storage; however, the long-term consequences of vitrification are uncertain and the process is expensive. Subductive waste disposal would require extensive research and development to implement, but this is a small price to pay for an effective solution to the as-yet unanswered question — what to do with nuclear waste? High level waste (HLW) increases by about 12,000 tonnes a year, equivalent to about 100 double-decker buses[6].

Over three million bundles of solid waste uranium fuel are now stored temporarily on site at Canada's twenty-two nuclear reactors, largely in concrete casks inside ordinary metal sheds on the surface. The waste can remain dangerously radioactive for as long as 100 centuries.

Another form of disposal is the reuse of some of the burned-out fuel rods and cells in breeder reactors, which squeeze out the leftover energy in discarded fuel cells and rods.

Climate change is undeniably happening as I write this: ocean acidification and oxygen depletion, habitat and rainforest

4   http://instituteforenergyresearch.org/topics/encyclopedia/solar/

5   https://www.nytimes.com/2017/10/07/business/energy-environment/ger
    man-renewable-energy.html

6   http://large.stanford.edu/courses/2011/ph241/ali2/

destruction, greenhouse gas emissions, rising sea levels, glacial melt, aquifer exhaustion and global warming. The "greenhouse effect," which occurs when the atmosphere traps heat radiating from Earth, is the main cause of the warming of the planet and is undeniably accelerating. How much of it is human-produced? Think about it: Eight billion people with all their energy needs and demands do have an impact. How can the world sustain a middle class, as we enjoy here in Canada, for all eight billion, and who is to deny the poor Chinese farmer a new fridge or tractor, and who to reject the need for heat, food or water to the cold, hungry and thirsty? We humans have built ourselves a progress trap; that is, we're too smart for our own good, and the future looks precarious at best[7].

Environmental concerns are at the top of the political agendas of most western nations, except in the present-day US, where the new administration is stepping away from previous commitments.

• • •

The first time I drove into Pátzcuaro in my VW camper, at the end of November 1984 (the Orwellian threshold), I stopped at the Villa Pátzcuaro Campground. The owner, Arturo Pimentel Ramos, turned out to be a passionate local historian, as well as a former regional tennis champion (thus the two tennis courts adjacent to the campground). Arturo proved to be a deep well of valuable information on the local history, politics, pageantry and architecture of Pátzcuaro. We spent many afternoons talking between games of tennis. Arturo was past sixty, while I was in my early thirties. He beat me every game.

The streets of the picturesque town were unpaved, and cars jostled for space with donkeys and *caballeros* on horseback. A lot of the houses were built with stuccoed adobe bricks and large sun-blackened beams. The gabled roof overhangs gave the earth-coloured buildings almost an alpine look, different from the usual

---

7   https://www.thegreeninterview.com/2010/09/05/ronald-wright-progress-traps/

box construction in rural Mexico. The reason can be found in the pine forests that grow at this altitude and supply ready building materials.

On that first trip to Mexico, I ended up staying four months, and I did pass through Morelia. My notes of the day read, *an urban gem of a city, modern and old worldly, classical Colonial and warm-hearted Mexicans*, and of Guadalajara, *The perennial city of flowers and art with a main square, an opera house and a cathedral to equal those in Europe.*

But my absolute favourite place in all of Mexico was Pátzcuaro. I stayed four weeks, walked the cobblestoned streets, marvelled at the diversity of artisan shops and family-run craft factories transforming wood, clay, textiles and copper into unique artifacts, utilitarian and decorative, some transcending craft to artistry. I never tired of the local *mercado* or hanging around the two main plazas, the Plaza Vasco de Quiroga and Plaza Gertrudis. I often sat for hours under the arches at one or another of the restaurants, sipping *cervezas* or coffees, reading and writing, or immersed in conversations with other travellers, all of whom seemed to have an abundance of time to spare. I have been back many times since then, and still love the quiet, picturesque town in the heart of Michoacán.

This story takes place before the cataclysmic events of 9/11, which changed the way governments deal with protest organizations of any stripe. It also happened before the Fukushima disaster of March 11, 2011, when, following a major earthquake, a 15-metre tsunami crashed into the coast of Japan. It disabled the power supply and cooling of three reactors, resulting in a meltdown and well over 1,000 deaths, and forcing 150,000 residents to flee the region.

Activist groups today are easily branded as terrorists, or simply ignored and marginalized by ridiculing their causes. The biggest demonstrations against the war in Iraq took place in Washington, D.C., in 2006. More than 200,000 people marched, but it barely made the news. The same is true for the Women's March in 2017, after Trump got elected: five million participants in all fifty states and on all continents. *Pay them no attention. Paint the demonstrators as freaks, radicals and unpatriotic* seemed to be the directive given to the media.

We live in a different and frightening world today, defined by the Internet, smartphones, YouTube and social media like Facebook and Twitter. Political campaigns are won and lost by computerized voting systems and populist movements controlled by massive web-based propaganda machines. Today's flippant remark is tomorrow's sound bite, seen by millions on their large and small screens. Movies and TV are opium for the masses, the news is scripted and propagandized and reality is made up of conflicting information, some fake, some real. It's a confusing world now, fragmented, torn and without spiritual and philosophical leadership or centre. It's like the mothership has abandoned planet earth and is drifting leaderless in a void.

Today, NNN would be smashed and broken up, divided and destroyed. No doubt about it. The world today is a much meaner place than just twenty years ago, and on both sides of the political divide the methods of control and propaganda have become much more brutal, intrusive and destructive. The radical, religious militants terrorize by kidnapping and killing indiscriminately, and the biggest military power on the planet has invaded, occupied and destroyed whole countries and regions, based on lies, deceit and hubris.

How does all that tie in to the cause of NNN? For example, there is one unifying thread that ties the invasion of Iraq and the fight of NNN together. It is energy: oil on the one hand, nuclear power on the other. The same goes for Iraq and the control of its oil, or the ambitions of Iran and North Korea to harness the power of the atom.

We need electricity for our modern way of life. Without it we're back in the Stone Age or the Bedouin tents of Arabia. Just where and how we produce this energy is of vital concern to everybody.

The fossil fuels of the twentieth century will be exhausted in another century at the current rate of consumption, which will only increase as more and more people want cars, fridges and big-screen TVs in the developing world — China, India and Africa. Unless we can replace fossil fuels with renewable energy sources and curb our voracious appetite for energy, we are doomed. Some may argue that's just the way to correct an out-of-control world-wide population explosion that has tripled from two billion to six billion in just thirty years and is forecast to reach eight billion by 2024[8]. The good news is that the rate of growth is declining.

We have the means and the technology to save this planet and the human species from self-destruction; all we need is the political will for a radically altered course. I'm talking about refocusing the political lens from an individual zoom to a wider focus, a common view where everybody is in the picture.

The members of NNN did just that in a small but skillful way. They didn't fight for personal gain or instant gratification, they fought for a better future, for a just process of consultation and planning, for a refocusing of the myopic lens of single issues to a wider, more inclusive vision. Thus, NNN's cause remains relevant and current. Just swap the nuke plant on Lake Patzcuaro for an oil well in Banff National Park or a coal-fired generating plant in Tofino.

As for the monarch butterfly sanctuary in El Rosario, its survival is tenuous. Although the sanctuary was declared a World Heritage Site by the UN, and the illegal logging of the pine trees in the area has slowed down, pollution, climate change, parasites and the disappearance of milkweed along the butterflies' migration route is threatening their existence, as is the increasing number of tourists flocking to the site. I believe the monarchs' saving grace is the remoteness of the sanctuary[9].

What once was a goat path up to the reserve is now a groomed and terraced walkway with railings and steps. The village of El Rosario has prospered with the growing popularity of the sanctuary and relies on the tourists. The butterflies return every year and still the miracle continues. On my last trip to El Rosario in the middle of March 2017, the monarchs were as plentiful as I remembered from previous visits. There seemed to be millions of them —

8   http://www.worldometers.info/world-population/
9   http://www.flightofthebutterflies.com/discovery-story/

airborne, in dozens of clusters hanging in the trees, and blanketing the open meadow just before the last bit of steep path. They were getting ready for the long three-generation trip north to Ontario, and by the end of March, they were all gone.

B.H. April 2018

Bruno Huber was born and raised in Zürich, Switzerland. He immigrated and settled in British Columbia in the seventies. He was the winner of the 'Höhnharter Wanderpreis' for Literature and he owned and operated a bookstore in Gibsons BC on the Sunshine Coast where he and his wife have lived since 1990. He divides his time between BC, Mexico and the Caribbean.

You can follow his blog: **www.brunospointofview.com**